WHAT SOULS ARE MADE OF

ARE MADE OF

• A WUTHERING HEIGHTS REMIX •

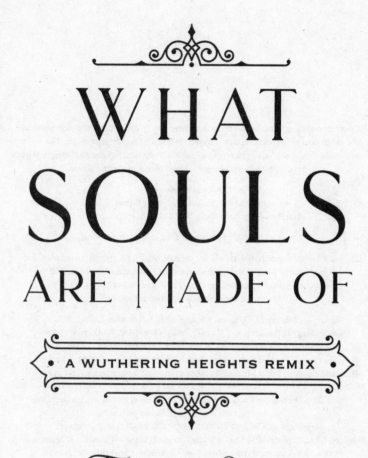

WHAT SOULS
ARE MADE OF

A WUTHERING HEIGHTS REMIX

TASHA SURI

FEIWEL AND FRIENDS
NEW YORK

A Feiwel and Friends Book
An imprint of Macmillan Publishing Group, LLC
120 Broadway, New York, NY 10271 • fiercereads.com

Our books may be purchased in bulk for promotional, educational, or business use. Please contact your local bookseller or the Macmillan Corporate and Premium Sales Department at (800) 221-7945 ext. 5442 or by email at MacmillanSpecialMarkets@macmillan.com.

Library of Congress Cataloging-in-Publication Data
Names: Suri, Tasha, author. | Brontë, Emily, 1818–1848. Wuthering Heights.
Title: What souls are made of : a Wuthering Heights remix / Tasha Suri.
Description: First edition. | New York : Feiwel and Friends, 2022. | Series: Remixed classics ; vol. 4 | Includes author's note and bibliographical references. | Audience: Ages 13–18. | Audience: Grades 10–12. | Summary: "Two lost souls cut off from their heritage find solace in each other in this remix of the gothic novel Wuthering Heights"— Provided by publisher.
Identifiers: LCCN 2021047407 | ISBN 9781250773500 (hardcover)
Subjects: CYAC: Identity—Fiction. | Racially mixed people—Fiction. | Illegitimacy—Fiction. | Belonging (Social psychology)—Fiction. | Yorkshire (England)—Fiction. | Liverpool (England)—Fiction. | Great Britain—History—George III, 1760–1820—Fiction. | LCGFT: Novels.
Classification: LCC PZ7.1.S873 Wh 2022 | DDC [Fic]—dc23
LC record available at https://lccn.loc.gov/2021047407

First edition, 2022
Book design by Michelle Gengaro-Kokmen
Feiwel and Friends logo designed by Filomena Tuosto
Printed in the United States of America

ISBN 978-1-250-77350-0 (hardcover)
1 3 5 7 9 10 8 6 4 2

*For the librarian who let me read the classics
in the adult section when I was eight.
This is all your fault.*

Chapter One

Heathcliff

Yorkshire, North of England
1786

FIRST COMES A BOY FROM nowhere. That's how it goes wrong.

Before he comes, there's a house on the moors and a family inside it: mother and father, son and daughter. All of them new to the village, or so people say. The family's only been around since the boy was toddling, the girl even smaller. The family's not generations old, settled here long ago, like the rest. But they fit so well that people most often forget it.

The Earnshaws? They're a strange lot, and new in these parts, but they're ours.

Nice, people call them. People don't know what nice is.

But the boy from nowhere doesn't fit. He looks like he doesn't fit: brown, thin, speaking a language no one knows. He brings nowhere along with him into the house. Memories of nowhere. Skin from nowhere, and language from nowhere. Reminders that *nowhere* is actually *somewhere*. Turns out, big unknown's got people in it.

Ghosts, too.

Turns out, you can run to the end of the world and it'll still find you. The thing you're running from.

Now the family's a mother and father, son and daughter, and a boy. Longer he's there, the more the nice peels right off the family. The mother dies. Then the father dies. And there's just a son, a daughter, and a boy. The son's angry about it. The son's vicious. He beats the boy, tries to thrash the nowhere out of him.

And the daughter . . .

Well. I thought she loved the boy. That's my own fool fault.

I walk. Creaking floorboards. Thud of boots on flagstones. Kitchen's never silent, never empty. The hearth's crackling. Cheery noise. Cooking knives are out, fresh-sharpened. My fingers twitch.

Maybe you don't know what tale we're in. But I do.

There's a boy from nowhere. Best he goes back to nowhere. Back where he belongs.

I pick up one knife and walk out the door. Walk down to the gate. Sky's turning gray for a storm. Someone's calling my name.

I don't look back.

It's good I forgot to thieve a gun when I ran. A gun's a temptation to killing.

No. The knife's enough.

The road here's narrow. Just a dirt track, cutting through gorse. No trees for cover. Still, I crouch low. Hope the gorse swallows the shape of me.

Light's fading. I walked a night, rain-drenched. Snatched seconds of sleep under tree cover, coat over my head. Walked a day. My feet ache. It feels good to be on the ground, finally not moving. Can't do it for long though, or I'll stiffen up. I think I've done about thirty miles. I haven't kept track. Haven't looked at milestones, though I've passed some. Haven't read fingerposts. I left home before I knew where I wanted to go. *Away* was enough.

A horse and cart pass by. There's a farmhand riding, bundled up in a smock. Broad hat tugged low over his eyes. He's whistling. He doesn't see me.

I let him go.

I'm good at being patient. Ground's wet under me, the way peat is always wet. I can feel the cold seeping through my breeches. But I don't move. I know how to hunt. I'm good at it.

Normally I hunt animals. But people aren't so different.

The sky is bleeding purple when a man walks up the dirt road. His hobnailed shoes thud heavily. He looks tired. Must be a day laborer from one of the farms nearby, heading on home.

I tense up. Waiting.

I don't have to do what I'm going to do.

I won't suffer for it, if I let the man go and keep on walking. I won't die out here. My coat is shabby, but it's decent enough. A castoff but a good one, strong wool, the kind that stays sturdy even when the wind goes knife-cold. My boots are decent. You need quality boots when you work hard, work outdoors. And me, I'm not allowed indoors anymore. Not often, anyway.

But I've got no food.

I know hunger. We're old enemies. That ancient dog's been biting at my heels for years. He's got sharp teeth, cold eyes. Once he's set on you, you can't shake him. So my belly's full of spite right now, and anger'll keep it going for a few days, but it won't be enough. Eventually, a man's got to eat. And if a man doesn't have food, he needs coin to get it.

So I wait. When the stranger's walked by me, I rear up. Get behind him, fast. He's got a sickle. I snatch it from him. Wrap my arm round his throat and show him the knife. He goes still. Easy as that, I've got my prey.

"Boy, I don't want any trouble," he says. He's breathing fast.

"Don't call me boy," I tell him. "Don't call me anything. Keep your mouth shut and give me all the coin you've got."

It takes him a moment to realize I'm not pinning his hands and won't gut him if he moves. Then he fumbles in his pockets. Hands me a knotted-up kerchief. I get it open. Inside there's just some pennies. Dull copper.

It's pitiful little. But I take it.

"The rest," I say.

"There's no more," he replies.

"I know there's more."

I say it low and steady. I say it like I'm certain. And sure enough, he shudders, and swallows, and says, "My shoe. In my left shoe. Have pity on me and leave me at least that."

I've got no pity, but reaching for his shoe will get me a kick to the skull. So I grunt agreement and let him go.

Some thanks I get for my kindness: he wheels round to punch me in the head. Grabs for my knife. It flies off. I duck and slam my fist into his belly. He gives a groan and stumbles back. I kick him hard in the leg. Kick him again until he tumbles and goes down. I hold the sickle to his throat.

His eyes are fearful.

"Take them both off," I say to him. "Both shoes. Now."

He doesn't move. I press the sickle down harder.

It draws blood, I can smell it. His breathing changes.

"Go on," I say, and lift the sickle away.

He scrambles up. Shoes off. I gesture at him to get back. He does.

I reach in. Snatch up the coin in the left shoe. Might be more in his stockings, but I don't ask him to take those off. I pocket the coppers, then pick up the shoes too.

"I'm keeping these," I say, and step back.

It'll take him time to get help, barefoot. The ground's cold. Sinks here, and goes stone-sharp there. I'll be long gone before he finds help.

"They're my only shoes."

"A pity," I say. "If you hadn't tried to fight, you'd still have them."

"Fiend," he spits out.

"I am," I confirm. "A fiend from hell itself, and if you speak of me to anyone when dawn comes, you tell them so. Go to the church and ask God to protect you from me, or I'll come for you in your nightmares."

I watch his face. He's bleeding from his neck—the cut's not deep, but it bleeds hard. Must hurt. He stares at me, trembling.

Maybe he sees me properly now. Maybe he knows he should be thanking me for letting him live. It's good I don't have a gun. Good I don't have the temptation. Because I'm angry, vicious angry. Not at this man. But I'd kill him anyway. I'd do it.

I wait him out. One breath. Two.

He stays quiet.

I nod.

"Good," I say.

A knife's better than a sickle. So I lean down and grab it where it fell. My hands are too full. Weapons, shoes. I'm not letting any of it go. I tuck the knife away and turn.

I start walking again. I don't go fast. I don't turn back either. But I'd hear if he followed. He doesn't.

Moon's rising. I slip off the dirt road. The grass is high here. Good enough to sleep in. But I won't sleep. Can't. And I don't try.

What do you think of it? What I did to him? I never know when you'll be moral. Maybe you're angry. Maybe you want to scold me for being cruel.

I wasn't cruel, Cathy. But you were.

It was all you. It's always you.

Cathy. The only reason I hurt the man is because of you. Because you said what you said, and did what you did. Because I left and had nothing to take with me. So if it's anyone's fault, Cathy, then it's yours. I've always been a villain, but you leashed me for a while.

Now you've set me free.

Chapter Two

Catherine

SICK AND FEVERISH, I DREAMED. The grass rustled around me. The heather sang like church bells. The moon was large, so large above me I was afraid it would fall from the sky and crush me.

I had run and run, shouting for him. I'd been trying to explain, to say, *Heathcliff, I didn't mean it! You don't understand! Oh, you fool, you fool, come back!*—but I couldn't find him, and I had gone too far in the pouring rain to go back home. My skirts were so heavy I stumbled and fell. My heart felt like a stone, too cold to beat even as my body burned.

There was a ghost following me. Her feet were backward and didn't touch the earth, because ghosts cannot walk on soil. I was lying on my side where I'd fallen, so I could see only her feet, gliding on nothing. Her feet were a brown like dusk, the soles painted red as blood or sunsets.

It wasn't the first time I had seen a ghost, so I was not as shocked as I might have been. Of course, worldly gentlemen will say ghosts are not real, and usually I would lie and say I believe them. But when one is gliding toward you on feet turned backward, you can't lie even to yourself.

She said something to me. Later, perhaps, I'll forget this.

Cathy, she said. *My Cathy. My baby.*

I could not cry, because the fever was too hot in me already.

Ma, I said. Why? I don't know. The fever was speaking for me. *Ma, please.*

She leaned down.

I saw cloth, pouring like milk or moonlight. And through it, I saw my own face looking back at me.

I squeezed my eyes tight shut, terrified.

Maybe the dream ended.

Someone found me and lifted me up. And after that—oh, I forget. I don't know. I don't.

Cathy. Catherine.

Miss Cathy.

Wake up. Wake up.

Please, Catherine.

Wake up.

Do all people dream old memories when they're deathly ill? I have never been so sick before, so I don't know. When I was carried into the warmth of the house, the candles flickering and the dogs barking, and the servant breathing heavily as someone shouted that the doctor must be called immediately, I thought I might die. I had been overnight in the storm and hadn't sheltered anywhere, only let the rain drench me. I was hot and cold all at once, teeth chattering. My skirts were so sodden I thought they might drown me.

While the fever held me, I dreamed of the same memories over and over again: Heathcliff standing in a circle of feathers under a crescent moon. Heathcliff pressing soil behind my ears. *For nazar,* he said. *Because the ghosts must be as jealous of you as I am.* The wind, wailing over the moors like song. Water, rolling and gray, lifting me up and down and up and down, until I grew sick from the sight and the feel of it. That is my oldest memory, my first memory. Gray water raising me up, then folding over me like a shroud.

The water is Heathcliff's oldest memory too. Isn't that strange? Sometimes I think it must have been Heathcliff's memory first and I stole it and convinced myself it was my own. But it *feels* like mine. I have never been more than ten miles from home, but I know the water all the same.

I stop dreaming eventually. The ocean swallows me and throws me right out.

I have never slept well. Big, colorful dreams always catch me when I begin to fall deep asleep and fling me back up to the surface. When I was very young I used to tell anyone who would listen to me about my dreams. Angels with six arms, and the sun like a great discus above them. Voices speaking in a language I did not know. I thought maybe it was the language of heaven, though our servant Joseph would scoff and say it was surely the language of hell, because I was such a wicked child, with no morals to speak of.

My brother was fascinated, at first. *What did the voices say? How did they say it?* Later he would pinch my mouth shut and tell me to stop talking about things I didn't understand.

The ocean throws me out, and the dream flings me out too. Flings me awake. I lie still with my eyes closed for a long moment and think about how warm I am now, and how hungry. I don't think I'm sick any longer. I'll live after all.

I force my eyes to open.

I am glad to be alive, of course, but I am also disappointed. If I had died trying to find Heathcliff, he would have been very sorry indeed when he found out.

Well, those ifs and maybes don't matter since I'm alive and well.

But now that I am awake, I realize that I am not in my home. This is certainly not my bed. My bed is an oak closet pressed up against a window. It is small and enclosed and safe. This bed is a grand, canopied thing. The curtains are a buttery yellow, and patterned with foreign birds, long-necked cranes and brightly feathered peacocks. On the wallpaper are little white pagodas, and ladies standing with parasols inside them. They wear foreign clothes and have foreign faces.

I slept in this room for more than a month when I was a girl of twelve. I was sick then too, but from a dog bite on my calf, and the very wealthy family who owned the dog took me in. The Lintons. All of them blond and genial and wealthy. One of their servants carried me up to this room and arranged the bedding for me as the two Linton children, Edgar and Isabella, watched anxiously. I stared at the curtains and the wallpaper and Mrs. Linton flitted into the room and around me like a little robin, all quick and trilling.

Chinoiserie, Mrs. Linton told me, very proudly, when she saw me peering at the walls. She said the style was from the Orient, and that was why the ladies holding their parasols did not look like us. She thought I had never seen anything like it before.

I did not tell Mrs. Linton that we had similar things in our own home. What was strange to me was that she did not lock them away, as we did.

I stare at those ladies now. My vision swims. It tosses the women about in a tumble, as if they are the ones on a harsh sea. What an adventure they appear to be having.

A figure appears at the door, and I am instantly glad to see a familiar face.

"Miss Cathy," Nelly says, pausing at the door. She looks relieved. "You're awake at last."

"Ah, Nelly!" I say, dragging myself up until I am seated. "What am I doing here?"

"You must not make so much noise, Miss Cathy," Nelly says severely. Nelly is only as old as my brother, but she always has a tight and worried expression on her face that makes her look like a grandmother. Today her face looks especially pinched, and I think somehow I've annoyed her already, even though

I've only been awake mere seconds. But she sits down beside me, and says, "Your brother asked me to come and watch over you, and help care for you until you are well enough to return home."

"Why am I here?" I ask. "Why am I not at home?"

"It was thought," Nelly says carefully, "that you would be better cared for here."

I don't ask who thought it would be better, and of course I don't ask why. I know exactly why. People know what my brother is like. They wouldn't have left me under his care, sickly as I've been. And people who don't know my brother very well still pity me for being the only woman in a household of men.

I am not actually the only woman, of course. I have Nelly. I am sixteen now, and nearly a grown woman, but Nelly has known me since we were both children, and she has bossed me about and looked after me from the very start. When I was sick as a little girl it was often Nelly—not my mother—who brought me my gruel or tucked me under the blankets to ward off a chill. She would take care of me.

But Nelly is a servant, so nobody thinks she is any kind of proper company for me, as I am meant to be a lady. I don't know who carried me here, sick and senseless as I was, but I can imagine what Mrs. Linton said when she saw me. *The girl needs a mother to care for her*, she would have said, wringing her hands. *And who better but me?*

But Mrs. Linton is not here.

"Has Heathcliff been found?" I ask. "Has he returned?"

"You chased after him," Nelly says. "You ran through rain

and storm. The doctor was afraid you would die for your foolishness. What were you thinking?"

"Has my brother sent anyone to seek him out?" I ask, insistent.

Nelly shakes her head.

"Has anyone tried to find him?"

Nelly sighs, and shakes her head once more.

My brother—Hindley—has not sent anyone to find Heathcliff. And Heathcliff has not come home.

My stomach feels leaden. I do not know what to do now, except sit silent and still, as Nelly exhales and takes my hand. Her grip is very firm.

"Miss Cathy," she says lowly. "You must not wail or complain. You must not speak of Heathcliff at all, here. The Lintons have suffered a terrible loss, and you must put their feelings first."

Nelly often does this, talking to me as if I do not understand how other people's feelings work. As if I have not comforted Edgar plenty of times when he has been miserable for some reason or another. She has often told me I am hard of heart, but I think it is quite mean of her to imply such a thing all over again when I am lying on my sickbed.

"Tell me what you mean," I say impatiently.

She clutches my hand tighter. "Mr. and Mrs. Linton also caught fever," she says, in that same low voice. I understand now that she is trying to be somber and respectful, and wishes me to be the same. "They have died. Your Edgar is Mr. Linton now. He and his sister are in mourning."

The breath leaves my lungs, all at once. "Both of them?" I say.

Nelly nods.

"I know how it feels to lose both parents, and to be alone. I'll be kind to him," I tell her.

"Very prettily put," she says. "You should say so to him yourself. And be kind to his sister too."

"I will," I say. "Of course I will. You think I'm so cold, Nelly, but I am not."

And suddenly, my eyes are streaming. I am weeping.

There is a pause. Then Nelly gathers me up. She is awkward, holding me, because it isn't how we are with each other, but she still does it. "Hush now. Hush."

But I need not hush. I should mourn. I am going to marry Edgar one day. We have agreed it, even if we are not formally engaged. We have an understanding, so that means I should understand how he feels, shouldn't I? His pain should be my pain, and I love him enough to grieve that he has lost his parents. And he and Isabella are so *soft*. The slightest inconvenience upsets them. They cry over the smallest hurts. A grief like this will drown them. I'll have to join them in those waters, or they will begin to think I am as hard-hearted as Nelly does. As my father did once too.

Nelly is still holding me. "Don't cry," she mutters. "It'll all be well, Miss Cathy. Wait and see."

Does she think I really mourn? I do mourn, a little. But it is Heathcliff I mourn the most. My tears are the same ones I wept when I realized he was gone. That he left without even saying goodbye to me. He heard—he was there when . . .

It doesn't matter. I won't think of that. Not now.

Where is Heathcliff? And why hasn't he come home to me? How could he have listened to my words, and taken them so seriously?

Surely he knows my heart better than this. He must.

Nelly may say what she likes. But it will not be well until Heathcliff is safe.

Chapter Three

Heathcliff

I'M SOFT.

Don't like that I am. Before, I didn't think I was. I despise people like that. Edgar Linton's soft. So pale and big-eyed. Never been hurt by anything but the fist I put in his face once, because he was bothering you, Cathy. Simpering over you. He cried then. Fat, miserable tears. Shocked. Like the world had never done him harm before and he didn't know what to do now it had.

I don't cry when I'm hit. I've learned better. Same as you.

Mostly I'm strong. Throw me out on the moors at night, I'll do fine. Give me an axe, tell me to set a fire, harvest peat, I can do it. I can work land. Want me to take a punch, and I'll take it. Pain doesn't frighten me.

But the city is hell. Never seen the like of it. Beggars in

corners. People shouting, screaming. Laughter too, and quiet talk, but even that is too much when there's so many people. My ears are ringing. Raw nerves are all I am, stumbling about, trying to find a place to stop and breathe.

I know about Liverpool. Or thought I knew. I know the ships dock here, carrying all sorts. Sugar, rum, tobacco. What Nelly bakes into the cakes, what Hindley drinks and smokes. It's all from here. I came from here too. Don't think I was carried over the water, though I keep dreaming of it. Gray, shifting. Enough to make me sick, like I'm caught on it forever.

Can't see the water. No sea and no river, not yet. The thick of the city's got me. But the city's gray and shifting like tidal waves. So many people and so much noise, lights spilling out of doors and windows. But the roads are filth. Suffering's all over. There's rats, mangy dogs. People who're all skin over bones. But there's money, too. That's why most come here—to make money, to know what being rich is. And some must get it. I see it round me. Ladies in colorful skirts. Carriages. Big signs over shops, painted up bright, selling hats and ribbons, sugar sweets. Things people don't get for need but for want, now they've got money to feed their wants with.

I see a tavern. People spilling out the doors, and candles lit inside. I'm thirsty. Near the Heights there's a spring. Clean, fresh water for drinking if it's boiled right. There's no water like that here. Only sick stuff, stinking and rotten. But I don't walk over to the tavern for small beer, the light stuff that'll fix thirst safer than water can. I go in, and it's all noise and bodies pressed up against me. I want to go straight back out, but I don't. I go and buy an ale. Proper ale. I don't hide that I've got a little coin.

It doesn't take long. A man sidles up to me. He's friendly. Asks me when I came to the city. I tell him today. Just a few hours ago, in fact.

"I came into the first tavern I saw," I say. I make myself sound nervous. I've been told I look sullen, angry, when I'm not thinking. But when I try, I can look different.

"Your first experience of Liverpool," he says, whistling through his teeth. "It must be a big shock!"

"Yes," I say to him. "A real shock. You get nothing like this where I come from."

His eyes rake me over. Maybe he's thinking I don't look like someone who comes from the same soil as he does. Or maybe he just thinks I'm a country fool, same as all the rest who come here looking for work and find drink instead.

"You're a young lad," he says comfortingly. "Everything'll be new to you. I remember when I was your age . . ." He trails off, and clucks his tongue against his teeth. "But you'll get used to the life here soon enough."

"You think so?" I keep an innocent look on me. Let him think I trust him. Let him think we're friends.

He smiles, and says, "Let's get you a better drink. Have you ever drunk wine?"

No. I've never had strong ale neither. But real wine's rich stuff. Costs good coin. I lick bitter ale foam from my teeth, lips closed. Think about what to do. Then I shake my head at him.

"Then let's get you a proper welcome," he says warmly, and slaps a heavy hand against my back. I don't shake him off.

He gets me wine. I try it, because he's watching. My head starts feeling light. But the way I stumble after him, that's for show.

I tip some wine away as I stumble. The less I carry, the less I'll have to drink when he looks.

He takes me over to his friends. They're playing cards. The deck is grubby, the red on the hearts and diamonds so bright it's bloodlike. They're playing a game. Lanterloo. Do I know it? They ask me. I tell them no. They all grin, friendly. We're all friends here. They say they'll teach me to play.

I sit.

We play for a while. Can't tip all the wine away, so I hold it up, pretending to drink. And then I drink a bit for real. One of them says, "Why don't we wager? Just for fun."

I agree.

We make bets. I win the first round. They all applaud me. A woman handing out drinks looks over and rolls her eyes. Turns away.

I smile at them. Let them think I believe I've won fair. That they're getting me nice and drunk. That I'll wager more and more coin. That they'll take everything I've got when I'm good and drunk and trusting. I know this sham.

The whole time, I'm watching them. Trying to trick them— that'll be a risk. I know it. But I can read them. The twist of a mouth. Way they hold their cards. There's answers in that, stuff that tells me who has a good hand and who doesn't. Who's lying and who isn't.

We're all friends here. We keep playing.

Two rounds later, I'm ready to strike. I wager like I did before. I lose once. They comfort me. Say it happens to everyone. Ask me if I want another drink. I'll win one more, then lose worse in a moment. But then. Then I'll surprise them. I'll turn their game on them and take all their coin from their hands. Show them I'm no easy mark. They're trying to con me, but I'm going to be the one to con them.

But first I try to make nice. I say I'll get the drinks this time. They protest. But I insist. They tell me I'm good, a good young man. I get up, taking most of my coin off the table. "So I can get you good wine, like you got for me," I say, earnest. They laugh. They don't think much of me. I go. Move through the crowd.

A hand grabs my sleeve.

"Don't fight me now," a voice says. But it's not a threat. It's not the fake friendly of the men, either. "You don't want to make them angry. And you're going to. The second you win, you'll have a knife in your belly, and no one here'll defend you."

I'm not scared of knives. But I'm no fool. I look at the boy who's got me. He's my age, maybe. Hard to tell. Bony-faced, tall, nose freckled. Brown as me, but different. African. He tugs my sleeve again.

"Come on," he says. "If you want ale, we'll get it somewhere else."

"I don't want ale," I say. "I want to win more money."

"Then win it from people you can fight," he says. "Not them. Come *on*."

Most of my money's in my pocket, but not all. Thinking of leaving what's on the table makes my teeth itch. But thinking of a knife in the belly gets me moving.

I follow him out. We walk fast together. Uneven streets, wet now from rain I didn't hear. Lights mirrored on it. Makes everything look strange. I think, if he's tricking me, I can take him. I've still got my knife. Sold the sickle a while back, when I was still on the road to Liverpool, but the knife's reliable. He said those men would gut me? Well, I can gut him too. He's given me ideas.

But he doesn't turn on me. He gets me somewhere I can see water. Not open sea, but a closed-up dock, keeping the water level under ships. I realize I'm looking at the Mersey. All river, no sea, though we've got the sea's ships in front of us. Still, the smell of salt's here, and something else. City smell. He exhales, all at once.

"James," he says, offering me his hand. "But you can call me Jamie. Everyone does."

I take it. We shake.

"Heathcliff," I say.

"Where did you learn sharping?" Jamie asks. "You almost fooled them."

Hindley taught me. He didn't mean to. He didn't like me, but he liked gambling. Liked cards and dice and drink, and sometimes I could observe a game or two. When he was really drunk he could be nice or deadly. I'd watch him: if his hand went for his cards, if he slurred out my name, I'd come sit. Cut the deck for him. Learn.

His friends all cheated him. Men from the village. Gentlemen from his school days. He didn't see how they looked at him when they bled him dry, hungry and disgusted all at once. But I did. And I learned.

I shake my head. "They would have knifed me."

"You asking me? Yeah, they would have done it. Isaiah and his men are okay sharpers, but you spend your time shamming laborers, and you get to be ruthless. Laborers are strong, and they don't like to get tricked. Sometimes they get violent." He flexes a hand to demonstrate. "So Isaiah's men know how to fight. You *could* be a better sharper, but you'd best learn to be smarter before you risk your neck like that again."

My stomach feels hot. I don't like being a fool. Don't even want to thank him, but I make myself do it.

He shrugs, scuffing a boot against stone. "We have to watch out for each other."

We. Like we're the same. I stay quiet.

He starts walking again. I follow. We walk side by side, mirroring steps.

"You're not a farmhand," he says eventually. "Not their usual mark. I knew it. Second I saw you, I knew."

"Saw," I repeat flatly. Think of my skin and his. "What did you see?"

"You've got scarred hands," he says, easy and quiet. Like we're friends, just talking. "Maybe you're running from a bad master? An owner? I hear law's changed on that, but you'd never know it here."

"I've got no master," I bite out.

"Says nothing about you if you do," Jamie says. "Or . . . did. You're here now. You don't have one anymore." He goes silent, thinking. Then says, "Are you a lascar?"

"Lascar," I say, like I'm his echo.

"A sailor from the East," he explains. "But if you don't know—I guess not, right?"

I didn't need it explained. I know the word. Been called it before. *Look at him, a regular dark little lascar isn't he?* Villagers over in Gimmerton, people sitting behind me in church—I heard it whispered about me. Dripping in my ears like poison. But right now, standing by the Mersey, the word *lascar* settles on me strange, like weight on my bones. I don't know what to say, but I don't need to. Jamie's gone on speaking.

"Maybe I'm thinking wrongly. Maybe you're a rich man's bastard, cast out of your home? No?"

I don't shake my head, don't glare, but he reads the silence all the same.

"Then you're just another laborer after all. No work in your old village, so now you're here trying to make your fortune." He exhales. "Ah well. That's dull."

He stops, turning on his heel to look at me.

"You need a bed, I know a lady who's renting one," he says. "Well. Half a bed. You haven't got enough for a whole one."

I lost coin to Isaiah because this stranger interfered. But I say, "You don't know that."

His mouth twitches. Almost smiling.

"Don't fight me," he cautions, and lifts a hand up. Shows me a palmful of coins. And I jerk, touch my pocket, and realize it's lighter.

"It's yours, it's yours," he says quick, and hands it over. Pours it out so I have to reach and catch it. Can't reach for my knife at the same time. Smart of him. "But there's a lesson for you. You can do numbers and shams. That's good. But you're too soft. You'll need to learn better."

He looks at me, waiting. Maybe he wants me to ask him to teach me.

I say nothing.

"Come on," he says eventually. "I'll show you what you can rent."

I've got pride. But I'm tired, head heavy. I don't say no. I keep on walking. Don't even turn back and walk away when he says, all casual, "Where are you from anyway? I can ask." Quick grin. "My da's a sailor. Kru, from the Pepper Coast. It's part of Africa," he adds when I stare at him. He says it like he's said it plenty before. Like people often don't know. "Ma's Irish. What about you?"

"I don't know," I say lowly. It's not true. Not a lie either though.

"Right," he says. He doesn't look pitying. Good. I'd have fought him, if he'd pitied me. "Well, maybe one day you'll figure it out."

I lie in my half bed. A stranger lies next to me, silent. Someone in another bed's snoring loud. I can't sleep.

My pockets are lighter, a frightening kind of light, because I paid for a month in full. This is the best I could get. Half a bed, in a house that takes men who aren't white. Aren't "properly English," is what the landlord said. So, this is where I'll stay.

I hesitated. Didn't want to pay so much. But the landlord said to me, "You can stay here, laddie, or you can stay in a cellar." He pointed down. Like I don't know where cellars are. "It'll only cost you a penny a night, if money's your worry, but you'll get dirty water up to the knee whenever it rains. Some places put beds high up on bricks, but not all, and that doesn't help the smell—"

"I'll take the half bed," I said, cutting off his words.

"Good choice," he said to me. I paid up.

The only light's from rushlights—reeds burning in holders. The sheets are musty. The air's got a thick smell, sweet mold, coal smoke. I lie awake and think. Can't stop thinking.

Cathy . . . Where am I from?

I shouldn't ask you. You don't know.

Most of the time, I never cared, not knowing. I wanted to be where you were. Home was the Heights. Home was *you*. But I wondered, sometimes. And now there's no you for me anymore, I wonder almost always.

When I was a boy, I lived in this city. I don't remember much now. But I was hungry. The kind of hunger that eats you. You start seeing your own ribs. You want to sleep all the time.

It was your father who found me, Cathy. Stopped dead in the

street. Looked at me, eyes big as plates. He thought he knew where I came from. It made him act strange. Made him carry me home under his coat, telling me he'd give me a new family. He fed me, too. First time he did, it made me sick. After that, he was careful. Small bites only. Meat pie, still hot—just a piece of crust, a sliver of the gravy from inside. A bit of bread. Maybe I don't remember my life, but I remember how good bread was.

He told me I'd get porridge in my new home. He told me what it'd be like. Milky, so thick you could stand a spoon up in it. As a treat, it'd have a pat of butter in it, he said. Or black treacle. Sweet, sticky. Hearing that made me hungrier. Made me eat my food fast again, not scared of getting sick.

I remember him watching me eat, like his eyes were starving for it.

He asked me my name. I didn't answer. Don't know what I would have answered now. That's long gone.

"Heathcliff," he said. "I'll name you Heathcliff." Ran a hand over my hair. "That was my firstborn's name."

I didn't ask if his firstborn was dead. Hearing him, I already knew.

He took me home. Tucked up in his coat, then let me tumble out. I remember how you looked at me. You and Hindley. Even Nelly, standing back like a good servant. All of you suspicious.

Your mother was angry with him. Took your father into another room. I was washed clean, Nelly reluctantly scrubbing me neat, dirt swirling in water. And you and Hindley were scolded for pinching me and laughing at me. You were sent to bed.

But me, I was left on the stairs by Nelly. She's more hard-hearted than she likes people to know. But she didn't think I was people then. She said I was a nuisance. Called me names. She thought I was from traveling people. Told me I should go away and find my own kind, because we weren't built for houses, only for stealing and running.

I didn't go. I waited. She left me alone, and then I walked over, quiet, following your father's voice. Listened, instead.

"He was hungry." Your father. "In India," he said, and stopped.

I thought, what does India have to do with me?

Your mother sighed.

"So natives starved," she said. "It is sad, certainly. But you take things far too much to heart."

"A man must atone for his errors," your father said. "Perhaps God sent him to me, an Indian to replace the ones the Company allowed to perish—"

"You don't even know if he's Indian," she said, sharp. "Poor creature, it could be anything. He could be an abandoned slave."

"No one treats anything valuable the way he was treated."

"*Escaped slave*, then. You should take him back and see if he belongs to anybody."

I heard a noise. Creak of a chair.

"You don't know what it was like, my dear," he said. "What we did."

She sighed again. "And how will you hide the truth about this child?"

"You bribe the right people, you can do anything," your father said. "It was easy enough before. A few parish records altered, a kindly clerk or two . . ."

"You had more money then. *We* had money enough to make things true. And still every day I worry about our babies. I worry someone will look at them and know. But they are so fair and so well formed. I am thankful for it. But he . . . he is so *dark*." Her voice lowered. "We cannot treat him as our own. And we cannot have him here. What if someone looks at him and . . . knows?"

So dark. It struck me hard, that. *So dark*. I'd kept back, but now I peered in. If I am so dark, I thought, the shadows'll hide me. The shadows and me are the same.

"I made a promise to love them," she said. Pale, faded woman. I thought, her children don't look like her. Don't have her thin nose, her thinner mouth. If I looked at their faces in a puddle next to mine—if water washed us all to shaky grays, turning our skin the same—we'd look more like each other than like her. "By my promise, I should drive that whelp out of my home."

Your father looked at her. Slumped in a chair, he raised his head. His face was stone.

"This is my home," he said. "You've said your piece. Enough now."

"I won't promise to love him."

"*Enough*."

I went back to the stairs. Sat there until dawn.

I've never told you, Cathy. Even after he died, and we sat and cried over losing him. I never told you. But he named me for his dead firstborn, so maybe you should have guessed. He took me in because of the dead. Because of ghosts. Because we were the same, Cathy. You, me. Hindley.

I don't know where I'm from. But I know where you're from. I know all your secrets.

Even the ones you don't know yourself.

Chapter Four

Catherine

EDGAR AND ISABELLA ARE MISERABLE. They are always miserable, of course, because they are in mourning, but they are especially miserable today, because I am leaving. They don't want me to go. Isabella clings to me, pressing her face against my shoulder. Even though I am older than her, she is taller and still growing, and has to stoop down to do it. Her curls tickle my nose.

"Don't cling so, Isabella," I say. But I hug her in return, and then brush back her curls so that I can breathe more freely. "I will only be at the Heights. I can visit you in the blink of an eye. You won't miss me at all."

"Can I visit you whenever I like, Cathy?" Isabella asks with a sniffle. "We can eat cakes and drink tea together and—Oh, you can show me your room, and the fairy cave you told me about. I would like that."

I can see Edgar over her shoulder. Our eyes meet.

"Catherine will come here to us," he says to Isabella. "We will have tea and cakes here. You're the mistress of the house now, Isabella," he goes on, when she continues to cling. "It will be good practice for you."

Isabella is calmed by this and is finally convinced to release me. Edgar moves to stand by my side. He looks very pale in his mourning colors, almost more sickly than I do. We must have made quite a strange sight to visitors who came with condolences: tall, weeping Isabella and ghost-pale Edgar, and me.

Maybe visitors thought it strange to see me sitting beside them, as if I were family, or already married to Edgar. It was improper, I expect, for me to be there at all. Edgar certainly thought so. He tried to convince me to convalesce in bed when visitors came, but I insisted that I would keep both him and Isabella company.

"I won't let you suffer alone," I said. "I should be there to grieve with you both. Don't argue with me, Edgar."

Even though Edgar hated to anger me, it looked as if he *would* argue. But when Isabella clutched my hand and begged him to let me stay—*Oh, please, please*—he wilted.

Visitors certainly gave me odd looks. But if they thought anything was amiss, they did not say it. Besides, it is obvious I have been ill. I have grown much thinner. When Nelly dresses me she must lace my stays tighter, or there is no support in them at all. And I am *very* good at grief. I sat by Edgar and

Isabella and wept when they wept, looking very sad and fragile all the while. It was very easy, really. All I had to do was think of Heathcliff and my eyes welled up for me.

"Catherine," Edgar says now, voice tentative, as if he wants to ask me something. But when I look at him, his eyes are only as sad as ever. He shakes his head.

"You'll be glad to be home, I expect," he says.

I cannot tell him the truth, which is yes. I shall be very glad to be home, but I am also full of dread over it. So I grip his sleeve instead, and squeeze, then release it. I smile at him.

"Let's go, Edgar," I say. "I don't want to keep everyone waiting."

Edgar was worried about me riding home, but I insisted. I am glad I did. I've missed the wind on me. It is cold and bitterly sharp, stinging my face. On horseback, I can see the way the grass moves with the wind, rolling like water—and the splashes of color that mark gorse and heather. Over my head the sky is cloudless, and birds are wheeling about. For the first time since I awoke surrounded by the yellow chinoiserie, I feel free again.

It isn't long before I glimpse the Heights. Set high, it is very dark against the blue sky behind it. But my heart opens at the sight of it, and even though my heart is full of an awful misery better left sealed, I can't help but smile.

I love the Grange very much. It's a beautiful place. I like to walk around surrounded by the long curtains and the fine wallpaper and candelabras as if I am bathing in sunshine. It warms you right through when you're surrounded by such wealth. The Lintons have heaps of it, and enough to spare for everyone, so I feel no guilt over enjoying it at all. But the Heights is home, and even when I marry Edgar, the Heights will keep all the parts of me that I cannot take with me. Most parts of me, really. I cannot be a talkative hell fiend, not fit for human company, always running barefoot on the moors, *and* be Mrs. Linton. I know that.

The Heights is all gray, austere whinstone; my home is neither as large as the Grange nor as small as any laborer's cottage. It is a perfectly respectable gentleman's home in size and shape, but somehow it has always been strange. Perhaps it is the gargoyles carved over the door, weather-beaten so that their faces are faded, nothing but flat eyes and gouged teeth, that make home look so very odd. Or maybe the way the house leans, like the trees do, as if the wind has made it bend.

When we were small I would sometimes tell Heathcliff that the Heights was a fairy creation, no different from the cave beneath the crags that we had so often explored together—built one night by unearthly, luminous hands and left behind for mortals to stumble upon. Sometimes I told him those tales by moonlight, or on the cold floor of my room with one lit candle set on the ground between us. The beeswax would melt and waft sweet coils of smoke like fingers between us, the flame turning Heathcliff's eyes as gold as a polished guinea. I told him so many times and so passionately that I truly believed it, and Heathcliff liked me too much to tell me that I was being a silly girl, telling silly tales.

Heathcliff has always treated everything I say as if it matters. No one else does.

Although I know better now than to believe the Heights is special, home still has the look of an enchanted ruin. Now I have come from the Grange, which is new and shining, I cannot help but notice how shabby home is.

There aren't many servants left at the Heights, but sour-faced Joseph—who beat me often as a child, and told me exactly how ungodly I was—is waiting with a few others, face pinched as ever. But he says nothing rude—says nothing at all, actually—so I am sure my brother has told him to behave. Hindley is trying to make a good show of it, I expect.

My little nephew must have watched our approach from the window because I hear a shriek of joy and then see him run out of the door.

I should greet the servants like a proper lady does, but when I dismount from my horse I lean down and press my face to my nephew's head instead. I suppose a proper lady would kiss him daintily on the forehead or the cheek—no, I *know* a proper lady would do exactly that, because I have seen how Isabella behaves.

Instead, I kiss him, and pinch his cheek, and say, "Well, have you missed me, then, Hareton?"

"No," he lies boldly.

I hear a noise from the door, and as Edgar dismounts and helps Nelly down too, I lift my head and see my brother.

Hareton may be all wild energy, but today Hindley is the opposite. He comes out of the house sedately, as regal as any

35

king. As if we will all wait for him. The servants, Hareton, me. Even Edgar, who is waiting politely enough, even though by his fine clothes alone you can tell he is too good for the likes of us.

We are not wealthy people. Not like the Lintons. I wear pretty gowns, it's true, that make me look rich. Silks and lace, hats with tall feathers, necklaces and other fine things. But a gown is an investment in all our futures, or so Hindley says. I must marry well, after all. But all the grand fortune my father earned from his travels abroad has been used up, mostly by Father. The few fine things we have left from him—silks and cottons and other strange gossamer fabrics, jewels set in gold, and little lacquer boxes—are all carefully locked away out of sight. Hindley cannot stand to look at them just as much as I could never stand to see them sold, so locked away they remain. I am not sure even Nelly has seen them.

Hindley is dressed neatly. Often when we are alone at home he sits in nothing but his shirt and breeches and mulls over his cups. But today his hair is washed and combed. His clothes are clean, too. I feel relief run right through me when he walks toward me and I realize his gaze is clear and calm, as if he isn't angry for once at all, and hasn't touched a drop of drink.

My relief doesn't last long, of course. Edgar has already forced a smile on his face despite his grief and is saying something polite—what, I don't know, but I suppose it hardly matters—when my brother abruptly cuffs Hareton around the ear. Hareton yelps and clutches his head. Nelly makes a noise too, but when I look at her, she has pressed her lips tightly together, looking away. I am sure she will comfort Hareton later, feeding him something sweet in the kitchen to soothe his hurt feelings.

"I told you not to run, boy," Hindley says gruffly. "What will Mr. Linton think of our family now?"

I feel Edgar look at me, even if I do not see it. But both of us are silent as Hindley takes me by the shoulders and looks me over critically.

"Well, you won't die after all," my brother says, sounding satisfied. "Though you've grown thin, Cathy."

"The doctor said I could only eat gruel," I tell him.

Hindley snorts. He doesn't think much of doctors anymore, not since the local physician let Hindley's wife die from birthing Hareton.

"We'll get you real food," he says. Then he pats my shoulder and releases me.

Nelly ushers me and a now sullen Hareton swiftly into the house, as my brother strides over to Edgar. The last I hear is my brother saying, "Linton, my condolences. Losing your family's a sorry business . . ."

And then the door is shut behind us by Nelly's firm hands, and she urges me equally as firmly to go and rest.

Despite Nelly's strict orders to go to bed, I walk around the house instead. I know Hindley will be some time talking to Edgar. Besides, I want to say hello to my own home. I skim my fingers across the walls. Tap my feet against the floor. Hareton trots after me, a stubborn shadow.

Home is where you go to bury things. I have always thought so anyway. At home I can be strange and foolish, angry and wicked, and tell stories that make Joseph mutter and stomp outdoors and Hindley threaten to take a switch to me like I am a child. Whenever I leave the Heights, I must leave all those pieces of me behind. I leave them in the gaps between the stones of the walls, where the wind creeps in. I leave them in the roots of the tree outside my bedroom window, the one that taps fingers against the glass. And I leave them in the books I keep by my bed.

It makes me happy, thinking that a wild version of myself still lives inside my home, even when I am not there. When I am elsewhere and being good, she gets to rattle around inside the Heights. I hope she breaks all of Hindley's wine bottles one day.

Eventually, Nelly finds me and hounds me to my room. I undress and clamber into bed. I am not remotely tired, but I do as I'm told, closing my eyes and curling up beneath the blankets.

I can hear it when Hareton creeps in. My bed is an old-fashioned type, a closet that closes up, so the only light I have comes through the window, or from my own candle. People can walk in and out of my bedroom and I can still be hidden away. Hareton scratches his fingernails at the wood, wanting me to let him in. I don't move.

"Shouldn't you be with Nelly?" I ask. "She'll be cross."

"Story," he whispers.

"I want to sleep," I say peevishly.

Hareton scratches the wood again, more harshly.

I sigh, and stare at the window. I can see the shape of the tree outside, the branches bare, a clouded brown through the glass.

"Fine. But you'll have to sit out there, and you'll get cold and uncomfortable, and I won't let you in here if you complain."

He agrees and sits on the ground with an excited scuff of feet.

I love Hareton, but I know I have very little patience with children. Sometimes I think of what it will be like when I am married to Edgar. I will have to have babies, I expect. Isn't that what wives are meant to do? But the thought of it makes my stomach squirm.

"Once," I say to Hareton, "there was no house here at all. And then fairies came, and plucked the grass, mixed it with dreams from little boys' heads, and began to make magical stones . . ."

Eventually, I hear Hareton begin to snore quietly. I stop talking. I'll have to wake him soon and give him to Nelly, or I'll be stuck with him, and he will have to share my bed. I can't leave him on the cold floor, anyway. But I decide he can wait a moment longer.

I unlatch the window. One thin branch, narrow like a spindle, quivers in the wind and bends in through the open window. It looks like it's waving at me. If I close my eyes tight at night, I sometimes dream that the shivering branches are hands tapping at the glass with sharp little fingers, scrabbling to get in.

I am good at telling tales. To others, or to myself, if there is no one around who will sit still and listen to me. Some of them are true, and some are not, but I am not always sure anymore which ones are lies.

I do know this: I know the Heights is not fairy-made. I know that Father bought the Heights with money from India. He made his fortune there, and then he came home, and brought Mother and Hindley and me here to live a quiet life outside of Gimmerton village, far away from his old one. He never cared for wealthy circles and friends, though I expect he could have had them once. By the time I knew anything of his past, most of the riches were gone.

Father always worried about fitting in. He warned me from when I was very small: don't tell anyone about the silks locked away in the house, or someone will call us a family of nabobs, and we will be mocked for our connections to India and never accepted. Don't speak nonsense words with Hindley, or people will think you're dim-witted and look down on us all. Don't run so much, Cathy, or folk will say you're wild and ill-mannered. Cathy, sit still!

I think Father was haunted by India. He would get a faraway look in his eyes sometimes and be overcome with a sadness I couldn't understand.

So it was very strange when Father brought Heathcliff home.

I think of the day Heathcliff arrived, now, and how Heathcliff looked: how small and thin he was, and how different from me. Because he was a boy, and poor, and hungry, and because he had skin like the warm heart of a tree, and thick, fierce eyebrows, and hair like nighttime. No one was meant to know that Father was a nabob, a man who'd made his fortune in India, but no one could miss that Heathcliff was a stranger. He even refused to speak English unless he was forced to, even though I was sure he knew it as well as I did. He flung strange words at us the way a hurt animal uses teeth and claws to keep your hands away from it. Everything that haunted Father was returned and alive in Heathcliff. And maybe that was why Hindley hated him, and even Mother too.

But I didn't fear him, and I had no past to haunt me. When I looked at Heathcliff, I just thought . . . oh, if I'm truthful I thought nothing at first. I was just angry that Father had come home so late. He had broken the riding crop I asked for as a gift, and I was pettily furious. But later, I looked at the anger in Heathcliff's face, and the pride in his chin, and the way he looked at *me*, and I liked him. I simply liked him. There was nothing that scared me about him. I liked him so much it was as if I had been waiting my whole life to meet him.

And if he is gone forever, if he never returns to me . . . I will spend my whole life waiting for him to come back.

I squeeze my eyes tight to stop the tears. I won't cry. Instead, I'll tell myself a tale. Something true.

I curl my fingers around a branch, the spindle-thin one that reached for me first, and think, *If there's any magic in this house at all, then it will bring Heathcliff home to me. It will bring him home.*

And there *is* magic. How else could he have come into my life in the first place?

41

Chapter Five

Heathcliff

IT'S EASIER THAN I EXPECT, getting to fight. I ask the man renting the same bed as me in the lodging house. He's scarred up, smoking a pipe. His name's John, and he was a soldier once. American, a loyalist, he tells me, one of the enslaved men promised freedom if he fought. He got his freedom, but now he's here—paying for half a bed. Getting work on the docks where he can find it. Though there's not much welcome for Black men, he tells me. Not on the docks, not anywhere.

"Or for men like you either," he warns me.

From the look on him—the way he holds his pipe, his frown—it's not the life he wanted. But he's practical, steady. He tells me he's done prizefighting before, so he knows where to go. This isn't legal fighting, John tells me bluntly, so fights move about. But those who want to know can find out where the next fight's going to be. News moves through taverns and gin shops, coffeehouses and dockside. John says he's good at getting knowledge like that.

"I know people. Plenty of people, and I get handed plenty of information I could do a hell of a lot with. The problem," he tells me, even though I don't ask, "is that I've got an excess of morals. And that's left me here."

"I'll take any information you want to share," I say to him.

He looks me over levelly, and says, "Let's stick to prizefighting, son. But I wouldn't do that neither if I were you." He puts emphasis on the *you*. But I wait, saying nothing, and he tells me where to go.

I'm at a warehouse near the docks. There's fish stored round here. Stinking, half-rotten, rheumy eyes on them. That's where I meet the men who run things. Who make blood sports happen, with dogs and roosters, and run fights between people. Eight of them, sitting on boxes. Arms on knees. Pipe smoke all coiling round their heads. They look like I expect. Friendly, but menacing friendly. You don't cross men like them.

One looks up, eyes going narrow, and another stands up. He's got a knife out. The rest go tense when he moves, some reaching for weapons. But one stays still. Hands clasped. Watching. He's got a blue sailor's jacket on and a kerchief round his neck. But he's no sailor. That's one to fear. That's the fixer—the one in charge.

"I don't know you," the man with the knife says. His nose is broken. Right cheek pockmarked. "What're you doing here?"

I stand tall. "I want to be a fighter."

Someone snorts and mutters, "You and every bloody child in this city."

"I'm sixteen," I say, though that gets them grinning. Mocking me. "Old enough."

The fixer says, "You're skinny." He says it all critical.

"Strong though," I tell him. "I can prove it."

Silence. They look between them. One chuckles, low. The pockmarked one with the knife puts it down and says, "Let's see, then. If you last a minute, maybe we'll see how you do in a proper match."

Everything about him is confident. He knows he can break me. I look at him, as he gets his coat off, rolls up his sleeves, and I know it too. But a minute's not so long. I get my fists up.

I last a while. But it's ugly. A fist grazing my cheek. Another going for under my chin. That'll break my jaw, I know. But I throw myself left. Drive my elbow into the side of his neck. He swears, then laughs as he grabs my hair, gripping me in a headlock. I squirm out.

Someone laughs again. "Like an eel," they say. "Look at him go."

I get free, but he shoves me down flat to the ground, getting my hands behind me. Pins me for a second, knee to the back.

There's a clap from someone. "Let him up," a voice says.

I'm let go. We stand.

The fixer in the sailor's jacket is still sitting, watching. He says to me, "That was two minutes. But you are too skinny, boy. You'll be stronger when you get older, maybe. Maybe not."

I think these men will turn me away. But then he smiles.

Pleased. "We always need someone who can take a punch," he tells me. "Someone who can lose when we tell him to lose."

I tell them, "I'm good at that, if I'm paid for it."

The next fight's that evening. The warehouse fills right up. Howling people making wagers. The fixer smoking a tobacco pipe. Me, taking off my shirt. Binding my hands up. I get told rules as I ready myself.

"Don't hit below the waist," the pockmarked man says, sounding bored. "If you go down on your knees or lower, you lose your round. You lose the whole match when you don't get back up for a new round. You understand?"

I nod. Say nothing.

He looks at the crowd, then adds, "But if the crowd's happy, there's no rules. And if you go down before round two or after, you won't get paid."

I look at the crowd. Most are normal—poor, tired, clothes shabby. I see mostly men. Some women. There are a few rich folk, hair high, clothes gleaming. They've got bloodthirst in their eyes. I know what the crowd's going to want.

"Fine," I say shortly.

The other fighter's bigger than me. He's angry.

"You give me a little boy to beat?" he yells at the man. "You know how stupid this makes me look?"

The pockmarked man doesn't care, only shrugs and tells him to make it quick, then.

"But keep it entertaining," he warns. That's what matters to him, to the whole lot of them. "People want a good time."

No one expects me to win. I look at the fighter, big and scarred and maybe ten years older than me, his nose cracked to one side, and don't expect it either. Fixer doesn't want me to win anyway. I'm here to lose. I just need to go two rounds.

Still, I try to hold my own.

I move fast. At least I'm quick. Dodging his fists. The first round lasts long enough the crowd's yelling and the other fighter's getting frustrated, pouring sweat, teeth bared. But he gets me in the end—a blow round the face where I'm already bruised. I go down. Knees hit the ground hard. He spits. The round's lost.

Second round comes, and he punches at me. Fists fast, aiming for my head. I weave away from him.

He kicks me in the leg, trying to get me off my feet. He gets my knee. I feel pain—a hot burst of it—but no one stops us. The crowd's yelling, screaming. Rules don't matter if they're enjoying themselves, and they are. I suck in a breath, and get myself steady. I don't go down.

I dodge him. Then I rear at him, fist tight. Get him hard in the nose.

Blood's hot on my fist. It feels good.

There's even more rules to boxing than I was told, if it's done to entertain gentlemen and ladies. When your father was still trying to make a gentleman's son of me, I learned that. They like to wager over sports that look fair. Fair even if there's blood and broken bones. You can punch here but not there.

Hurt someone like this, but not like that. I guess blood's better for gentlemen when they get to say how it's spilled.

But here's sport for normal people. And they know there's no such thing as fair. I hear cheering when I get the bigger man, when he stumbles back, swearing, clutching his face. But they scream even louder when he rears up and hits me hard in the gut. When I go down, he kicks at my head, and no one stops him. Crowd's so loud their noise is drowning me. I've got to get my arms round my own skull and wait it out, until the boots stop.

I don't get up for the next round. And then it's done.

I get coin though. "Come back again and you might get more," says the pockmarked man. Behind him, the fixer nods.

I tell him I will. I wait until I'm outside to double over. Breathe through my aching ribs.

After I lose, I go walking. And thinking.

I've been hurt plenty. Punched. Kicked. Threatened with a knife. A gun. Once, a broken chair leg. All Hindley, during his rages. That's familiar.

Being hurt by a stranger felt new. He didn't hate me. Just wanted his money. He was vicious, but so was I. It felt . . . cleaner.

But pain's pain. Not long before I start limping. My ribs hurt. Face feels hot from swelling up. Now that my heart's not pounding for the fight I'm getting tired, and there's a mean feeling in my chest. It was a cleaner kind of fighting, but I'm still angry over it. I should have done better. Should have punched harder. Should have aimed for the fighter's gut first, his shoulder second. I saw how he held it. Hunched. Hiding an old wound.

Next time I'll be better. The crowd—they'll look at me and think I'll lose. Wager against me. Maybe they'll laugh. I don't care. Next time I'll know I could have won, even if I lose for coin. Even then.

I should go back to my half-rented bed, but I don't want to. I think of lying flat and hurting and angry, listening to the man on the bed to the left snoring. I think, and keep on walking somewhere else. Where, I don't know yet.

City's big and small all at once. Houses on the main streets are all clean and tidy. The courts of poor homes, tall and narrow and stuffed with people from cellar to roof, are hidden behind them. But street-facing or court-hidden, the houses have all got the same smoke round them. Same noise and same clothes hung out drying, strung over alleys dark as pitch. No paving on those alleys. Slip through one, and the walls close round you. You're in a road so black and narrow that you could be anywhere and nowhere.

Nowhere. I laugh to myself. Stuff a hand between my teeth, muffling me quiet.

Nowhere.

Makes sense, doesn't it? I'm right back where I belong.

Cathy. Do you remember when I tried to run the first time?

I remember. Not all of it. Some though. I remember . . . misery. Feeling homesick. The Heights wasn't home then. Liverpool was home. Maybe I craved running down dark alleys the way you crave running on the moors, seeing with your feet, the wind on you. But all I remember now is craving and not having. Missing something.

First night, Nelly left me on the stairs. But the second, Nelly was away, sent off for a day or two because your father was angry with her. He gave me a room. All mine.

"This is your home," he told me. But I thought I knew better.

I waited. Night was deep when I got up. I would have thieved bread from the kitchen, but I was scared of the dog.

So I just ran.

It was a good night for running. No rain. Not too cold. I remember the stars. Don't think I'd seen them so bright and clear before. Sight of them made me stop before I even reached the gate.

Maybe that gave you time to creep out after me. You were so quiet, Cathy. I didn't hear you until you were right behind me.

"Stop," you said. Stamped your foot. Dull thud—barely any noise at all, because you'd got no shoes. Your feet were bare, mud on them, ankles white like bone. "Stop! You can't go!"

But I'd already stopped. I was looking at you.

"If you go," you said, "you'll become a ghost."

"Die," I said. Throat scratchy. I hadn't spoken proper since the first night, when I'd screamed my lungs out, keeping you all distant by shoving words at you that you didn't know. That made your mother's face go all tight, fearful. I shouted so many words I don't know anymore. Language I've lost. "You mean, I'll die."

"Nooo." You stretched the word out. Your eyes were so big, black as anything. "You're a stranger. You don't know here. You'll get lost and then you'll wander the moors forever and ever, and some nights I'll hear you wailing." You cupped your hand round your mouth. Wailed out. I heard it echo back and forth, stretching out like an animal noise.

You took a step toward me. Mouth still open, feet making no sound. You could have been a ghost if you hadn't been the most alive thing I've ever seen. Flushed face. Hair all tangled up, wind in it. Made me want to reach out. Touch.

I didn't though.

"I've seen ghosts before," you confessed.

Maybe you lied. But me, I believed you.

"Seen ghosts who . . . scream. And their feet won't touch the ground, they're all backward—"

I said a word, one I knew then. It's gone now. Sore absence is all I've got, like a milk tooth lost. But you stopped breathing for a second. You said it back. Nodded, slow.

"Yes," you said. "Those kinds of ghosts."

It was like we'd always known each other, Cathy. Like what came before didn't matter. Maybe that's why I don't remember now. Why there's only dark and nowhere in me, before you. You came and found me, and I let the rest go. Easy as that. All my life led to you. To a word I can't remember, and you reaching out. Grabbing my hand.

"I'm going home," I told you, even though I didn't want to. Not anymore. "My ma . . ."

I didn't finish. Wind was howling. It stole my words right away. And what the words were, I don't know anymore.

I only know you looked right at me. Gripped on tighter. "We'll make this your home."

So we walked. You and me, searching. I didn't know for what. You did. You crouched low by the fences and clucked your teeth. Reached down and lifted a feather up.

"Lapwing," you announced, all serious. "Pigeon's better, but we'll make do."

You tucked it in my jacket. Right over my heart. Said, "Soul's can't go if there's feathers." And I'd never heard that, but I nodded. Believed you.

Nights and days went. You and me found feathers in the barn. Outdoors, caught in high grass. From shot-down birds, fresh game hung up for plucking and butchering. Hindley glared. Nelly muttered. But your father was pleased we were becoming friends.

No one caught us, two weeks later. Moon was full, and we went out. Crouched under the tree at your window. Buried feathers in a circle right there under it, peeling up dirt with our fingernails. You bit off a lock of my hair. I stayed still as you took it. You cut your own too, your teeth white on your brown curls. I would have done it. Leaned over, torn it for you. But you didn't ask. You twined them together, black and brown. Then we buried it in the middle.

"There," you said. Voice all satisfied. "Now you can't go."

Some might say that was a child's game. But I know better. Something settled in me. Put down roots.

Cathy. I shouldn't be able to run from you. My soul's bound up at the Heights. That's true enough. I got tied there, with soil and feathers. Stories and words we shouldn't have rightly known. With you.

But I've still run. And every step I take pulls another root out.

Nowhere spits me out. It's sudden. I wrench one foot in front of the other, and the dark ends. The road widens up. There's lights. I look around me.

I thought the city was all the same. But here's different. Big buildings. Posh stone, the kind that's got a gleam on it, all soft yellows and shining whites. People move easy, laughing, smiling. Carriages gliding like birds on water.

So. This is what wealth looks like.

The Lintons are one kind of rich. Big lands, big house. But this isn't one big house. Not even one street. Rich here's different. I see carriages painted up gold. Fine-dressed men. Got on powdered wigs, black buckled boots. Women in big skirts, silk and ribboned up. The kind of silk even you don't wear, Cathy. I'd steal it for you, if I could.

I don't see any brown skin. Everyone's pale. Whiter than the stone round them, whiter than fresh milk. No one here's bleeding from a split lip or limping either. I can't stay here. Got to keep moving, and fast.

Being here makes my teeth hurt. It's hunger, that hurt. I want it like bread, like porridge still stove-hot, butter- or treacle-rich. I want to be wealthy. Want money, and the right to be in a place with wide roads, walking like they belong to me.

I just got beaten for measly coin. But I don't want scraps. I want *this*.

I get to a square. It's big, paved gray. A building's ahead of me, bigger than any I've seen. I go to it. Read the name over it. *Playhouse Theatre*.

I limp away from it. Keeping my distance. Like I'm not fit to be near it.

I stop by a night house. Kind of tavern that never sleeps. But the ones I've known stink of ale, beer, gin. Old, settled-in smell, kind that can't be washed out. But this one's shining. Oil lamps hanging. Doors spilling open. A statue in an alcove's out front, carved out to look like some wealthy man. He's got a severe face.

A beggar's playing a pipe under it. The music's winding. Gets under my skin. But I won't part with coin, so I don't look him in the eye. I keep on.

My limp's getting heavier.

The music stops—one long, slow note that quiets. I hear scuttling. Quick footsteps. Feel a hand on my arm.

"Bhaiya," the man says. Then something else. Something I don't know. I catch snatches. Half words, like echoes. "Wait—"

I wrench away from him. It's not hard. He's older than me, I think, but small. Wiry. Doesn't seem like he wants a fight, because he lets me go.

He says more words I don't understand. I tell him so. He blinks and makes a noise. Apologetic. Don't need a shared tongue to understand that. But he's still looking right at me, still got his eyes fixed. Deep brown. Narrowed.

All that sorry noise, but his eyes are judges.

He says something else. Another language I don't know. Never heard so many worlds out of one person.

I shake my head. "I know English. Nothing else."

The sorry noise dries up fast. He sucks his teeth.

"You came on a ship?" he asks me. "Which one? Who is your serang?"

"Serang," I repeat.

The word itches something in my skull. A lascar word. Don't know how I'm sure it is, but it is.

Or maybe I do know. Maybe I knew the second Jamie asked me if I was one. I've got lascar blood in me.

The beggar—the lascar—is looking at me and measuring me up.

"I'm no lascar," I tell him levelly. "I'm from here."

I could tell him I come from soil, not sea. If I'm from across waters, I don't know about it. All I've got is half memories. Guesses and ghosts.

I could say, *Give me another language. Stick a few more words through my ribs. Let's see what gets my heart bleeding. Help me work out what I am.*

But instead I stay unfriendly, mouth flat. Lips tight over my teeth, so he knows I've got no welcome for him. "What do you want?" I say.

He hesitates. Regretting bothering me now, I expect. A man like him should know better. If he's been treated how I've been, he knows how hard people can be.

But he doesn't go. He pats down his jacket. Up, down. His pockets are empty. He reaches for the kerchief round his own neck, knotted up the way sailors wear them. He takes it off. Then he offers it up. When I don't take it, he touches a hand to his own cheek. Mine's sore. Might be bleeding a little.

"You've been beaten," he says.

This is the second time a stranger's fixed on me and tried to help me. But Jamie wasn't pitying. This one is. My stomach's twisting. Shame's part of it. I don't need looking after. But anger's in it too.

I'm not weak. I could show him. Scare him. My fingers are twitching, knife hungry. I could prove I'm strong.

But I don't lie to myself. I want some kindness, even though it makes me angry, wanting it.

Truth is, only you've been kind to me for years, Cathy. And even your kindness has sharp edges.

Maybe his does, too. Thinking that calms me. I take the kerchief. Press it to my face hard enough to sting. I pull it back. There's blood on it.

"Thanks," I say curtly. I offer him a coin, because a trade's a trade, and trading makes sense.

Him shaking his head and stepping back—that doesn't.

I don't like pity, if that's what this is. I grit my teeth and my cheek goes hotter, deep pain echoing down right through me.

"Don't worry about me," I say, though I don't much care if he does or not. "I chose this. I got paid."

His face does . . . something. Whatever it is this time, it's not pity. He turns the pipe between his fingers.

"You need help," he says.

"I don't." Words come out of me abrupt. Sharp. I scrunch the kerchief up tight in my fist. Got to send the feeling in me somewhere.

His forehead wrinkles. "If you need help," he insists, "then you go to Mrs. Hussain. She knows everything and everyone."

Behind him, distant, people are spilling out of the theater. All laughing, all dressed up. Music seeps out after them.

"Theater's over," the man says, stepping back. He lifts up his pipe. "I've got to work. But you go to Mann Street and ask for Mrs. Hussain. Remember."

Hussain. Haven't heard a name like that before. But still, my brain burns. Ghosts and guesses all over again.

I won't go. But I nod all the same. He nods back and jogs away.

Another man's waiting for him by that statue. Didn't see him before. He's all silent, arms crossed. Tricorn hat with coin in it on the ground right in front of him. Keeping watch, I expect. Protecting the money. He's brown, too. Younger. More like me. He doesn't nod.

I look until the crowd closes up round them. All silk skirts and powdered hair—that's all I see now. The music starts up, tinny pipe noise. I turn to go. I'm tired now. Ready for my half a bed, and sleeping until the pain wears thin.

The kerchief's still in my palm. I open my hand. Cloth's stained with my blood and it's cheap quality—faded, washed out from time, and salt water. But the cloth's strange, like I've not seen before. Stitched all over, white threads making it wrinkle up same as if it were some padded cloth for the insides of a coat, or one of Cathy's thick underskirts. But it's light, airy, and the pattern on it's meant to be seen all swirling. Curls like strange feathers, orange and red.

I think it must have traveled a long way. Across oceans. And I stare down at it before I tuck it away. Right over my heart. That's where feathers go.

Chapter Six

Catherine

"THAT BOY WAS A CURSE," Hindley says. "And I'm glad he's gone. You should be glad of it too, Cathy."

I put down my spoon. The stew is good, still piping hot and everything I'd dreamed of when I'd been on my enforced medicinal diet of gruel with a side of more gruel. But suddenly I am not hungry anymore.

It's taken Hindley far longer to bring this up than I thought it would, but I am still not prepared. I have tried to be. I had nothing else to do while lying in bed than think about what I would say to him about Heathcliff.

How can I be glad, when half my soul has been ripped away from me? I want to say that to Hindley, but I cannot. Hindley would . . . misunderstand. He's never understood how it is between Heathcliff and me.

"When Heathcliff comes back . . . ," I start.

But I don't finish, because Hindley gives a snort. It's an ugly noise, and his mouth twists into a petty sneer as he makes it, as if he thinks I have said something particularly childish.

"He won't come back, Cathy," he says in a very relaxed sort of voice.

I know it's not because he *is* relaxed, or feels nothing over Heathcliff's absence. Hindley feels deeply about everything, so much that he's always trying to drown all that emotion out. But right now, he's clearly feeling only smug joy and wants me to know it. "He knows if he shows his face here again I'll kill him."

"You won't," I say, even though I should not. My tone is too fierce for Hindley to take in the mood he's in, which is a joyful cruel mood that could tip into something much worse with no more than a change in the wind. Joseph scowls at the floor and slinks out of the room, muttering something about prayer. Nelly does not go—she will not go while Hareton is playing on the floor with one of our dog's puppies—but her eyes do widen at me in warning.

I have never let warnings stop me before. And I must keep on talking because Heathcliff will come back. He *will*. So I say, louder than I did before, "You must welcome him back, Hindley, because you owe him a debt. You told me so."

"I owe him nothing."

"If Heathcliff had not been there, Hareton would be dead and it would be your fau—"

Hindley slams his hand so hard against the table I hear the wood crack.

The mood darkens immediately. From the corner of my eye, I see Nelly pluck Hareton from the floor and carry him from the room. There is only Hindley now, and myself.

"I should take a switch to you, Cathy," he says, nostrils flaring. "If you behave like a child you should be treated like one."

"Someone should look for him," I say.

"*Cathy.*"

"You may hate him all you like, Hindley," I say, my temper rising, "but he doesn't deserve to be left with nothing!"

"Nothing's what he started with, isn't it? He had nothing, *was* nothing, before our father dragged him into this house and gave him everything." Hindley slowly uncurls his fist, which is bruised already, gone red. "He's had enough from us."

"You took away everything Father gave him," I bite out.

When Father was alive, Heathcliff was my equal in every way. And then Hindley took away his best clothes, his bedroom, his life, and made Heathcliff less than a servant. Unpaid and unloved, and reliant on Hindley's cruel charity.

"I fed him, didn't I?" Hindley demands, eyes blazing. "Kept a roof over his head? Didn't I do that?"

"And beat him," I say. "You think I don't remember the time you broke his arm?"

"That was correction," he says, "for bad behavior and a wicked nature. He should be grateful for that too, and so should you."

"I am not grateful," I say, fighting back tears. I hate that when I am angry I often cry, but what can I do? I won't stop defending Heathcliff, and I cannot defend him without feeling all my fury. So I let the tears fall and keep on talking. "Father would be *ashamed*."

Hindley looks at me. There is a blank, flat look in his eyes. Abruptly, he reaches for a plate. Lifts it up and throws it hard at the wall. It explodes into a thousand pieces. The noise makes the dog yelp and run, her puppies skittering after her.

"Say what you like," he grits out. "It changes nothing. He'll have no welcome here."

My heart is pounding, but I do not think this is fear, or even anger. Every part of me is alight and blazing, all of it for Heathcliff's sake.

The worst thing you can do is show Hindley you're afraid. It is like blood to hounds. So I do not.

"Give me money, then," I say. "If you won't seek him out, then let me go find him."

He stares at me. As if he doesn't understand.

"Hindley, give me money and allow Nelly to come with me. If not Nelly then . . . another chaperone. One of the women from the village? Oh, it doesn't matter. Just let me find him. If he does not have a home to return to then he deserves to have the money it takes to build a new one. You may not want to honor your debts, Hindley—"

He reaches across the table, smacking his palm over my mouth. I don't know if he intends to do it hard but he does. Hard enough that my lips sting against my teeth, and my eyes burn.

"Shut your mouth, Cathy. Be silent, for once in your life. God, will you risk a beating for that dog?"

Heathcliff is not a dog. I wish Hindley would not call him that, but he does it so often. Every time he calls Heathcliff names, my stomach turns and my skin feels hot. It is anger and shame and sickness. I bite Hindley's palm for it, and he swears, and snatches his hand back.

He should be happy I didn't draw blood.

"You animal," he starts. But I lean across the table, a palm on each side of the cracked wood.

"I am an animal, and you're an animal too," I tell him, voice a low hiss. "If Heathcliff is an animal, then we are, aren't we? We grew up together. He's as close to family as someone can be."

He grasps my jaw and forces it shut, so I won't say anymore and can't bite him either. He looks at me with that flat stare again.

"I am different from him," he says. "And different from you. I own the Heights. I own everything. What do you have?"

I say nothing. He smiles, but he's not joyful anymore, not smug. There's only malice there.

He lets me go.

"The money's mine," he says, sitting back. He sprawls, loose and easy, because he knows everything in the house is his. Including me. "And I won't spend it on him. The only thing I'll spend on him is a bullet. Now, eat your food, Cathy. And keep your mouth shut."

Slowly, I sit back. I look down. The stew has spilled over the table. There is a little left in the bowl.

I pick up my spoon. Lift it to my mouth. But I can't eat.

I throw down the spoon and stand. Hindley reaches a hand out to grab me, but I dart away. I'm glad the table is between us.

"Oh, you can throw things, but I can't? Fine, then," I say. "Fine, I'll throw myself. If I can't even throw a—a measly *spoon*, if all I have is myself, then, then—"

I don't finish. My air leaves me all at once, like my anger is a fire that has seized it all up for itself and left me nothing. Before I can say something else I'll regret, before I can tell him I will break myself if I cannot break anything else, I turn on my heel and run.

I storm out into the night. I hear him yelling, and all I can do is bite my own tongue to stop myself screaming back at him. My eyes are streaming again. I hate him.

It's dark outside, and cold, but I don't stop. I keep on walking, faster and faster until I am practically running, and my lungs are full of ice.

I know I won't find Heathcliff like this. I know. But that doesn't stop me.

Ever since Father's death, Hindley has been growing more and more monstrous.

Before Father died, Hindley was away at school. Those were good years where it was just Heathcliff and me, wrapped up in each other, not caring about anyone else. No matter how anyone scolded, we just went our own way, doing what we pleased.

One August day when it was especially hot out, we hunted grouse from dawn until the sky was purple with sunset. Heathcliff was a fine hunter, and he should have shot a good few grouse, but he didn't kill anything at all in the end, because we got distracted arguing with each other over the last oatcake we'd carried out with us. We tussled and rolled down the nearest hill, and then Heathcliff chased me about. After that, we couldn't remember where we'd left the rifle, so we had to go and hunt it down instead of birds.

That evening, Father scolded us soundly. Heathcliff was very contrite, because he loved Father and hated disappointing him. I complained that we'd done nothing wrong. I complained so long that Heathcliff kicked me in the shin to shush me, and Father shook his head and rubbed his knuckles against his forehead.

"You are a trial to me, Cathy." Father sighed, sinking back into his armchair. His face was very gray, I remember. He took his kerchief and mopped his forehead, which was damp with sweat. "Ah, what did I do to deserve such a fiendish daughter?"

I apologized to him very sweetly, because I did not like to upset him as soundly as I clearly had. I got on his lap, and kissed his forehead despite all his sweating, and told him some nonsense tale until he fell asleep right there in his chair.

I did not know he was sick. I should have. But I only had room in my heart for myself and Heathcliff, and I didn't see what was right in front of me.

Father was dead by morning.

I don't know when he died. It may even have been when I

was sitting on his lap, believing him asleep. But I know Joseph found him in the morning, still in his armchair, unmoving and cold. After that, there was nothing. Just grief, ringing bells in my ears, and the house full of noise. The next thing I knew, I was kneeling on the floor of my bedroom with my eyes shut so tight they ached, and Heathcliff was kneeling in front of me, whispering my name over and over again.

"Cathy," he whispered again. "Cathy, Cathy."

"Heathcliff," I said back eventually. My voice wobbled like a spinning top. "Leave me alone."

He didn't. I felt him press his thumbs gently over my closed eyelids. Then my cheeks. "Cathy," he said again. "Come back, Cathy."

It was like being woken up.

I opened my eyes. Everything was blurry to me, all soft and strange. But Heathcliff was there, and he looked like he always did, though his eyes were red.

"What is heaven like, do you think?" I asked him. I didn't trust the vicar, or Joseph, or even my sermon books to tell me the truth. But I trusted him. "Do you think Father will like it?"

"I think it's full of angels," Heathcliff said.

I swallowed. My voice didn't want to work. I had a throat full of snipped wings, and no words could fly out around them.

"He'd like angels," I replied eventually, voice thick. "Maybe heaven's a place just like here, with the same sun and the same green fields and even the same cattle. But with angels instead of us."

Heathcliff nodded. "Maybe," he said.

Father would love that, I thought. No fiendish daughter. No disappointing son who never came home. No cares or worries. But terror gripped me hard at the thought of it.

"I wouldn't like to go there," I blurted out. "If there are only angels in heaven, I wouldn't like to go at all. I wouldn't go."

"That's where souls go," Heathcliff said, brow creasing. But he didn't sound sure. He didn't trust Joseph's lectures any more than I did.

"Not mine," I said, feeling suddenly sure. I wouldn't go where there was no Heathcliff. I wouldn't. "And not yours. Say you won't go, Heathcliff. Please?"

He nodded. There was a black, intense look in his eyes— almost murderous, it was so fierce.

"Mine won't go if yours won't," he told me. "Where you go, I go too."

"Promise."

"Cathy," he said. "I promise."

Hindley came back for Father's funeral and ruined our peace. He'd been bitter when he'd left, but he came back loud and hateful, and he brought Frances with him, his wife who was silly and pretty and cruel. Perfect for him, really. Or at least he thought so. Hindley liked to sit with her on his lap by the fireplace. They would coo at each other like lovesick children. Heathcliff and I laughed about them, because they were so ridiculous, and because we needed *something* to laugh about.

It was so grim, being under Hindley's power. The years went like this: I would clean up Heathcliff after a beating, washing his wounds with a little water and cloth. He would sit obediently and let me do it, but he would always insist on making sure I was unhurt first. If his face had been hit, I would have to show him my own face, turning it from side to side so he could look at me. If Hindley had twisted Heathcliff's arm, then I would have to shove up my sleeves and show Heathcliff my own. He believed if Hindley hurt me, I would not tell him.

He was right, of course, but I still told him it was silly of him, and that he shouldn't worry. He didn't listen to me.

"I'm glad you bruise easier," Heathcliff said, more than once, when I showed him my knees, my arms, so he could see I didn't have the green-and-purple marks of a beating, like he did. That I was *safe*.

"I don't bruise easier," I always told him. "It just shows more on me. Yours are hidden, because no one wants to see them."

It was true. If Heathcliff was hurt or miserable, no one wanted to know about it. They wanted him to be strong and stoic, and so he was, I suppose. It's not as if he had a choice. But I saw his hurts. I always did.

Sometimes I let myself touch his hurts a little longer. Hold the cloth too long against his cheek, his chest, his shoulder. I'd linger. And I'd say, all soft, "It still hurts you, even if some can't see it."

When Frances died after Hareton was born, it was like grief peeled all the remaining goodness off my brother, until he was nothing but cruel nerves and impulses. He drank and he drank, and gambled with his friends late into the night, and beat Heathcliff even more harshly. He'd have beaten Hareton too, if Nelly hadn't loved the boy and hidden him from my brother.

But Hindley almost killed him, all the same.

It happened only months ago. I wasn't there to see it, but Nelly told me later, in a grim little voice, as she chopped the vegetables for the stew—how drunk Hindley had been, raging over some loss at the gambling table. He decided that we had all turned on him, and caught Nelly hiding Hareton in a cupboard, where she'd hoped he would be safe. He threatened Nelly with a knife. And then . . .

Then, Hindley was striding up the stairs. Holding Hareton. And somehow, he dropped him. Somehow, Hareton tumbled, and would have broken his skull and died.

But Heathcliff caught him.

I know Heathcliff regretted it after. He told Nelly so, but he didn't want to tell me. He avoided me for a while, but I caught him alone and asked him to stop and talk to me. And he did, though he kept his back to me as if he couldn't look at me, as if he was ashamed.

"You can tell me anything," I said. "Just like I can tell you anything, isn't that true?"

For a long moment he was silent.

"I caught Hareton by mistake," he said. "I'd do anything to break Hindley's heart. Small and decayed as it might be." I watched his shoulders rise and fall, as he inhaled and exhaled a slow, controlled breath. "If someone had asked me . . . if I'd known. I would have let the boy fall, Cathy."

I took a step closer to him. I asked him to turn and look at me, but he only shook his head.

"I know he matters to you," Heathcliff confessed. "Hareton."

"You matter more than anyone," I said. And because we were alone, just the two of us standing on the landing, I placed my head against his back, right between his shoulders. He stiffened, then relaxed and tipped his own head back so it was resting against my hair. He smelled like the outdoors—like sweat, but also heather sweetness, and something like an echo of salt water.

"You wouldn't really have let him fall," I said.

"I would have."

"Hareton's my blood," I told him. "And he annoys me so much, Heathcliff, I won't deny it. But he's mine. Don't you think he has eyes just like mine? I think he does. And our faces are the same shape."

"Skin's just skin," Heathcliff said. "It doesn't mean anything."

But we both knew skin meant a great deal. We both knew that if anyone knew the way we were—the way we compared hurts and bruises, or held each other just like this, when we were alone—skin would mean everything.

"He's mine," I said again.

After a second, I felt him sigh and tip his head forward. I hated the feeling of him pulling away, so I put my hands around his arms. He let me.

"Yours," Heathcliff said, soft. "Well, then I'll leave him be."

I claimed him, so I knew Heathcliff would never hurt him. I knew if Hareton fell again, Heathcliff would catch him. Just like he'd always catch me.

But who is there to catch Heathcliff? Have I let him fall?
I am afraid, so afraid, that I have.

The ground crunches beneath me. It hurts, and it is cold, wet. I am not in my proper boots, only little silk slippers. Still, I get further than I thought I would.

"Miss Cathy!" Nelly yells. She's running after me, hiking her skirts up with one hand. "Where do you think you're running off to? At this hour?"

"I am going to Heathcliff," I tell her. "Isn't it obvious, Nelly? Where else would I go? And no one else is going to help him, are they? Certainly not here. None of you care about him at all. Not a single one of you."

"This is nonsense," she says stoutly. "You can't help him like this. You'll need coin and someone to go with you. Why, you've never been beyond Gimmerton! Be patient. Convince your brother."

Oh, how cruel of her. She knows Hindley cannot be convinced. She just wants me to come home and be still and quiet and cause no trouble. It makes me seethe. What good will it do if I am biddable? Why should I have to be obedient here, in my home, which carries the wildness in me in every brick and stone?

"I would rather go look for him with nothing but the clothes on my back than wait here for help that won't come," I snap. "I would rather die searching for him than sit quietly waiting for him to return. I would rather be a ghost, Nelly, than a living thing that doesn't try to save all that matters to her."

"Miss Cathy, talk sense," Nelly says. "'All that matters to her'? Don't say such things."

"Heathcliff is all that matters!"

"That isn't what you said before he ran off," she replies, suddenly sharp, something awful flaring up in her face. "And he left because of it."

The words hit me in my stomach. They steal my breath from me.

"All the more reason for me to find him," I cry out. "Nelly, I—"

"Hush, hush," she says, touching a hand to my face. I think she is trying to silence me, even if she does not cover my mouth. It's warning, not comfort. "Joseph is coming. Walk back home with me now."

I wrench my head back. "You can't tell me what to do or not do," I announce. "You're not my brother or, or family of any kind. You have no right to order me about."

She flinches, as if I struck her. "I may not be family, Miss Cathy," she says, "but I grew up right alongside Hindley, and right beside you. I am owed your respect if nothing else!"

"Do you think it's fair that you must call me *miss*?" I ask. "That I wear pretty gowns and you do not, even though we grew up just the same, in the same house on the same moors? Do you think it's fair I can treat you as I do, or Hindley can treat us *all* as he does, just because of an accident of birth?"

"So you know you're not acting reasonably," she mutters,

grasping at only one thing I've said and ignoring all the rest. Typical Nelly. "Does that mean you'll repent your rudeness and behave?"

I shake my head and laugh, a wild kind of laugh.

"If I were Hindley this would never have happened," I say. "I would never have treated Heathcliff the way he does. I would . . . I would have the Heights. It would be mine, Nelly. And it would be Heathcliff's too. I would never turn him away. But nothing is mine. If I were not a girl—"

"Hush," Nelly says again. She is looking right through me. I know my emotions irritate her, and she wants to be back indoors, back with Hareton, wherever she hid him away. But I did not ask her to come after me, and if she insists on staying, she will have to witness this.

I cover my face with my hands and howl.

I do not want to be a girl, I think. And I do not want to be a woman, either. I have been playing a game all these years, wearing fine dresses and smiling widely at Edgar, all of it because it made people smile back at me, because it made me fit in. Even loving Edgar is like wearing a stiff and pretty gown, or powdering my hair—it is a thing I've put on. But the real me is underneath it. The real me is only there if you peel everything else off.

I hear the crunch of boots, and then Joseph is there.

"Inside," he says, and grabs my arm. "Now."

Joseph drags me back inside by the wrist. He releases me so swift that I stumble forward and almost trip into the table. Old brute. He must love all of this. I know he does. Any excuse to judge the sinners, that's all Joseph wants.

But Joseph does not gloat over me. He steps back into shadow, eyes glittering and malicious, as I start to shake, from my toes to my teeth. Nelly follows me in and says something about a warm pot of tea to drink. Sugar to settle me.

Hindley is watching. He's still seated at the table, with his red knuckles, his jaw clenched in fury.

"I don't want tea," I say tightly, even though my teeth are chattering. "Or ale. I don't want anything."

I just want Heathcliff.

Hindley and Nelly share a look over my head. I see them do it. I don't know what the look means, but as Nelly ushers me to sit down, Hindley's jaw relaxes slightly.

"I won't kill him," he says eventually. He sounds exhausted, as if all the anger has finally drained out of him. "Damn you, Cathy, but you're not wrong. I owe the devil a debt. If he ever shows his face here again, I'll give him his due."

Chapter Seven

Two weeks come and go. I'm starting to understand the city is no different from the country.

Every place has its rhythms. At the Heights, it's the creak of wood and chill of stone in high winds—the way the house shifts and breathes like it's living, sound changing from morning to night, winter to summer. It's how we all watched Hindley. Watched his face, his mood. How much he'd drunk. Thinking, how quick would he turn angry? When would he fling his cup against the wall, or look for the gun Nelly hid away beneath the stairs?

The moors had a way, too. How birds moved before rain comes. Color of the sky at dusk.

Here in the city, the rhythm's the lodgers sharing the same damp room who wake, groaning, before dawn to work on the docks. The hours the streets are full and heaving. The way they clear and go dead quiet between the end of day's work and start of night's drinking, before sunrise comes all over again. I get to know it by walking. Always walking. Watching through the hours, and learning that way.

I go fight one more time. After I lose three rounds like I'm told to and get my payment, I go walk again, crossing the city. I watch people move about. This time, no one stops me. I get no pity. That's good.

I can't keep on doing this. Money's not good enough in fighting. One bad bout and I'll break something I can't afford to. One hard punch, and maybe I won't get up. I need proper money. Work on the docks is better paid, but men who look like me aren't always wanted. And even if you get work, it's got dangers. The stuff that pays best needs an apprenticeship, and I'm too old. Sixteen's a man. I can't be a shipwright or joiner now.

And I don't want it anyway. I want something that's going to get me real coin. And something that'll get the violence out of me. I've got too much anger, and it won't lie still. It needs a way out.

I go dockside, even though I've been warned to keep away. Men staying at the lodging house told me the navy's always on the lookout near water—prowling dockside taverns, keeping an eye on dockhands, merchant sailors coming home, any man or boy who looks fit enough for work. No one wants to work on navy ships. That's what they told me. Merchant ships are better. Privateering's good money. So the navy press-gangs men, drags them shipside even if they run or say no and takes them to war.

"Not boys like you, mostly," they said, looking me over. "Mostly English men. But maybe if they're desperate for bodies they'll take a lascar too."

I am English, I wanted to say. But it never matters what I say, so I didn't.

I'm no lascar, but I do look like one.

I wash blood and dirt off me, waterside. I keep an eye out while I do it. The kerchief's enough for me to wipe my hands, face. But while I keep an eye out and wash, wounds hurting, I think too.

The water's got the look of ink under my hands. It's not safe for drinking. If I could, I'd boil it up before washing. But part of me wants to taste it. All I've drunk is tea, small beer, weak ale. I miss water. I wonder if this water'll have salt in it, the sea caught up inside it, carried over by ships.

Cathy, you know the spring right by the Heights. An easy walk, down the slope if you know where to look, or follow its noise. The water is sharp, clear. Boiled or not, it tastes sweet for drinking. Plenty of times after I was banished from the house I ended up kneeling by it in the dark, washing off blood from a beating. I remember how it made me feel less human, doing it: bathing my hurts under night, crouched in soil, the rest of you snug in the house.

I stopped feeling animal-like, the way I did then, when I started finding jugs of water in the stables on bruising nights. Sometimes warm from the hearth. Sometimes cold. I knew you'd left the water, Cathy, or bribed Nelly into sneaking it out. I knew then you'd seen my hurt. Watched me from a window maybe, you trapped on one side of the glass, me on the other. And you'd done for me what you could. You always did.

Remembering that leads my head somewhere sweeter. A good memory. How when we were smaller, before any death or before Hindley had power over us, we'd take off our stockings and get our legs bare before splashing through the spring. You'd tie your skirts up over your knees, the way you'd seen women working outdoors do. You made a big show of saying we mustn't get dirty—*Mother told me I mustn't play outdoors in the sun, Heathcliff, and she'll find out if our clothes get wet!*—but then you dragged me under the water by my hair, laughing vicious.

I still dream of that, Cathy. But when I dream, we're older. More like we are now. I dream you with your long curls soft with water. Water on your eyelashes, your mouth. I dream of you leaning down. Your mouth smiling. Your mouth lowering to mine—

I banish the thought. Splash dark water over my face again. The cold shocks me back to now. Liverpool, the Mersey below me. My bruises, and what I've got to do.

I know this city now. Know how it works. And I know I can't be a lone animal here. That makes sense. I needed people in the Heights too. Needed you to comfort me, Cathy—needed the way you took my hurts up like they were your own. I even needed Nelly's way of listening to me—always judging, always hard, but practical too. Steady. She'd never let us go hungry.

Not me, not you. Definitely not Hareton. And she'd never let Hindley go as far as killing a man either.

I can't thank her for that. Without her, he'd have been hung long ago.

By the time I'm near enough clean, I know what I'm going to do.

You wouldn't think it, looking at me, but I'm good at vanishing. Maybe I don't remember how things were before your father saved me, Cathy, but some things live inside a man. Knowing how to be silent. Empty tunnels where language should go. How to survive a place.

Can't change my skin, of course. Or my face, my nose, my eyebrows. Every part that folk have commented on. Joseph calling me fiendish. Hindley calling me devil. My skin made your mother worried I'd give you and Hindley away, Cathy. That someone would look at me and know we weren't so different.

Your father brought me into the house, but he worried too. I knew it. So he told me how to dress. To talk. Said, "If you look like a gentleman's son, Heathcliff, then you'll be treated as a gentleman's son."

So, I tried to be a gentleman's son. I put on good clothes your father gave me. Brushed my hair and tied it up right. Learned to read and write and count, and pray in Gimmerton Kirk beside the rest of you, like I was family, not servant or stranger. But people still looked and talked, and I wasn't a gentleman's son. There's no parish birth records, false or real, saying I've got respectable blood. So I stopped trying to be worth respect I wouldn't get, and instead learned how not to be seen. Sit still in church, look like you're not looking or listening or feeling, like you're furniture, and people stop looking and listening and feeling about you too.

It served me well, when your father died, and Hindley took over things. When he hounded me out of the house. Turned me from your father's servant to . . . nothing. Not even a servant. Just a thing, stuck in the garret, or exiled out to the stable. Not liked, and not wanted. It served me even better when Hindley's wife died, and he turned to drink. Drink, and his fists, with me.

Only you always saw me, Cathy. No matter how still I got, how much I faded, you'd see me. All I had to do was breathe, and you'd look. Fix your dark eyes on me, and smile.

There you are, your eyes would say. *I see you.*

I move with the city. Take myself back one night the way I came in. Past lodging houses and tenements that never would have taken someone who looks like I do or had my lack of coin. I go where I met a boy who sent me somewhere they *would* take me.

I hunch my shoulders. Lower my head. Move through the tavern, the crowd and the noise, letting them cover me up. Jamie's hard to spot. He's good at blending into the background too. But I see him because I'm looking. And he sees me because I shoulder my way through the alehouse until we're face-to-face.

For a second, he doesn't know me. Then his eyes widen.

"You," he says. "What're you doing here? If Isaiah sees you, you'll be in real trouble."

I doubt that. Isaiah saw me once. I look different now. If Jamie can vanish, fade away, I figure so can I. Besides, the fighting's changed my face.

"You're all minced up," Jamie says, like he's just noticed it.

"I'll be fine," I say. Bruising fades. I don't think I've broken anything. "I came here looking for you."

"Me," he says. He suddenly looks hunted.

"I want to talk," I say. "Some other place. Like last time."

"What about?"

"Your work," I say. "What you do."

He doesn't answer. The hunted look gets stronger.

"I want to talk about it somewhere else," I tell him. "But I'll ask here, if you prefer."

Talking about what Jamie can do—the way he can lift coin right out of a purse, a person none the wiser—seems like something no one should talk about in a tavern. Thieves make people angry.

He must think so too, because he nods and strides out. I follow.

We don't go dockside this time. We just walk. Aimless.

"I helped you," he says, low. "And you threaten me?"

"I didn't threaten you."

"If you'd started talking about what I do, in *there* . . ." He exhales through teeth gritted tight. Then he shrugs. Says flatly, "It's my fault for showing off. So. What do you want?"

"I'm strong," I tell him. "Good in a fight. Ruthless, if I need to be."

"It looks like you've lost a fight," he points out. "And lost badly."

"I was paid to lose. And I'm better when it's not a fair fight. When I can sneak up. Use my knife."

He laughs. "You're telling me you're good in a fight when you cheat? Who isn't?"

"I'm telling you I can get things done," I say. We keep moving. "I'm telling you I'm strong. Useful."

"Useful to someone who isn't me," Jamie replies. "You've got the wrong idea about me."

Don't think I do. Not fully. But I wait as he thinks and kicks a rock across the road, into a wall. A cat sitting on the window above it startles at the noise, rears its tail up, and skitters away. Jamie gets a guilty look on his face. Swears under his breath.

"I didn't mean to scare it," he says. Then he looks at me. "I pick pockets," he says. "I steal. But I don't get violent unless I've got to. I don't *like* being violent. Why else would I have helped you, the first time? I didn't want you hurt. So you being tough, that's no good to me."

He looks at me, searching. I don't know for what. But I say nothing.

"Being tough isn't enough," he says finally. "You've got to be *smart*."

"I am smart," I say.

He makes a noise like he doesn't believe me, low in his throat, and I go on.

"I came back to see you, didn't I?"

"You came back," he agrees. "You came to ask me for help."

"To tell you how I could be useful," I reply, keeping my voice even. "To tell you why we should work together."

"No, you came for my help. You came because you're not coping on your own. Getting hurt. Not making enough to live on, I bet." That searching look is on his face again. "It's your pride that makes you want to be the big man, helping me and not getting helped *by* me," Jamie stresses. "But you need me, and that's why, if I help you, you've got to listen to me. You've got to learn from me, and do what I say. Can you do that?"

I say nothing as I think. But I take too long to answer, so Jamie speaks again.

"I can't have someone who likes fights bringing trouble to me and my friends," he says. He says it seriously. Like he wants me to understand it. "I've got to put my own lot first. And I can't have someone who isn't useful. And being a fighter . . . you can see. That's not useful to me."

"Teach me how to be useful, then," I say evenly. "I learn fast."

His mouth quirks up. He's still guarded but . . . a smile's good.

"You don't know how to make people like you, do you, Heathcliff?"

"I'm not interested in being liked," I say swiftly.

"It's easier to trust someone you like. Easier to want to include them."

"Better to be honest than to lie until you're liked," I say stiffly. Besides, no lie I've ever told has made anyone like me. Hindley, or anyone else. I figure, someone like me only gets liked by some miracle, or by money.

If I were rich—*when* I am rich—it won't matter that I'm harsh. That I wear my anger heavy on me. That most parts of me don't fit anywhere, don't make people feel easy or friendly. I saw it with Hindley. If you've got land and money, no one cares that you're a monster.

"It'd be smarter just to lie," Jamie says. "Maybe that's something you can try."

"I'll do my best," I say, and Jamie laughs, big and loud, throwing his head back.

"There you go," he says when he calms down. Grinning. "That was a really good start. We'll make a sharper of you yet."

Chapter Eight

Catherine

NELLY AND HINDLEY CONSPIRE TO stop me from running away again. I tell them I won't, but they don't seem to believe me. In fact, they're acting very strangely, and I cannot make sense of it. Hindley was not angry at me when Joseph dragged me home, which was strange enough. But he does not grow angry later either, even though I am waiting for it. Instead, he avoids me and is polite when he can't avoid me. He and Nelly encourage me to stay in bed and go only for the shortest walks, in dull circles around my own room. They insist the windows remain shut and fire always be lit, for fear I'll catch a chill and die suddenly, I suppose. I have never been so coddled, and it's stifling.

When I grow restless, they allow me in the kitchen, where I can pet one of the dogs as long as I do not get "excited," as they call it. But I am not allowed to help with any chores, and when I complain of boredom, Nelly fixes me with an extremely harsh look that I don't like at all.

"If you hadn't run off into the cold again, perhaps your brother would think you were fit and healthy once more and would leave you to run wild," she lectures. "But until you're well enough to put our fears at ease, Cathy, you'll simply have to be bored."

I hate it, but Nelly isn't entirely wrong. I am not well. I don't regret trying to search for Heathcliff, and I don't regret my anger, not even the smallest amount. But my recovery from the fever that kept me at the Grange has been ruined. I am not deathly ill like I was when I dreamed of gray waters in Mrs. Linton's chinoiserie room, but I am shaky. My heart feels like a little bird that rattles against my ribs when I breathe.

It takes me some time—more time than it really should—to realize that it isn't my illness that has made Hindley so meek and strange. I don't realize the truth until the day that Joseph is lecturing me about some wickedness I have done—feeding the dog one of my oatcakes, I think—when Nelly glares at him and says something about not disturbing my mind's calm. Then, I understand.

They think I have a sickness of the mind, too. Hindley is afraid of disturbing my temper, in case it kills me as any cold wind might. It is the kind of thing the doctor once said about Hindley's wife, when she was particularly sad, before Hareton was born. A frail woman's mind must not be disturbed. It must be treated gently and handled with care.

Perhaps Hindley spoke to the doctor after all, despite his dislike of him. Or perhaps Nelly insisted, because the way I yelled at her had frightened her so. Nelly has a lot of sway over Hindley when he is not in one of his dangerous moods. But it does not matter how they came to believe they must be careful with me. All that matters is that I'm furious. How *dare* they.

Hindley can be angry whenever he likes. No one says Hindley cannot be angry. They wouldn't dare. He may break crockery or furniture, or beat Heathcliff, or threaten Nelly with a knife; he may raise his fist to me, or call me names, or make little Hareton sob in terror, but no one thinks he cannot be trusted with all the things he has—this house, our father's money. All of us, servants and family, under his thumb. But if I get angry, or if I risk my own safety, my own life, for something that matters, when I have nothing I own and nothing I can risk *but* my own life? Then I must be watched more closely even than a child.

It's not fair, not fair at all.

But I cannot change how things are. So I pretend to be obedient. I lie in my bed with the shutters closed around me and my candle lit, and I pick up one of the books I keep on the window. Most belonged to my mother once, and some belonged to Father. Now, of course, they all belong to Hindley. But Hindley has never cared for reading, so they are really mine.

Father was rarely proud of me. He did not really like me, if I am truthful, because I was so noisy and wayward and did not like to sit still and peaceful beside him, like Heathcliff did. But he was proud when I took an interest in his books of sermons.

"Theology will do you good, Cathy," he said, patting my hair. "Faith will soften your temperament."

My poor father. I did not take the books to read them. I took them because I wanted paper. I took because I knew no one else would have even the littlest bit of interest in opening up books of dour sermons, and that would keep my own secrets safe.

The book I open now is one of the prettiest, bound in a very fine marbled red leather. Inside, the pages are faintly yellowed, dusted here and there with mold spots from being pressed too long against the window. I turn to the center of the book. There, around all the printed words, are my own words. My own writing, neat and small and spiraling into every bit of empty space, filling it up.

I begin to write some more.

I prefer to be outside running or climbing, or getting into some kind of trouble, rather than sticking my head inside a book. But there are times I can't. Like now, when I am locked up as well as any prisoner.

Today, I write about Hindley and Nelly furiously. I write every awful thing I am thinking about them but can't say. Then I draw them: Hindley scowling. Nelly bent over in the kitchen. I make them look as sour as they have behaved, so that if any traveler stumbles on my book in a hundred years they will know that Hindley and Nelly are joyless prunes with no happiness in their hearts.

I write my fury out in little gasps of ink. It is like what the doctor does when a body is feverish and sick—he lets out blood to get rid of sickness. But I let my own out with ink, just enough so that I can sit still and sweet and make everyone stop treating me as if I will shatter.

When I am done writing and I've exhausted the worst of my anger, I begin to write my own name, nice and slowly, in the looping cursive I was first taught by my father when I was small. I find it soothing. Cathy. Catherine. Catherine Earnshaw. Over and over, I go.

Then I write Heathcliff's name. Very carefully, with little flourishes around the *f*s, and the *l*. The way I've always written it.

The first time Heathcliff ever saw his own name, I was the one who wrote it for him. We were sitting next to each other at the kitchen table. It was after breakfast, and the hearthstone was still giving off wafts of smoke and heat, smelling of peat, but we sat so close together it was like we were both trying to get warm. I was kicking my legs back and forth, jostling Heathcliff's leg every time I moved, but he didn't complain. He just watched quietly as I wrote out each letter. I sounded them out so Heathcliff could follow.

I wrote his name far more elegantly than I'd written my own, putting in loops and swirls like I'd seen in some of Father's books. I think Heathcliff knew I was making a special effort.

"Beautiful," he said, when I was done.

"You think your name's beautiful?" I asked, and laughed.

"No," he said. But he didn't tell me what he'd really meant. He just smiled at me. The smallest smile I'd ever seen, like a little flame struggling to stay alight in wind.

Father had told Hindley to show Heathcliff how to write his letters, not me, but my brother had been terribly sullen about the whole thing and refused to do it and had stormed out of the house early in the morning to go hunting instead. By then, Heathcliff had been living at the Heights for a few months, and Hindley had cultivated a real hatred for him. I know he had twisted Heathcliff's arm at least once, hard enough to stripe the skin red. Heathcliff had made me promise not to tell Father.

"I'll get my own revenge," Heathcliff had said. And when he'd convinced Father to give *him* the best pony in the stables instead of Hindley, I'd thought that was only fair.

Secretly—well, not that secretly—I was happy Hindley was gone. I wanted to be the one to teach Heathcliff. I had decided he was going to be my friend, and I was doing everything in my power to knot his heart round my fingers. The smile made me feel like . . . oh, like light was dancing through me. Like maybe I'd done it.

"Do you want to try?" I asked him.

He looked at his own name. "Show me your name too," he said. "Write me *Catherine*."

I wrote my name too like he'd asked, so close to his that it was like they had been crushed into one name, one name for one soul.

Catherine Heathcliff.

I don't write that now. If ink is like bloodletting, I think that's blood I can't lose. Not yet.

Instead, even more slowly still, I write: Catherine Linton. Catherine Linton. Mrs. Linton.

Linton.

I feel steadier, as I hold the book open upon my lap to let the ink dry. I know what I have to do now, or at least, I think I know what I must try.

Nelly told me to be patient and good. To not act rashly. I will take her advice now, because I have no other choice. But I will do it my own way, and spend a little of the closest thing to coin that I have.

I soon convince Hindley that I should visit the Grange again. "What if Linton forgets about me and suddenly decides to marry someone else?" I ask.

"The boy's in mourning. He won't be marrying anyone for a while yet," Hindley says. "Suddenly or otherwise. He's too proper."

"*Proper* mourning takes a long time. All the more reason to remind him I'm waiting for him."

Some people mourn more swiftly, and change out of their dark clothes as soon as they're able. Hindley certainly did when Father died, though he mourned lavishly enough for his wife. But I know Edgar isn't like that. I know Edgar will wear black and grieve as long as a respectable man should, because it is what his parents would have wanted, and he loved them.

"A gentleman won't give you up if you have an understanding," Hindley mutters, but I must worry him enough that he agrees to let me go without much fuss.

Nelly dresses me up finely. At home, I dress simply in a

typical kind of day gown and cap, but I always dress properly before visiting the Grange. I always have my hair up, all my curls made tidy and pretty, and don a proper silk gown, so that I look like someone who *fits* in the Grange. Even when I was there recovering from my fever, I was the best-dressed invalid there ever was. Now, I make a special effort, and even put pomatum and powder in my hair so that I look especially nice.

When I arrive at the Grange with Nelly, Edgar is waiting. It is a very bright day, and the sun makes his hair shine golden and his eyes look even more blue. He is smiling, so I smile back at him.

"Where is Isabella?" I ask.

"Inside," he tells me. "She's organizing tea and cakes for you."

"Just for me?"

"For all of us," Edgar corrects himself, still smiling at me fondly. "She wanted to direct the servants herself, so we must give her a little time, if you'll allow it."

"She doesn't need to please me," I say airily. "But I suppose we can give her some time to prepare. Shall we walk around the grounds?"

Edgar hesitates. "Your health," he says carefully. "I was told you've been unwell again."

I scoff and link arms with him. "Are you saying I look sickly? No?" When he shakes his head and protests, and stammers something about me looking very lovely, I smile at him and say, "We can walk around indoors instead, if that will make you worry less."

"I'd prefer it." He sounds relieved.

So we walk inside. There is a library I like especially, and I make Edgar take me to it. I have never read any of the books here and I am not interested in trying, but I like the gold on their bindings, and the way the leather smells. I like how the room is as grand as the rest of the house, but somehow quieter. There is a large window that looks over the moors, and if you stand by it even for a moment, you can see the light shift across the gorse, rolling like a strange and slow wave.

Edgar stands by me, as Nelly settles herself on one of the chairs and gets out her knitting. What a good chaperone she is. He tells me something about how it is to run a household all on his own, and I manage a sympathetic noise, although I am not terribly interested. I turn my head from the window as he talks and look at the corridor, where I can hear quick foot-steps tapping out a rhythm. After a moment I see one of the maids scurrying along the corridor, carrying a plate piled high with sweet things full of currants and dried fruit. The smell wafts over to me and makes my mouth water. I doubt Isabella is doing anything like work to prepare the tea and cakes, but I know how fussy she can be. She'll be bossing the maids around terribly. We may have to wait a while yet.

Nelly makes an especially loud clink with her needles. I look back at Edgar, and see him looking at me.

"You seem distracted, Catherine," he says gently.

I make myself beam at him. I put my hand around his wrist. In my own head, I scold myself. I am meant to be myself again—charming and pleasing—and I am not managing it at all.

"I'm sorry," I say. "I'm just—oh, my head is full of worries. Nothing like your own, of course."

"Your worries matter too, Catherine," he says earnestly. "Never doubt that."

I meant that mine are more important than his, but it's probably better that he doesn't know that. I don't bother to correct him.

I lower my eyes and look at our feet. My heeled shoes, covered in pale silk, silver-buckled. His gold-buckled boots. We look so perfect, as if we have never walked on dirt before. I take a deep breath.

"Heathcliff is gone," I blurt out.

"That servant boy? He ran away?"

I nod. I don't say, *I made him run*, even though the words crowd up behind my teeth.

"I am sorry," he says, and he almost manages to sound sincere, even though I know how much he hates Heathcliff. "I know how much you care for him."

He doesn't know. I have tried to explain it to him, but he always looks so confused.

It's better that he doesn't know. If he truly understood how it is between Heathcliff and me . . . well. Perhaps he wouldn't want to marry me anymore. And I dearly want to marry him. I want to walk with our arms linked in gardens that belong to him, in the shadow of the grand house that belongs to him too.

I want that life. I want to carve myself to fit it, so I will be safe and warm and fed forever.

"Do you remember the first time we met?" I ask him.

"I do," he says, eyes soft. "I remember it very well indeed."

"I was only . . . oh, twelve, I think. And I peered into the Grange window, and saw you and Isabella fighting over your new little puppy, and I laughed at you." I laugh again now. "I was such a wild thing! When the guard dog caught me when I tried to run away and bit my foot you must have thought it had caught some kind of monstrous creature!"

"I did not," he protests. He is blushing, his cheeks flushing red in a way mine never do. "I'd never seen anything like you, Catherine." His voice goes shy. "You were—so bright and so pretty. I liked you immediately. You're . . . you're still so bright and pretty."

I blush, even if my skin doesn't change as dramatically as his does. I know my face feels hot. I think of kissing him—maybe just kissing his cheek, but even though Nelly is probably not looking at us, I can't forget that she's right behind us and listening even if she's not watching.

"I remember you were very handsome," I tease. His blush darkens.

It's a lie, of course. Edgar *is* handsome, but I barely looked at him when we first met. For one, I was twelve and wasn't looking for a fiancé or a husband. And second, all I could think about was the pain in my leg, and the dog that looked like it wanted to bite me again, and Heathcliff who wasn't allowed to follow me indoors. When the Lintons took me into the house and cared for me until I was well, they left Heathcliff outside in the cold. I remember he yelled my name. His eyes were so wide, more scared than I'd ever seen. But the Lintons threatened him until he ran away, back to the Heights without me. One of the servants muttered cruel names at him. We both looked wild, both had dirt on our feet and our hair tangled, but because Heathcliff was dark they drove him off, and because I was light and they knew me as the Earnshaw girl, they took me in. I remember that.

I only thought Edgar was handsome later. When he started being nice to me.

"Do you remember that Heathcliff was with me?" I ask.

Edgar looks confused for a moment. I suppose it is confusing, that I've moved so swiftly from calling him handsome to speaking of Heathcliff. But then he says, "Was he?"

"Yes."

He shakes his head and says, "I truly don't. I suppose I only had eyes for you."

I should blush again, or compliment him or—I don't know. Laugh, I suppose. Something pretty and bright, since that is what he likes about me. But I only bite my lip and look at him and think, *How can he love me if he can't see Heathcliff? Heathcliff is me.*

Edgar only sees part of me. He's always only seen part of me. I feel strange, realizing that. Of course, I have only ever shown him my best face, but I . . . I thought, perhaps, he knew the rest of me was still there.

It's as if part of me has fallen and is fading away, as easy as any shadow-thing under fierce sunlight.

"I want to search for Heathcliff," I murmur. I try to keep my words soft so that Nelly will not hear them. "I worry about him."

"You have a good heart," Edgar says, his expression going ever so tender. "But he'll be fine, Catherine. I'm sure."

"You could help me search for him." I hear Nelly cough and rustle in her seat. "Or you could send someone out to look for him. I'd be *so* grateful, Edgar."

"I'm sure your brother already has sent out a search party," Edgar says, even though he should know Hindley better than that. He swallows and says carefully, "He wouldn't like me to interfere with his household, I think. It isn't . . . gentlemanly."

Has Edgar tried to interfere before? I wonder. *Has he tried to protect me, or do something for me? Or no—perhaps his father did?*

He gives me a look that is keener, a little sharper than most I've seen on his gentle lamb face, and then he looks away from me.

"Boys like Heathcliff are good at surviving," Edgar says. I think he means to be comforting.

Boy. Heathcliff is Edgar's age, or older.

I had no help from Hindley. I will have no help here, either. But I do not scream or berate Edgar.

I think of what would happen if I did. I think of him recoiling from me, in concern or in horror. I think of him handing me back to Hindley. I think of how my brother would lock me away, and how my life would grow smaller and smaller, until there was nothing of it but my room, and Hindley's stormy rages, and the promise of nothing good. No hope. No future ahead of me, only a colorless nowhere, with no love in it.

Bitterness swirls in me like poison. But I smile, and link my arm with his, and say, "I'm sure you're right, Edgar."

We go and sit with Isabella. The sugared tea is sweet on my tongue, and the cakes sweeter. I think of the first night I was carried into this parlor with a dog bite on my leg and was offered a little slice of a currant scone by Edgar, his hands trembling. And how—how I put it onto my tongue, and it was like a vow I had made, a fairy thing. I had eaten here, and tasted sweetness, tasted what it meant to be rich, and now I could never run again for the craving of it, even if it would one day strike me dead.

Chapter Nine

Heathcliff

JAMIE TAKES ME TO AN alley. Looks left and right. Seeing no one, he says, "Wait here."

He grabs the window ledge. Hauls himself up. I watch him go, climbing window ledge to window ledge, gripping exposed brick with his hands and boots. Then he's on a sloping roof and gone. He moved so lightly he didn't even kick off any loose tiles, and from where I'm standing all the tiles look loose, the brick crumbling. Looks like the whole building's ready to fall over.

I wait for Jamie. I wait, and I look at the building and wonder how long it'll last, how long until the whole thing collapses right in on itself.

I hear a clink. Boots on tile. He jumps back down.

"They're ready to see you," he says. He's been sweating. I

watch. He takes off his cap. Pats it against his own head, dabbing up sweat. Smiles, mouth closed. Then tells me, "They weren't happy with me. But they'll come round. Follow me up, and don't take them too seriously, all right?"

I nod, and follow. Climbing a building like this isn't much like climbing up a tree to Cathy's window, but I spent plenty of time on the crags too. They weren't safe—uneven, liable to split your skin with their sharp edges, and if you tumbled you might die. So I don't fear this climb.

Jamie takes me to a break in the roof covered in a piece of wood. We squirm through. He leads me down into a room, ceiling low, floorboards bending under me. It's small, the room. Walls feel like they're pressing down on me, though they're wide enough for two beds shoved close, a curtain hung up between them. Curtain's faded, gone rust-colored. There's a table shoved in front of a door nailed shut. The people living here aren't meant to be, that's clear enough.

Three people watch me slip in. Another boy, wiry, small. Must be good for pickpocketing, to be so small. Two girls, both sat on the second bed together, hands wrapped over each other's, tight.

"That's Hal," Jamie says, nodding at the boy, who nods back. "And Annie, and Hetty."

"Very nice to meet you," Hetty says, offering me a nod. Her jaw's hard—set so even though her welcome's polite, her face isn't. I nod back.

"Same to you," I reply.

Annie's pale as milk. Even her hair is near white. I notice

it, because Hal and Hetty are something else, brown but not like me, and not like Jamie. Don't know what, and I don't ask. That's none of my business. But then milk-pale Annie gives me a look, says, "Anne. I'm only Annie to my friends," and I hear the Irish in her voice. It sinks into me.

All of us here—we've got somewhere else in us.

"Anne," I repeat. Nod. She nods back, all regal.

"Jamie says you need help," Hetty says. "You need education."

She goes silent. Waiting. She and Anne look at me, judging. Hal's quiet, looking back and forth between us.

I say, "I can't keep prizefighting."

Hetty looks me up, down. Purses her lips. "I can see that."

"I need a living that won't kill me," I tell her. "I asked Jamie to help me."

"Took advantage of his kindness, you mean."

"I offered him a fair exchange. Offered him my strength. My knowledge."

"We don't need someone who fights. And we don't need to learn fighting. I'm sure Jamie told you."

"Everyone needs someone who can fight," I say evenly. "But I don't mean teaching you to punch."

Her eyebrow quirks up. Like maybe I'm saying something she wants to hear more of. "You think I can't punch?"

I ignore that challenge. "I can read. Write. I'm good with numbers."

They go silent.

Anne and Hetty don't look at each other, but they're still

clutching hands. I think they're speaking that way, how hard they're holding each other. The way Anne moves, shifting to sit straighter.

"I'm a sharper," Anne says. "And Hetty too, sometimes. We know our numbers. But writing, reading . . . Well, now. That's different."

If there's one good thing Earnshaw did for me, it was getting me to learn my letters. He taught me some—slow, patient, him sitting by me. Though you taught me most, Cathy. Me next to you, watching your fingers move. You, writing out my name. Teaching me who I was.

Most don't get the chance to learn. But they're clever enough, these four, to know that without their letters, life's always going to cheat them.

"Teach me how to cheat at cards and pick pockets, and I'll teach you reading," I say levelly. "And if you need someone who'll fight, I'll give you that too."

"Generous of you," Hetty says.

"I want to live," I reply. "You can help me do that. I won't beg, but I'll pay you fair."

Jamie's got his hands in his pockets next to me. Waiting. It's not him who gets to decide, I can tell now. The young one, Hal, sits quiet. Watching.

Hetty purses her lips. "Come back," she says. "Tomorrow. After midday. Not earlier. And we'll start lessons."

I nod. "I'll need chalk," I say. "Something to write on."

"Then you'd best bring that with you," she says. "Consider that part of your debt."

Jamie exhales. "You'll have to leave by the window again," he says, and goes to shove the wood slat back.

We both slip out. Make our way down, crossing tiles, sliding along guttering until we hit the ground.

"Tomorrow," I say. "I'll see you then."

"Tomorrow," Jamie agrees. He looks relieved.

My lessons start like this:

Jamie gestures at the table. It's got one chair. I look between it, the beds, and say, "Where do you want me?"

Hetty sighs. "Stand. Jamie, you stand too. You're going to be our practice. Get your coat."

Jamie goes obediently, grabbing a coat from under his bed, then standing. Then he says, "Right. Heathcliff—Hal's going to show you something useful. Hal?"

Hetty and Jamie direct, but it's Hal who gets out a knife and shows me what's to be done.

They teach me how to pick a pocket, using just hands. How to cut a purse or pocket at the base so the coin'll slip straight into your waiting palm. Jamie's coat is especially for this, with more pockets sewn right into it for cutting. "Some people hide their coin better than this, inside their shirt or jacket, but you have to start somewhere," he says practically.

After Hal shows me what to do, he gives me the knife.

Turns out, even if you're already handy with a knife, it's not simple work.

"I've seen a trick with a long piece of wire," Hal says after my third failure to do it the way Hetty likes. He's got a high, thin voice. Birdlike. His hands go up. He draws them wide. I watch him play at holding wire—how he'd unspool it if he had one in his hands. How he'd shape one end into a hook. "You wait until your mark's standing still, distracted—country folk new round here are the best because everything's strange and shocking to them—and then you take your wire and just . . ." He mimes hooking something out of a pocket and lifting it up and out.

"Hal's never going to try that though," Hetty says, warning in her voice. But it's not a violent thing, that warning. It's got care in it, like Nelly telling Hareton not to touch the cooking fire so he won't get burned. "You do it wrong once, and that's it. The jail's for you, or you'll be beaten by a mob until you're dead. Unless you've got a good talent for running."

"You don't want to try to fight," Jamie cautions. "Not over picking pockets. It's tempting, because of your knife." He lifts up the blade that was in my hand a second ago. I didn't even feel him take it. He spins the hilt between his fingers, grinning a little. Smug. "But if someone catches you, you'd best just run. Run like your life depends on it."

"Dead men move slower than live ones," I say to him.

Hal laughs. Cuts the noise off, shoving his hand over this mouth. Anne and Hetty are stone-faced.

"True," Jamie says easily. "But making one man dead always seems to make the other men who saw you do it move faster. I'm not speaking from experience," he adds, real quick. "But you see things, when you're in the business long enough. Kill one man, get a hundred more at your back. That's the way of it."

We try a bit longer, getting me to learn the right tricks. Anne frowns, eyes going narrow. Says, not to me it seems, but the whole room, "You've broken your fingers before."

I've had my fingers broken. It's different. But I nod.

"It'll make it harder," she says. Something like concern runs over her face when she looks at my scars; my one finger, twisted a little wrong. "Much harder."

"Harder doesn't mean I can't," I say. And I practice a bit more after, just to prove it.

After that, I get my chalk from my pocket.

The table's bare, and no one complains when I use chalk on the wood. They just gather round. Watching.

I've never been a teacher. Doubt I've got the skill for it. But I made a promise. I'll try.

Squeak of chalk on wood. All four of them leaning forward. Jamie's got his arm on the table next to me. No one's been this close to me for anything but fighting since . . . You, Cathy. Since you.

I swallow. Then I tell them, "We'll start with letters, one by one."

Slow, so they can learn how it's done, I draw an *A*.

I come back. Over and over again.

Sometimes I go fight because I still need coin. If I'm told to lose, I lose. Then I wash blood off my knuckles by the water's edge and look at the scars on them, old and new. I let myself be glad I haven't broken any bones. That I'll survive another day.

The four of them in their stolen room, I get to know them. I don't plan to. I don't want to. It's still no business of mine, and knowing about people's lives just gets you tangled up with them. So I don't ask, but they talk, all of them. So it happens anyway.

In between thieving practice and lessons in letters, when Hetty watches intently and Hal holds the chalk clumsily in his hand, and Anne mouths words, following along, I learn them.

Hal's got no family anymore, but his mother and him were brought here by the merchant who thought he owned them. When she died, Hal decided to leave and make his own way. Anne crossed the sea for work. Hetty's father came from Malaya, a lascar on some ship that landed and left before she was even born.

"But he told Ma where he came from, so I know too," Hetty says easily. She's still stern, but she's getting relaxed around me. She's not so sure I'll turn on them anymore.

I want to ask about her father. About lascars. Want to say, *I think my father was one too. But I don't know. Not for sure.*

I don't ask.

They're not my friends. I don't need any friends.

Maybe once I could have had some. There were other children at the Heights, now and then. Working, mostly. But they weren't there for play and didn't want to make friends with me. Only you wanted that, Cathy. You were enough. For a while.

But after you got bitten by that dog—after you got stuck at the Lintons'—you came back changed. Stuffy, tidy. You looked like you were afraid to touch me and get dirt on you.

You were twelve, and I was near enough—or so we guess, without knowing when I was born. Twelve, and until then we'd been like people tied together. Sometimes, I'd sneak into your room at night. You'd tell me tales—strange things, a lot like lies. And I'd flick my fingers through the candle flame on your window, fast enough to not get burned and not snuff the flame out, and listen. Sometimes I'd go slower and slower. Waiting until the heat singed.

But we spent more time together outdoors than in the house. It made Hindley blood-spitting angry. But it was like finger through flame. A game to see how long you can touch fire before you'll burn's not much different from a game where you see how long you can run wild before you'll get beaten. We'd run all the time, down hills and up. Climb like we'd got dogs at our heels. Laughing, me and you, but like Hindley was a ghost or a gun at our backs.

Once, we stopped. Went still, falling down in long grass when we'd run so long our legs were aching and bodies sweating. You made me put my head on your lap, Cathy. Your skirt smelled like lavender, sun. You combed my hair out, gentle with your fingers. It made me feel all calm.

"What do you call the sea?" you asked suddenly.

"Me?" I didn't open my eyes. I knew why you asked. The grass 'round us was bluish green, wind making it move like waters did in our dreams. "Sea or ocean or water. Same as you do."

"You knew other words once. I know you did."

"I don't know them anymore."

"How could you forget?" You didn't sound like you were accusing me. You sounded curious.

"Easy," I said. "I wanted to."

Then you went quiet. I felt you shift. You let my hair go. "Don't get up," you said when I started moving. "I'm making you a gift."

I stayed still. Maybe I slept. But I woke up proper when your hands got on my hair again, setting something on it.

"There," you said, pleased. "I've made you a crown."

I sat up and touched it. Heather crumpled against my fingers. Green and purple falling over me. I swore at you, and you laughed.

"Careful." You giggled. "Careful, you're going to break it. Heathcliff, *no*, don't take it off!"

Later, I crept into your room. The two of us in your oak closet. Sheets warm from your body, and the smell of wood and lavender water all around us. You were already half sleeping, so you just put your head on my chest when I lay back. Listening to my heart, I think. There'd be no stories that night.

"Samudra," you whispered. Your voice was sleep-thick, your eyes half-open. Don't think you were really awake anymore.

"Are you dreaming, Cathy?" I whispered back.

"That's what the sea's called," you slurred. Sighed, and sunk down against me. "That's what I dreamed."

I watched your eyes close. Your breath go easy. I thought . . . Oh, Cathy. I thought right then, we must have been made for each other. Maybe not on purpose. Don't know if I believe God's as kind or as cruel to do something like that. But the world wounded us both, maybe long before we were even born. And whatever wounds we had, they'd shaped us to fit each other.

I put my fingers through yours. Even sleeping, you held me so tight your nails left marks.

We were both wounded and wild, before you met the Lintons. You didn't pretend we weren't.

But after, you were different. Me, still ragged, dirty, alone. And you . . .

Perfect. But you were always perfect to me, Cathy. Now you were perfect to everyone else.

You prattled on and on about the Lintons. Their big house and how nice they were. All their fine food and the way Mrs. Linton wore her hair and painted up her face. And you talked about Edgar Linton. Told me how he followed you, how sweet he was. How he brought you gifts. You laughed over it.

It made me jealous. Anything you want, I want for you. I always have. But that didn't stop me wishing you didn't want him.

I asked you once, when the anger got too high on me, and I couldn't stop myself, "Does he know the truth about you?"

You frowned at me, confused.

"What truth?" you asked.

I stared at you. My mouth wouldn't move.

How could you not know?

When your parents were living they didn't whisper as soft as they thought they did over India. Didn't hide their worry over you and Hindley. And you and me, Cathy, we had words in common, words I must have learned from my father. Words you must have learned somewhere, from someone. *Samudra*, you'd said to me. That was no thing you'd dreamed up. When we were out too long in the sun, your skin went golden, warming brown like bread, not burning. You knew your family had secrets and you had to keep them. You knew not to tell anyone about the chests of cloth and gold. Trinkets from India, locked up. You knew there was danger if you let anyone remember your family hadn't always been in the Heights, in the same stone house high up on the moors. You knew there was a lie wrapped round you. You had to know.

I kept staring at you. You stared back.

"Heathcliff," you said, sounding frustrated. "I don't understand."

I remember—I turned away. Looked down at my hands. Felt shame run through me, a hot knife through butter.

"It's nothing," I muttered, and stomped off. Leaving you.

It took me a while, after that, to understand why I felt like I felt.

You didn't want to know the truth, Cathy. Some part of you saw it, the same way you saw ghosts, and buried feathers, and dreamed strange things. Some part of you *knew*. That there was nowhere in you, the same way as there was in me.

And you turned from it, turned to the Lintons, and pretended there wasn't.

Hal says to me, "I want to show you something."

There's only us in the room, sharpening up two knives. The others are out—Jamie seeing his family, and Hetty and Anne gone somewhere else. Hal didn't know where. Just shrugged and said, "Doing sweetheart things."

Then he looked at me, looked careful like he was weighing me up.

So I shrugged back and said, "You'll get further in your letters than they will, then."

And he relaxed.

"I don't want to learn," he tells me now.

"Fine," I say, and put the knife down. I start rolling up my sleeves so I can slip back out through the window and head off. But Hal shakes his head.

"Don't go away yet." His voice is thin, but sure. "I want to show you a thing."

He takes me out the window anyway. Shoves the wood back in place and doesn't take me to the slope roof and down to the road. He goes the other way instead. The roof's narrow here, but he moves across it light as air, like he's built for it.

"Be careful," he calls back to me.

I think of saying to him I don't care if I fall and break my head, but I don't think he'd laugh the way you would, Cathy. So I don't. I just follow.

He shows me ways to cross the city. Through chimney smoke. Sky wide and close.

The roofs aren't even. Not the same height, and none of them safe for people. But Hal shows me if you're careful, quick on your feet, there's paths taking you right near water. We climb up, feet gripping onto grooves and cracks in stone, and get on a flat roof. Hal makes me crouch. Points out the docks. Church spires. The river leading to ocean. The water, shining oily gray and green and blue.

"Down there, the roads are for work," he says, pointing down at the people walking under us. "Up here's safe. Up here's mine."

Why show me, then? I think of asking. *Why risk what's safe when you know all I want is to keep myself alive?* But I don't.

"Thank you," I say instead.

He looks at me. And I watch as his mouth shapes up a smile.

Anne and Hetty are back before we are. Anne's fixing her hair, putting her straw cap neat in place.

"Did you both have fun?" Hetty asks. She's not asking me. Her eyes are on Hal, mouth puckered up. Concerned.

"We did," Hal says. And then he goes over to his bed, and sits, and pulls out some socks that need darning. He keeps his head down, focused.

We watch him get a thread through a needle's eye.

Then he says, "It was good."

Then Hetty and Anne look right at each other. Hetty shrugs, and Anne nods back and sits herself queenly at the table.

"You still want to try card tricks?" Anne asks me, out of nowhere.

I nod once.

"Come sit," she says.

I sit, and she gets out a deck of cards from her skirt. Starts to shuffle it, quick and neat.

"There's a tavern," she says. "I work there sometimes. If you learn properly, you can come with me. But if you cause trouble I won't ask you again. Do you understand?"

"I do," I tell her.

"Say it back to me, then," she demands.

I stare, keeping my eyes fixed on hers. Not as challenge. Respect.

"I'll learn, same as you learn letters," I say. "I'll work hard. I won't cause trouble."

Anne says nothing. Her nostrils flare. I don't know what feeling she's holding back.

"Trust that I don't want jail or a hanging," I say levelly. "Trust that I want to make good money. So I'll listen."

She keeps eye contact. Fans out the cards.

"It's always just been us," Anne says. She says it serious. The cards are all in front of her now—fanned out, black, white, red. She wants me to know something. Something she's not saying.

I wait.

"Jamie's parents love him," she says finally. "But mine are so far away they're good as gone. And Hal . . . Hetty and me are all he's got. We're family. And we take care of each other."

"I don't need family, Anne," I say.

She frowns and looks down. "Take the cards," she says. "Let's see how you shuffle the deck."

I go for the fanned cards. She clucks her tongue like I've done something wrong.

"Call me Annie," she says casually. "And let me show you how to do that right."

Later, I go back to my lodging house. Jamie says I can sleep on their floor if I want. I've done it a few times. But today I say no.

I go up the lodging house stairs. I've eaten nothing, but I don't feel hungry. My head, my stomach—all of me's full of what I've learned. Tricks that work for different games, different decks. Faro, whist, piquet. Ways to remember cards with your hands. How to mark them, ways no one else will see so only you know what's coming next, using black dots, clean water, a splash of India ink on card backs. Diamonds, spades, hearts.

Ways to make a mark trust you. Ways to trick someone not by cards but by your smile or your charm. Anne—Annie—says that's not my strength.

"But we'll try to teach you," she said. Looked me over keenly. "Maybe there's other ways to trick a person than smiles."

John, who shares the bed with me, is facing the other way already, feet by where my head will go. He's smoking a pipe. Watching me.

"You're not much around anymore," John says. He's giving me a narrow look. Like he's suspicious of something.

"More room in the bed for you, then," I mutter at him, taking off my boots. My feet ache.

I lie back, not bothering to undress. Close my eyes.

Strange to be watched. Strange to have someone care if you live or die.

There only used to be you, Cathy. I always thought that was enough.

Now I'm not so sure.

Chapter Ten

Catherine

AFTER SEEING EDGAR AND ISABELLA, I feel empty. There isn't much point anymore in trying to convince Hindley that I must see Edgar, if Edgar cannot give me what I want. So I stop trying to be good, and eventually Hindley seems to stop worrying over me anyway.

I still try to keep out of his way, but the problem is that we're both restless at night and both like to wander. Once, I even hid in the room where the trunks of treasures from India are kept. *Treasures* makes the room sound very grand, but it is not. It's dust sheets and one small window that lets in only the weakest light, and trunks full of things that have not been touched or worn for more years than I have been alive, I expect. I sat under the sheets with the chests, and breathed dust, and thought about not being.

Sometimes, I just walk along the corridors, or go down into the kitchen and pet the dog and prepare leftovers from the pantry for myself. Usually I can slip away down another corridor or into another room before Hindley sees me, but he has caught me a few times anyway at night. He went very pale the first time and had to swallow three times before he could shout.

"You're worse than the mouser," he spat. "Always turning up where you're not wanted."

I've never brought anything half-eaten or half-dead—or both—and laid it at his feet, as our old cat has done many times. But I suppose that shows what Hindley thinks of me, doesn't it? His feral little sister, always carrying something unpleasant with her wherever she goes, thinking it will be a gift. The mouser carries mice, and I carry . . .

Oh, I don't know. Myself, perhaps. There's something that sets Hindley's teeth on edge about me. Maybe it's the Heathcliff-ness of me. Now that Heathcliff isn't here, there's no one to make me look softer. I often thought people believed me cheerful and sunny simply because Heathcliff carried his own rain cloud with him wherever he went. Even gray days—and often I feel as if I am a very gray day indeed—look very fine when you set them against a moonless night.

"Did I scare you?" I asked, and Hindley cursed me and dragged me back to my own room.

But now, it is not night, only very close to it, and when I creep down the stairs that creak uneasily beneath my feet, I can feel something. It is like the air is heavy. My spine prickles. I feel like a hare at the end of a hunting rifle. There is danger about, and my body knows it, even if my fool self keeps on walking toward the kitchen to eat as if all's well.

I find Nelly hiding Hareton in a cupboard. He has his favorite blanket in his hands and is sucking on the cloth and making it dark with his spit. Nelly looks at me sidelong and mutters, "You should go back upstairs."

I can hear glasses clinking about, and braying laughter.

"Does he have company?" I ask tentatively. Sometimes my brother has friends from the village come visit. Gentlemen, most of them, all of them with deep pockets. They like to gamble. So does Hindley, but he is not very good at winning. He is always miserable after a game. Always a little poorer. One day, I expect I will wake up and learn that Hindley has gambled the Heights away entirely, leaving us homeless.

"He does," Nelly confirms. "So you'd best go to bed."

"I'm hungry." There is an instinct in me for trouble that I should not listen to, and that instinct wants to swan into the kitchen and carve some bread and cheese, calm as you like, as if I am not afraid of Hindley's moods at all.

"Cathy," Nelly says. She says it cold and steady. No *Miss Cathy* this time. "Get to bed."

I hear more laughter, and it makes the hairs rise at the back of my neck and on my arms, as if my body is a little animal and is rightly afraid. I look at Hareton, and then at Nelly, and I say reluctantly, "I can hide him in my room."

Hareton stares back at me with huge eyes.

"No," Nelly says slowly. She looks me over, up and down.

Frowning. "No, don't worry yourself, Miss Cathy. I'll keep Hareton safe and sound."

She doesn't trust me. I suppose I have never done anything to make her think I would be good with Hareton, but somehow it still shocks me. Like the world has stumbled sideways.

I go to my room.

Hours later, I hear glass break. And another loud noise, like a rifle shot. I wish Heathcliff were here, but I am also . . . also glad he is not.

Sometimes, when Hindley got his rifle, he'd look for Heathcliff. And I'd watch out the windows as Heathcliff strode out across the heath in the dark night, because he'd have no safety anywhere in the Heights. Not even in the stables, nor the dairy. He wouldn't come back until morning, on a night like this one.

Once, he was a true fool and didn't run far away. He climbed up the tree by my window and crouched in the branches. Tapped hard on the glass. I thought it was the branches against the glass at first. And then I realized it was him and scrambled to get the window open, panicked.

"Heathcliff," I hissed. "What are you doing here?"

"Hiding," he said, like it was obvious and I should know it. "Talking to you."

"You should be—oh, you should be anywhere but here," I said sharply, trying not to let my voice rise.

"I was thinking I don't like leaving you alone, nights like these," he said. "I was thinking, I don't trust Hindley."

"Hindley would never hurt me."

I heard a crash from downstairs. Flinched. Heathcliff didn't say anything about it—not about Hindley's brutishness or my fear—which was unusually nice of him. Instead, he said, in a voice that was a scrap of something dark and velvet, "Imagine I'm just an angel guarding your window."

The moonlight was liquid over half his face, making it shine. The other half was all shadow. I looked into his moonlit eye, which gleamed like a night creature's, and said, "I don't care for angels."

"Just a man, then," he said. "But a man that's got wings. That can carry you away if there's danger. That won't let you get hurt."

"A man sounds better," I whispered. And I kept my window open all night, listening for the warning creak of Hindley's footsteps on the stairs, even as Heathcliff and I whispered nonsense stories to each other, our hands tangled.

Tonight, I dream of Heathcliff. Of opening my window and holding out my hands and being carried away, stars raining over us, all slippery light.

Later, Nelly calls my name and wakes me from an uneasy sleep. By the time I open my door she's gone, but there's a hunk of bread outside wrapped in cloth. I snatch it up and close my door and eat half crouched on the floor, crumbs gathering on my knees. And then when I am no longer hungry, I crawl back into my cold bed and dream.

Morning comes fast.

I know Hindley will wake late today and everyone will be

quiet as mice so as not to disturb him. So I decide to take advantage. I feel trapped and decide I will go outdoors. That is the only thing I really decide. After that I trust my instincts. My body knows where I should go, even if my tired mind doesn't.

Quietly, I get up. I have a mirror in my room. I stand in front of it as I dress. It's clumsy work, trying to dress without someone to help. When I was a young girl, my clothes were all practical, with stays I could put on by myself, but now that I am sixteen and a lady my usual gowns are far too tricky for me to manage easily on my own. Too many things to lace and tie, and most of them behind my back. I try to fumble with the laces for a long minute, and then I become horribly frustrated and swear the way I have heard Joseph do when he thinks none of us are about to notice his sins.

I look at myself in my mirror—my face silvery, and my hair loose, and my body a long thing with no proper clothing to give it the right shape. And then I remember.

I have some of Heathcliff's clothes. I put them here long ago, when he outgrew them. He said nothing when I took them, only gave me a long look, and said if I wished to know how to wear a waistcoat properly, I need only ask him. I have kept them in my room since then, hidden.

I take them out now. A shirt and breeches, both covered in neat darning, because Heathcliff had to fix tears in them so often. A coat that I know became a little too small for him years and years ago, but he wouldn't part with, in case his best one became damaged and he had no replacement for it.

I put it on. It's far too big for me; the sleeves and shoulders drown me.

I feel a little silly doing it but . . . I turn my head and press my nose to the collar. It doesn't smell of him anymore. It just smells of wool, a little damp, and faintly of the lavender I keep in my trunk.

I sit at my mirror and pick up my comb. I brush all my curls out, stroke by stroke, until my hair is a storm. It's as close to Heathcliff's sleeker hair as mine will ever come, I suppose. I tie it into a queue with a ribbon.

I look into the mirror. I don't look quite right. I stand up tall and hunch my shoulders a little, as if I am not sure if I want to vanish or want to be seen. I firm up my jaw. Tighten my eyebrows, pushing all my anger up to my face. Then I look again.

I look a little like him. Like Heathcliff.

I think I like it.

I have to wear my own boots, of course. I don't have any of Heathcliff's, and they would be far too big anyway. So I slip into my own, and I lace them up. I have a little bread left from last night, so I eat that while standing, shoe leather warming to my skin, and then decide I'm ready enough.

I don't try to go out the door and risk being caught. I open my window instead. It's good I'm small, because I can squirm through the frame and cling on to the tree outside. I've done it plenty of times in my normal clothes, and it's even easier dressed liked this. I climb down and land on the soil. And then I start walking.

The sky is blue, smeared with watery light. I raise my face up to the chill and make my way out, away across the wide moors, toward the crags I can see in the distance and the strange cave that lies inside them. My place, and Heathcliff's. The fairy cave.

I walk and walk—and climb, the stone cutting into my hands, my boots creaking as I go. My breath puffs out of me. I'm nowhere as strong as I was before the rain, and my fever, and what has come after. But I still make it there.

The entrance of the fairy cave is part of the crags, and narrow. You have to turn sideways to get in, the stone wet around you. But once you're inside . . .

I make my way in. It's so still here. Water running gently down stone walls, which are white and marked with strange things. Circles and gouges.

I look around and hug myself. Wrap my own hands into the coat that Heathcliff once wore. And I breathe. And I remember.

I was fourteen when Edgar and I began to fall in love. It was great fun, falling in love. Laughing over each other's jokes, and walking arm in arm, and trying to steal kisses. We didn't have much luck, though. We were always carefully watched to make sure we'd behave.

We managed it once when we succeeded in running from our chaperones. We were laughing, and Edgar clutched my face in his hands and nudged his mouth against mine. It was clumsy and . . . nice. Fun. When it was over, I thought, *Oh. I suppose I can do that again.*

Sometimes we would walk around the lawns of the Grange, and I would imagine being mistress of the house and how nice it would be, to be rich and loved. When Edgar brought me roses cut from his mother's garden, the thorns all carefully scraped off, I would thank him and raise them to my nose and think of all the flowers I would plant instead. Wild things that would overgrow everything. Things with sharper thorns, that would bite hands that touched them. Maybe I would breed a new kind of rose. Hardier and crueler.

That should have been a good time. But it was not, because as I began to build a grand future, Heathcliff began to slip away from me.

Heathcliff was sullen, most of the time. Always working, because Hindley didn't like seeing him rest. Truthfully, Hindley didn't like seeing him at all. There were some days that I would only see Heathcliff through the windows, just a small figure with hunched shoulders, carrying sacks or tools across the distance. But when I did see Heathcliff, I always tried to coax him to smile or laugh like he used to when we were small, before Mother and Father died, and the dog bit me, and the Lintons took me in and taught me what being a lady meant.

Once, Heathcliff got fed up of my prodding and said, "If you want to make me happy, Cathy, you'll come with me."

"Where?"

He shrugged. "Don't know."

"You don't know?"

"No."

"Heathcliff," I whined, jabbing his arm with my finger. When he shook his head, I tugged a lock of his hair that had come loose. He scowled but didn't pull away, so I tugged harder.

"Why won't you tell me?" I asked. "You're just trying to annoy me, aren't you? Do you *like* seeing me angry?"

"I like it when your face goes red," he said very seriously. "It makes you look like a strawberry."

"I hate you," I said without meaning it. I saw a smile tug the edge of his mouth—just tug. And it made my heart somersault, giddy. "If you don't know, then why don't we just stay here?" I asked.

"And do what?"

I hesitated. There was nothing we could do that Hindley wouldn't interfere with. I looked into his eyes, and he looked into mine. Then he nodded.

"Let's go to the fairy cave," he said.

I knew he was daring me. I could see it in his eyes. The fairy cave was a long walk from home. We used to go there all the time, when I didn't have to worry about being chaperoned, or about keeping my clothes clean and neat, or my hair high and curled, like a proper lady's should be. If I went now I would be in trouble. Heathcliff would be in worse trouble.

But I missed him. I missed him so much. And I hadn't felt uneven stone beneath my feet, or wind on my skin, in so long.

"All right," I said. "Let's go."

It should have been dark in the fairy cave. It had been so dark when we entered, like going down a tunnel that led into another world, where there was no sun, no moon or stars at all. But the light had followed us in, the thinnest strand of it, and the white stone made the light spark into dozens of smaller flecks of light. We were haloed like angels, and all of Heathcliff's curls were sun-drenched, turning his black hair a brown that shone like brass.

It almost hurt to look at him. I don't know why. I only know my heart ached like it was being split open. Like something was unfurling inside it, petalled and strong. So I turned away and looked at the cave walls and the light spilling over them. The little gouges in them, deep cups, ringed by fanning lines.

"Look at all these marks," I whispered, awestruck. I kneeled down on stone. My skirts were already dirty from the climb. What was a little more now? I was already in trouble. "How clever those fairy hands must have been, to carve such strange things!"

"If I were a fairy, I'd do more than carve some marks in walls," Heathcliff said.

"Maybe they did a great deal more but it's all gone," I said, determined not to let the tale go. I could hear him walking behind me with steady, even footsteps. He crouched down beside me, his hands clasped in front of him.

His wrists were bare. I remember that. His shirt wasn't long enough at the sleeves, so I could see the skin the sun hadn't touched, and the way it grew darker at his hands. There was soil under his fingernails.

"Your hands are dirty," I said. "Did you get mud on them when we climbed?"

He looked down and turned them over. "I must have, I suppose," he said. "But don't worry. You're still shining clean. Maybe you're too much of a lady for the mud to dare touch you."

"How silly," I exclaimed. "My skirt is absolutely ruined, and we both know it."

"Of course," he said, faintly smiling. "It's your skin it won't dare touch."

I wasn't sure if that pleased me or scared me—scared me that I had become so different from the dirty, wild little creature I'd been as a girl without even knowing it—so I brushed back my curls and said airily, "I can't help being perfect, Heathcliff."

He exhaled. That was how he laughed, sometimes. Without any sound, something small and private just for us.

Then he reached his hand for me and touched his fingertip behind my ear.

"For nazar," he said, pressing the dirt on his skin behind my ear. I let him.

"Nazar?"

"The evil eye," he said, which didn't mean anything to me. "To protect you from jealous folk. It's something I remember."

He didn't say where he remembered it from, but I hoarded up the word and the memory like gold.

"There's no one to be jealous of me," I said. "There's just you here. And me."

"Not true. There's ghosts. They must be as jealous of you as I am."

"Why would *you* be jealous of me?" I asked.

"Because you never have to be away from you," he said seriously. "You get all your brightness all the time, Cathy. The rest of us only get pieces." He paused, and his mouth was . . . soft. A little open, around his breathing.

"Sometimes I think I'm starving, when I'm away from you," he told me quietly. "Like I need your light to live. Maybe that's jealousy."

A shiver ran right through me.

"We used to know the same words, once," he observed.

What a strange thing that was for him to say.

But it didn't shock me. It wasn't the reason my breath caught in my throat like a bird tangled in a net. It was his hand on me that made the breath go strange in me. Just his fingertips and nothing else, pressing the skin behind my ear. But he wasn't letting go. He was stroking the skin, little strokes, like gentling.

I tried to imagine what it would be like if he moved his fingers against my head and tangled them in my hair.

I thought of the kiss with Edgar. The clumsiness of it. The pleasantness. There was nothing pleasant about whatever this was, this thing I could feel running between us, like water, like the memory we both shared of waves underneath us.

"Close your eyes," I whispered.

He closed them. He had very thick eyelashes, very black.

I leaned into him. Pressed my thumb against his lower lip. He still had his eyes closed, trusting me.

I wanted to kiss him so much. I wanted to take his face in my hands and kiss him so I could pour all the feeling in me into him, and he could pour feeling back.

I touched my mouth close to his own. I was so close that I could feel his breath. And smell his skin, which was like . . . oh, like salt and heather. Like home.

My thumb was between us. So even if our lips touched at the edges, even if I could feel his breath, and count his eyelashes, we were not kissing. We were not, but it was so sweet. I wanted to run my thumb over his lip and kiss him properly, like we were sweethearts. Like we would marry one day, and nothing could stop us.

I drew back.

I had no dirt on my hands, but I touched my fingers behind his ear all the same. He let me. He was looking at me with open eyes . . . oh, I can't even describe his eyes. Dark and wide, the kind of dark that enfolds you.

"For nazar," I said softly. "Because. It's the same for me."

Oh. Oh, why did I come here?

I know why. I know why.

At some point, I kneeled. And my legs hurt and are cold but I keep kneeling, because I am crying too hard to stand. I was kneeling when I kissed Heathcliff, too. Or almost kissed him. Does the difference matter?

I weep and weep and weep. I can't stop it. I don't even know what I'm weeping for. I just keep thinking of Heathcliff and our almost kiss. I keep thinking of words, half words, forgotten words. Nazar. That isn't English I know, but how do I know it?

Is this something else I stole from Heathcliff and decided was my own?

Isn't Heathcliff mine? Aren't I his? Is that why I feel like only half a person, like he took something with him? Wearing his clothes, tying my hair like his . . . I know it is a childish thing to do, I know it makes no sense. But I want him back so much. And I want the Cathy I was with him.

I used to write it in my books: Catherine Heathcliff. I wrote our names together once to teach him his letters, and after that I couldn't stop. As if I could take his name and stitch it to my own so I could become his and he could become mine in a way I know he can't.

"I bound you here, Heathcliff," I whisper. Because I did. Bound him in shorn hair buried in soil, in feathers, in names sewn together. And here, inside the fairy cave, with the walls dripping water and the light shining above me, the sound of my words bounces and echoes and sounds like more voices than my own.

"I bound you, so you must come home to me. Or I shall haunt you until the end of both of us. I vow it."

Chapter Eleven

Heathcliff

IT'S LATE, NOW. GETTING TO the time when the taverns and gin shops start filling up.

I look out the window, smeared almost black by night and grime. The candlelight looks back at me, glowing red. It flickers, so I turn, and there's Annie waiting. She's dressed up to charm her marks, in a gown that's got ribbons, a feather in her cap. She's got her cards ready.

"Daydreaming?" she asks.

"No," I tell her. "I'm ready."

I've learned plenty of tricks since Annie started teaching me. When she thought I'd learned enough, she set me and her up against Hetty.

"Trick her with me, and you can do your first sham with me," Annie said.

I never properly tricked her. Hetty always knew what I'd do. Besides, she knew all the same tricks as Annie. The way you can say what a card is with a blink, or your mouth open or closed, or shifting in your chair. The marks on cards, Annie's marks, telling you what they are from the back. But eventually Hetty decided I was good enough anyway, and told me so by warning me exactly how she'd gut me if I did anything that got Annie in trouble.

So far, we've had no trouble at all.

In one tavern, near the theater, Annie, Hetty, and me shammed a drunk theatergoer out of good money. He laughed over it, not knowing I was a sharper or that he was being tricked. "Next time read my fortune, eh?" he said to me.

After he was gone, Hetty looked over at me and rolled her eyes. That made the anger pinching me ease almost as much as the coin did.

Tonight, it's just me and Annie. Hetty's miserable sick, nursing a stuffed nose in bed.

When Annie's sharping, she's not so solemn or haughty. She goes charming. It's a trick, same as cutting a pocket or skirt lining and lifting out coin. When likely marks look over, she smiles or laughs, or tosses her hair about. When she and Hetty work alone, they make a game out of it—two smiling, happy girls who want to try cards, looking to have fun. Sometimes men ask if they've played before, and they say no, but they would like to learn.

So they pretend to learn. Then they clean up, taking the money for themselves.

Now it's me and Annie. I can't do sweet and laughing, so we do a different play. One where she flirts and teases, and I look sullen. Don't know why, but it draws people in.

The tavern where Annie's playing cards today isn't like normal. It only looks rough. The wood looks old, but it's good quality. The windows are dingy, but someone's made them so. The floor's scuffed, used-looking, but someone keeps it properly clean. I've never seen an alehouse or tavern with a floor that doesn't stick to your boots.

Here, the drinkers aren't normal people either. They've all got money. They try and dress like they don't, but you can see it if you look, and you don't even have to look that close. Good-quality cloth in their clothes. Not patched or mended. Powder still in their hairlines. The muck in their boots is all new, not stained in from walking through the same sewage round here, day in and day out.

"They want to slum it," Anne explained to me, when she was getting ready. Putting paint on her face, Hal holding a small cracked mirror steady so she could do it. "It's a good place to work, because if I flirt a bit and make them feel special, they won't mind losing a bit of money to me, and they can afford to do it."

"I don't think they'll want flirting from me," I muttered.

And Annie cracked a real grin, cackling out a laugh. "You're just going to the wrong places," she said. "Bless you. But if you ever want to flirt with a gent, you let me know. I'll show you how."

The tavern fills up. We make a show of drinking. The owner knows and takes a cut, as long as we drink and get people to do the same, whether they're marks for a sham or not. Annie laughs and chatters. I just try looking like I don't want to gut anyone. I drop half the drink away, Annie doing the same. We play a game or two, not cheating. Just settling in.

The night goes on. Candles get relit. A group of men stride in. Boots thumping. They've got the look of rich folk pretending to be poor, but most of them are big. Muscled like fighters. The crowd opens for them. They go to the best table, over in the corner. The people sitting there take one look and get up. The newcomers order ale and start smoking pipes. I think they won't be bothering us.

Then one turns and sees us. He nudges the man next to him.

Annie stiffens up. *Not them*, her shoulders say. *Not them*.

But one comes over. Sits himself down. The rest stay where they are, in shadowed seats, smoking pipes over mugs of ale.

Up close, in candlelight, I see him proper. My heart thumps.

He looks like me. He's Indian maybe, or something like it. He looks at me, then Annie, smiling like a cat with a mouse in its jaws. I know that look. I saw the mouser at the Heights playing with her food plenty of times.

One second passes, then Annie makes her smile brighten up. Flicks back her curls and says, "Do you want to join our game, friend? I'm teaching this one the rules of piquet." She prods my face with a finger. Playful. "He's not very good."

"Is he your sweetheart, lovely?"

Annie laughs. "Silly! Do I look like I have a sweetheart?"

"You look like you could have a dozen sweethearts if you wanted to," he says. Someone listening starts laughing.

I don't laugh. Annie doesn't laugh either. I try to be calm. How can Annie and the rest say they hate violence when they've got to deal with folk like this? My teeth hurt, I'm gritting my jaw so hard.

My knife's still in my coat.

"We're family," I say. "I'm her brother."

"Brother?"

"Half brother," I say shortly. "Come on," I say to Annie. "We'd best get home to Mother."

"Sit down," he orders. "*Sit*."

"We do have to go," Annie says nervously, and some voice across the room says, "You're scaring the girl." Trying to warn them off.

"You're trying to cheat me," the man says. The mood of the room goes ugly. He points at us. "You two. You're trying to cheat at cards."

Annie gives him a confused look. For once, she's not feigning. We've done nothing yet.

"Fight me," he says, standing so he's looming up. Blocking the room right out. "You." He points at me now. "Get up and fight me, if you've got any honor."

People are watching, not sure what to do. Usually they'd be jeering for a fight, but the wrongness has got them on edge too.

I get up.

"Go home," I say to Annie.

She frowns at me. "No."

"Go home," I say again. "What would Mother say if I let you get caught up in a fight?"

Her eyes flash. But she gets up, and the man lets her.

I take off my coat. Roll up my shirtsleeves.

"If you wanted to fight," I say low-voiced. "You only had to say so, friend."

"I want to fight," he says back. Grinning. Malicious. "Friend."

He aims a punch straight at my skull.

I duck. He brings his knee up hard, trying to break my nose, but I see him move and I grab a chair and shove it between us. The wood cracks and knocks me in the face, but it's better than a knee to the nose. And it hurts him too. He swears, tripping a step back. That's good. That gives me long enough to lift the broken chair up and slam it at him. He's too tall for me to get the face, so I go for what's between his legs.

The noise he makes is a scream like I've not heard before.

"You little bastard," he snarls. Then he lunges for my throat.

I can't get out the way. But I've still got a broken chair leg in my hands. I hold it up to his throat.

He freezes. Sharp stillness. If he hadn't stopped, the wood would be in his neck. If he hadn't stopped, I'd be a killer.

I meet his eyes, and bare my teeth. Smiling.

"Done?" I ask.

He looks like he's not sure. Like he might keep fighting me anyway. But through the noise the crowd's making, someone speaks up, and the crowd goes silent.

"Stop," they say. They say it calm. "Bring him here, there's a boy."

I think the *boy*'s meant for me, but it's the man in front of me, chair leg at his throat, who answers.

"Come with me," he says. "My master wants to meet you properly."

Killing him would do me no good, so I lower the wood. I follow him to his master.

The master's sitting at the corner table. Smoking his pipe. He's got gold in his coat, and gold shot through his waistcoat. Silk stockings under those breeches. Gold-buckled boots. His hair's eye-watering white.

"You seem like a strong one," the master says. Cultured voice. He's half in shadow, but his eyes gleam like ice. "Come here. Stand closer."

I go. I stand closer. My heart's still hammering. I'm bleeding from my mouth.

"I have," he says, "an offer of employment for you. Would you like to make your fortune, boy?"

Yes. Don't even need to think to know that's what I feel. But I don't say so. I'm not such a fool.

"What employment?" I ask.

He tells me, as he taps ash from his pipe, "Keeping order."

I wait. He says nothing more.

I tell him, "I'll think on it."

"Good boy," the man says. He smiles at me. The light gives his mouth more teeth than what it needs. "You think on it as long as you like. But I'll need an answer tonight."

Edgar Linton wouldn't think for a second. He'd be right out the door. Black wood swinging shut behind him, sucking cold air between his teeth. *Foul men*, he'd say. *Ruffians.* I can see it, in my head: his white face gone blotchy, the way it goes when you rile him right up, get him frothing like a yapping pup. Pale, soft hands trembling. He's never even thought about doing wrong. So he'd go.

But Edgar Linton would have died in that fight. And me, I'm no soft-handed gentleman. Put me in good clothes, brush my hair, do what you like. That won't make something gentle out of me. I've got hard hands. Five scars on my left knuckles, finger twisted wrong on the right. Hindley broke it, and it healed crooked. I broke it again on purpose, and you helped me set it right, Cathy, but it's still twisted, still twinges and turns slow. Hindley beat me enough that I'm the same as your books, Cathy. Peel back the skin, and there's words written in there that shouldn't be.

Hindley called me dirt. Filth. Savage. Brute. He called me a lot worse, when he was in his drink, and Nelly had run away with the baby, and you were locked tight in your room, brushing your hair furious until it turned to clouds. Brown going crackling black. And me, with my lip split and jaw smarting, wondering if this time he'd get his gun.

He tried to knife Nelly once. When he held it at her face, she bit the blade between her teeth, and he was so shocked he let it go. Me, I would have ripped the hunting knife out of his hands and stabbed him through. That was why he always went for fists first with me.

Later you'd come find me in the barn. Creep down the stairs, cupping the candle. Jump over the eighth step, which creaked.

I liked the sight of you—the moon behind you, candle in your hands, hair stormy. Liked when you said we could kill him together someday, the two of us.

"You don't want him dead," I said to you once, my voice low. "If you did, I'd have killed him a long time ago."

You looked at me, all serious.

"I do want him dead," you said. "I do. Right now, I truly do. But, Heathcliff, tomorrow I'll wake and Hareton will be playing and Nelly will offer me breakfast, and Hindley will be sleeping, and this will all seem like a bad dream. And I will think of how fine it is, to live in our little home, with the moors all around us and you with me, and I will not hate him anymore."

I asked you, not that time—what would you do if he hit you too? How would you stop me killing him then?

You shrugged. Cracked your knuckles. Stretched your fingers.

"Where else," you said, all reasonable, "could we live?"

If I take what I'm being offered, I might end up dead. But I might make a wealthy man out of me. No one cares if you're dark if you're rich. Nelly said to me once, you could be the son of an Indian queen. A Chinese emperor. And what makes an Indian prince better than a lascar's son but coin? Enough money and you can buy anything you like. You can make a home wherever you want to.

Cathy. You, and me, home. I could buy that.

"I'd like some work," I say to the man. I say it calm. "If you're offering. Whatever you're offering."

"Good. Meet me here tomorrow morning," he says. "Let's talk business. Like men."

Chapter Twelve

Catherine

THERE'S A NEW GOUGE IN the parlor wall. I know it was made by a rifle. Gambling must have gone very poorly for Hindley to shoot the wall, ruining his dead wife's favorite wall hanging.

I want to pretend to myself that the hole is like the little carved marks on the walls of the fairy cave. It's the kind of tale I would have told Heathcliff once. *It could be a fairy's work*, I would have said. And Heathcliff would have touched the gouge where the bullet had gone in and would have said in that cold, certain way he did, *Fairies or no, Cathy, your brother will pay for this one day. Mark my words.*

My stomach lurches. I can't pretend. I take some oatcakes from the kitchen and then I go back to my room. I will need a proper meal at some point, but I don't think I shall try and have one today. Hindley is going to be awful, I am sure, if he catches sight of me. So far he has not.

I got home without being seen, after visiting the fairy cave, and climbed back into my room through the window. If anyone came to wake me in the morning, I saw no sign of it. I should have been relieved to be in no trouble, but I wasn't. I already had trouble inside me, and the trouble's still there. It hurts like sickness, but I know it's not. It's guilt.

I have done nothing to get Heathcliff home, or see if he's safe. I have argued with my brother and tried to cajole Edgar, and I've managed nothing. The most I've done is make myself ill.

What does me running out on the moors until I get feverish do for Heathcliff? Nothing. But what else can I do but howl and run and scream for him? I have no money, and no knowledge of the world at all. I can read Hindley's mood like I can read the skies—I always know when a storm is coming. But I wouldn't even know how to begin living in the world beyond Gimmerton.

But that isn't the real reason I haven't saddled my horse and raced off after him. I think it's because deep down I know the truth. Even now I don't want to think it or look at it but I know:

It's my fault Heathcliff isn't here. And I am absolutely the last person he would want to see.

This is why. This is my shame:

Edgar asked me to marry him. He asked me in the Heights, in the parlor, so earnestly, so sweetly, and my heart bubbled inside of me. He said he would speak to his parents and make everything formal and proper, but he wanted to ask me first, to hear me say yes in my own voice and see my face with his own eyes. It wasn't like a Linton to be improper even in a small way, and it made me feel special.

Of course I said yes. I was triumphant. I finally had him and all my dreams with it.

But I also felt sadness too, and I didn't want to look at that feeling. Didn't want to touch it, squirming the way it was in my chest. But it refused to let me ignore it. Even as I cajoled Nelly into sitting with me and told her how excited I was to one day be Edgar's wife, I felt the sadness rise up and force words out of my mouth.

"Heathcliff," I blurted out. "Do you think he will be happy for me?"

The look Nelly gave me was very judgmental at first. But then her expression smoothed and she said, "Why do you love your Edgar, Miss Cathy?"

I told her why. Because he was handsome. Because he was kind. Because he was rich, and young as me, and we would be happy together. Because I liked how it felt to be with him. Safe and steady, like the world couldn't hurt me.

"Is that all?" Nelly asked.

"All?" I repeated. As if that was not everything I could want.

Loving Edgar was—well, it was freedom. And I was not often sensible, but I knew I could not stay here at the Heights. I knew what Hindley was. I didn't know what would happen if I did not marry and I stayed at home, only that even thinking of it made my breath run short and terror fill my head. Terror for me, but also for Heathcliff, who had no one to love him but me. Who spoke of killing my brother. Who had no hope at all—only anger, and his own bones, and a hunger for things he couldn't have.

"And how do you feel for Heathcliff?" Nelly asked, after a moment.

"He is too low for me," I said immediately. "He is beneath me. I couldn't possibly marry him."

And oh, how bitter it was that Hindley had made things that way! But he had stripped Heathcliff of all the fine things our father had given him, and what was Heathcliff now? Less than a servant. Nelly and Joseph had more power than him by far, because they had a place and a role, and Heathcliff had . . . nothing. He was an outsider. Not someone I could kiss in a fairy cave or anywhere else for that matter, not without the both of us being thrown from the Heights and starving to death somewhere. We had no money and no skills between us. What hope was there?

But his lowness—it didn't change his soul. And I knew from the second we stood together when I was only small, alone at night outdoors, and spoke of ghosts and buried feathers, that his soul was mine. My soul was his. But it wasn't an exchange or debt between us, it wasn't a vow made before God, the way marriages are. We were *one* soul, one ancient thing that had been split in two halves and been searching for the other piece of itself for centuries upon centuries, and now we had found each other. I am Heathcliff, and Heathcliff is me. What was marrying Edgar, compared to that?

I tried to explain it to Nelly. I tried to spin all that feeling and truth into words, to explain to her how loving Heathcliff was something written into me, something everlasting. I went on breathlessly as she stared at me, not understanding my heart at all, even though I poured it out to her.

"When I am rich," I said in the end. "I will give Heathcliff anything he wants. I'll give him the finest future he can dream of."

I could not marry him. What of it? I would still love him. He would still love me. And because he was written into me, into my bones and my soul, no matter what he did or I did—even if I became Mrs. Edgar Linton and he went away, or married some other girl—we'd be part of each other. That's what I told myself. And we would both be free from all the dark things we were afraid of here in our own home. Hindley would never be able to hurt us. And maybe one day, maybe somehow . . .

I couldn't even finish the thought. There was no point in dreaming of having more with Heathcliff when I knew I never could. Dreaming of angels or fairies couldn't hurt me. But dreaming of being able to kiss Heathcliff or love him? That would be like driving a knife into my own heart. My own heart that had his name written into it tangled up with my own.

Nelly was staring at me. I thought it was another of her judgmental looks at first—and I was going to scold her for always asking me how I felt, and then thinking less of me for it—but then I realized she looked very pale. A guilty, frightened kind of whiteness.

"What is it?" I asked, alarmed.

She swallowed. "Heathcliff."

Her gaze flicked over my shoulder, and I turned and saw the door a little open, a shadow spilling through it. And even before Nelly began to tell me that Heathcliff had heard me speak, had listened with his face growing stormier and stormier and then turned on his heel and left so swift it was like he was running from his own death, I knew he'd heard me. I *knew*.

"When did he go?" I demanded. "Did he listen to everything? Or did he . . . ?"

"He left early," she said in a tight voice. "Right after you spoke of his . . . his lowness."

My blood ran cold.

"Why did you not stop me speaking?" I yelled at her. "Why didn't you stop him?"

Nelly shook her head, which was no answer.

"Do you *want* me to suffer?" I asked, already crying. "Did you want *him* to suffer? How could you . . . how could you . . . ?"

"Cathy," Nelly said. No *Miss Cathy* this time. She stood up at the same moment I did. But she was too late. I was already running to the door. Already throwing it all the way open and running down the corridor, calling Heathcliff's name. But there was no sign of him.

The kitchen door was open, the cold wind blowing in. I knew Heathcliff was gone.

He heard me call him beneath me, and low. He'd heard, and he ran.

So I ran after him in the rain. Ran and ran until my body gave up.

And now I am here.

Alone. Without him.

It is like the real Cathy is fading away day by day. I can spend time with Edgar with no trouble at all. Slipping into that skin is so easy. I only have to smile at him, or tease Isabella until she laughs, and I am Catherine Almost-Linton. I am sunny and bright and lovable, but ladylike of course—always perfectly ladylike, my ringlets never misplaced, my skirts shining.

The minute I am in the Heights—no, the very second—I am just Catherine Earnshaw again. It is like all the strength leaves me. I am just ugliness and grief.

Going to the fairy caves awoke something inside me. It is the same thing that awoke when I pressed my thumb to Heathcliff's mouth and almost kissed him. Like a flower opening up to the sun. Or a tree bending into a new shape from the wind. But what's bloomed is useless to me and won't be any use to Heathcliff either.

I am starting to look forward to the day that Edgar and I marry. Then I will be Catherine Linton all the time. This girl who feels so many things and hates herself will be gone. I won't feel like this, and that idea sounds wonderful to me.

I go to bed and dream of being Catherine Linton. I dream of the corridors of the Grange, and the roses in the garden, blooming pink and red. And then I dream of the chinoiserie room, and all those women under their parasols turning toward me, foreign flowers in their hair and their eyes steady, judging me as Nelly's do. *Cathy*, their eyes say. *Cathy, Cathy, you fool. You can't run from yourself.*

And then, I think . . . perhaps I wake up.

I don't know if it's another dream to follow the first or if it really happens. It feels real enough, when I open my eyes in my bed, and hear the wind singing outside, and decide to get up. No one will be awake. I know that. There's a way that night feels, when it's very deep. It goes very still, and the air feels somehow colder, so cold that you can breathe out and watch it flower into wisps in front of you.

I open my oak closet. I open the door. I stand in the hallway. I am not even holding a candle. Everything is dark, the kind of dark you can't find outdoors on the heath, where there is always moon or starlight to help you see. Indoors, with curtains shut, the dark is like . . . like cloth, pressed up all around you. Even the air is heavy.

But even though it is dark, and I should not be able to see a thing, I am sure there is something watching me from the end of the corridor. I am sure it stands at the top of the stairs . . . although stands isn't quite right, truly. I know its feet don't touch the ground.

I start to walk forward.

I can hear it breathing, or hear myself breathing. Something wheezing and strange. My heart hammers in my ears. The air gets heavier, heavier. But I don't turn and run back to my bed. I am not that sort of person, although perhaps things would be easier if I were. I hold my arm out. Out, out . . . until my fingers graze cloth.

It's almost like grazing air. The cloth is so soft, finer than water. My arm is lead, and I cannot move it. The cloth shifts as the wearer shifts, gliding forward with a chime like shells or bones. I feel skin under my hand, cold and gossamer.

I dart forward and put my hands around its throat.

The cloth over its face melts away. I still see nothing, but I feel the bones of the ghost's neck, and see the black where its eyes must be. Its hair tickles my arms, curling exactly like my own, and my whole skin skitters as if covered with a dozen spidering hands.

My feet are numb under me, like I am not touching the floor at all.

I am a ghost. I am a ghost. Heathcliff is gone, and all the parts of me that I shared with him are fading like dust. I am a ghost, and I can't find my way home, because my home has run from me. I am a ghost, and I have a ghost's neck in my hands, and I don't think I can breathe.

Cold is creeping through me, from my hands through my arms to my lungs. I can't breathe. I feel the ghost lean forward into my grip. I see a face staring into my own—

I wake in my own bed. Gasping.

If I was sleeping, I am sure I am truly awake now.

I wrap myself up in a shawl. It is knitted and soft, an old one that belonged to my mother. After she died I often wrapped myself in it and tried to smell her on it—the rosemary she kept with her clothes, and the warm scent of baking bread. That's all long gone now.

I go into the corridor, holding my candle. I can see warm light from downstairs. I go down and realize the light is coming from the parlor.

We spend most of our time in the kitchen, because the fireplace is nearly always lit there, and the hearth is large and very warm. The dogs sleep by it, and Hareton is nearly always playing on the floor at a safe distance, with Nelly keeping a watchful eye on him as she works. The parlor is more formal, reserved for special occasions and visitors, and for Hindley when he wishes to spend time alone, because the hearth is so much smaller, and the room is always subtly too cold.

Tonight, the fire's lit, but the floor is ice under my feet. Hindley is slumped in his chair, his sleeves rolled up. His arms are pimpled with gooseflesh. His head is lowered. I swallow.

"I saw a ghost," I say.

I don't know why I say it. Hindley already thinks I am all nerves and that I'm fragile. But it feels important to say it—it feels like I *must* say it, like it is what the ghost wants, and so I do.

Perhaps there is something mad in me after all.

Hindley looks at me. The fire's dying. The room is so dark, all I can see is the orange light reflecting in the whites of his eyes. Does he think I am mad? Perhaps he would be right to. But the truth is you cannot live as I have and believe there is nothing under the surface, that there is only God and the green grass and nothing else that drives a man. I saw it when my father carried Heathcliff home like devils were chasing him; I saw it in my childhood dreams of strange-tongued angels, and I saw it in the fairy caves when Heathcliff and I almost kissed, and I saw it when Heathcliff left, and I have seen it tonight.

There are ghosts, as sure as any of us have souls that go on even when the body is long gone. And there are ghosts *here*, in my own home.

"I saw a ghost," I repeat, because he hasn't answered and I think perhaps he hasn't heard me, or is pretending he hasn't—and no matter how wise it would be to walk away and leave him, I hate being ignored more than anything. "I saw it and I murdered it."

"You can't murder the dead," Hindley finally replies. He sounds very tired, which makes sense, it being as late an hour as it is. But his voice is also not slurred. I think perhaps he has not drunk anything at all, or his head has cleared in the hours he's been asleep. "I should know. I have tried plenty of times."

I don't know what he means, so I say nothing.

"Your ghost," he says. "Was it Father, come back to scold you for being a wicked creature?"

I shake my head.

"No?"

Hindley exhales and leans forward, crooking a finger at me. "Come closer," he says.

I walk to him. My feet are bare, and the floor still feels so cold.

He takes my face in one hand when I am close enough. He

draws me down so he can look carefully at me. He's silent for a long time. There are circles under his eyes, so dark and large they are like smudged ink.

"Sometimes," he says eventually, still holding my face with his fingers. "When there's only candlelight, when it's dark . . . you look just like her, Cathy."

"Like who?" I ask.

"Like our mother," Hindley says.

No one has ever said I look like Mother.

"You've got the same nose," he says. "Straight and strong. The eyebrows. The smile, though you never show it to me anymore." He taps my nose, hard enough to sting. "She had a jewel right here. I remember—she didn't like getting too much sun on her because it made her skin go dark and brown, but early morning she'd go out. The light would glint off it."

"Mother was fair," I say, voice shaking like a leaf, like the words are falling from me and drifting away. I don't know what to say about the nose jewel, so I only say what I can. "She burned in the sun."

"One of our mothers was," he says. "Not the one who birthed us. Not the one who haunts us. No." He taps my cheek then, right over the bone. "She was dark like him."

The way he says *him*, I know he means Heathcliff, and my stomach does a strange somersault.

"Did your ghost look like you, Cathy?" Hindley sounds curious. "Was it our mother, trying to drag her children down to hell with her?"

"No," I say tightly, but I am lying, and he knows it.

"I hate your face," he whispers bitterly, and settles back in his armchair. "When I see ghosts, it's her I see. And when I look at you, I see her too. The dead are everywhere."

I take a step back. I can't truly feel my legs.

"I never planned to tell you," he murmurs, as I take another stumbling step back. "I thought I could spare. But you . . . ah, you're a fool girl, Cathy. A frivolous, silly fool. There's too much Indian blood in you by far. Father should have caned it out of you when there was still hope." He closes his eyes and tilts his head back against his chair.

"No hope," he goes on as I walk away from him, faster and faster. "No hope at all."

I run up the stairs. I run so fast the stairs make a noise like crashing thunder, as they do when Hindley storms up them in a rage. But I am not in a rage. I am crying, but I don't know why. I have left my candle, but I throw the curtains open, the windows. The moonlight spills in, and I can see the carpet and the walls and the ceiling and see that my mother's ghost is nowhere, nowhere, long gone, leaving me behind.

Chapter Thirteen

Heathcliff

I DIDN'T GO STRAIGHT HOME after seeing the rich man sitting in the corner. Annie was waiting outside, half hiding. She hadn't left. She'd listened. I could see the knowing in her eyes. She told me I should come with her.

"You should speak to Jamie," she said.

But I shook my head and said I would go on my own. She pursed her lips but didn't stop me, only drew on her cloak and hurried off, like hell was following her.

Now I'm walking. Seems like, every time I get hurt, I go walking like I'm a ghost that can't find its way home. I pass a building with the door caved in. There's bullet holes round the frame. The road is full of women, some clutching children, some holding knives or pans, pacing, swearing. There's one crying, kneeling on the ground, saying, "They took him, took him. What will we do now? How will we live?"

Some other women hush her, but I hear enough to know that a press-gang's been by and forced a man out of his own home. He belongs to the navy now, and the woman will be lucky to see him again for a long time.

I keep on going.

It's almost daylight when I stumble back to the lodging house. There's someone outside, leaning against the wall, cap low over their eyes. I know them by the shape of their shoulders. The way they're slumped.

"What're you doing here?" I ask Jamie.

He lifts his head up. His eyes are red. Doesn't look like he's slept.

"I've been waiting for you," he says. His voice is scratchy. "Annie told me you got in some trouble."

"Not trouble," I tell him. I don't go closer to him and don't go in. I just stand looking at him. "I got an offer."

"An offer like that's trouble," he bursts out. "You think a rich man coming round our neighborhood and watching a brown boy get beaten by his men for fun is safe to take coin from?"

"What do you think happens at boxing matches?" Blood, sweat. People screaming with laughter. Even rich gentlemen and ladies, eyes wide with bloodlust, watching close. "I don't mind fighting for someone else's fun if it gets me something."

"Don't go back," Jamie says. "Don't do it. That offer's cursed and you know it."

"I won't turn down an offer that could make me rich."

Jamie laughs hollowly. "You think he's going to make you rich? When we first met, I thought you were just green and didn't know how the world is, but maybe you're simply not very smart."

Jamie's not usually the kind to throw barbs. It stings when I'm not bracing for it.

I didn't even know I still had places in me that could be hurt.

"I think," I say slowly, "that some merchant may believe he can test me and use me, but that's his weakness. I think if he lets his guard down that's his fault. So if I get the chance to destroy him and take all he's got, I'll do it. But first, I've got to say yes and pretend I'm trustworthy."

"Can you hear what you're saying? Can you . . . ? Hell," he swears, and presses his hand to his head, like he wants to clip me round the ear but he's forcing himself not to. "That's not how the world works, Heathcliff. People like us don't destroy people like them. *We* get destroyed."

"Maybe *you* can't. But I know exactly what I'm capable of."

We're not the same. Jamie's got a good heart. He's got people he cares about. And me . . .

That isn't me.

I think things I haven't let myself consider, since I asked Jamie for help, and packed my rage away. I think all the dark thoughts that come so easily to me, always: of how easy it'd be to destroy Jamie and the rest and take everything they've got. They care about each other too much. All I have to do is tell the building's landlord what's happening in the nailed-off attic, the one the landlord probably thinks is too small and cold to be used for anything. Then Jamie and the rest would have no home.

And I go darker still: Hal's a runaway. They say on the docks it's illegal, having slaves now, but I've seen the papers. Rich men are always looking for what they think they own and won't let any measly law stand in their way. If I threatened Hal, then Hetty, Annie, and Jamie would all fold like wet cloth, doing what I want. I could control them. And their pain and anger . . . that'd just make them easier to twist and turn.

Thinking it makes my stomach knot. It runs through me like poison.

I wouldn't do it. Not can't—I *could*. But I don't want to, that's the truth. I owe them too much. But the fact I can think it at all, see those paths branching out in front of me . . . that shows what I am. No good. Cut me open and I'm rotten.

Jamie's looking at my face. He still looks angry, but the edges are gone from it. Something in my expression, I don't know what, has changed him.

"I don't know what kind of person you think you are," he says. "But you're wrong."

I know what I am. I got called brute and monster, got made low and barely human by Hindley, by villagers in Gimmerton, by what was in Edgar's disgusted sidelong looks. By you, Cathy, in the end. I know what Hindley calls me doesn't make me what he says, but sometimes a man has to look at himself clear-eyed, and I always try to. Underneath what was said to me and about me, underneath the way Hindley would turn on me like my bones were his for breaking, underneath all that . . .

"I'm cruel," I say bluntly. "When people hurt me, I don't want justice, don't want them to feel an equal hurt. I want them to suffer a thousand times more than I do. I dream about it all the time. I'm angry. Sometimes all I want is to cause pain so everyone feels like I do." I can't stop now that I've started. I keep talking. "I don't have patience. I hate weakness. I hate most other people. Some days I wake up and all I want to do is get blood under my hands and a neck under my boot. I want the dark pleasure of being a man in power. That's not what I think I am. That's what I *know* I am. You think I can't deal with a rich merchant? You think I can't bow and scrape in front of him, then slit his throat? I can. That's just the kind of thing I'm good at."

"You've been teaching us to read and write," Jamie says fast. "No one asked you to do that. But you did it. You don't argue or get vicious when Annie gets sharp or Hetty tells you what to do. You're not like you think."

"Being good when it benefits me doesn't make me good. You've only seen one side of me. Now you're seeing another." I shrug. "If you don't want to be around the person who'd go off with a merchant and do his dirty work, then you don't need to be around me. I don't care."

Jamie's laugh is ugly. "Sure you don't. Sure." He straightens. "You know there's gangs in the city, don't you? Not gangs like us. Proper gangs. If you'd gone to them and shown them you were good at fighting, they'd have taken you. You could have been angry and vicious and caused pain all over the place, as much as you could dream of. You could have made all the coin in the world—or at least, more than you can make with us. Because we're nothing, Heathcliff. Just four nobodies trying to live and take care of each other."

He's walking up to me, until we're near nose to nose.

"If you're such a monster, why stick with us?" he asks. Says it like a challenge. "If you're so cruel, why be our friend? Why bother at all?"

"I'm not your friend," I say harshly. "If you think I am, then you're a more trusting fool than I thought."

"Heathcliff," he says pityingly. "You don't know what you are. You've got no idea."

I was ready for him to lash out at me—I can see how angry he is. But I wasn't ready for whatever this is. I don't want him looking at me anymore.

"I'm going," I say. "And you can't stop me."

Jamie grabs me hard by the arm, and I swing my other hand up and punch him in the stomach. He doubles over and lets go of me. I hear him struggle for air, then get one big lungful in. "Fuck!" he yells.

"Bother me again and I'll break your nose," I warn.

"Why not just knife me?" Jamie demands. "That's what cruel, people-hating you would do, right?"

"You want me to knife you?"

"Don't *you* want to knife me? Go on. Show me what you are."

I'm getting a headache.

"I'm not knifing you to prove a point," I grind out. "But I will beat you if you don't shut up."

"Fine," Jamie says. "Beat me, then." And he barrels into me.

I go down, and then we're rolling on the floor, not fighting proper but punching and kicking like children. I get him in the side of the face with my knuckles. He kicks me. I bite his arm, and he swears and says incredulously, "Are you an animal?"

I answer by punching him again.

It finishes when someone flings open a window and screams at us to shut it. We end up sitting on the ground, even more bruised up than before. Jamie wipes blood from his lip. He laughs once, then wipes his eyes with his other hand.

"You going to change your mind?" he asks.

I say nothing. Keep saying nothing.

"Fine," he says eventually. "Go and meet him."

He stands up and starts limping off. Then he turns back. I'm still sitting on dirty ground. I look back.

"You're not a bad person, Heathcliff," he says. "Or at least no worse than anyone else. Annie says the scars on your hands. She said . . ." He stops. Swallows the words. Says instead, "You're not evil. What you do when people treat you ill, when you're just a child . . . only the worst folk would blame you for that."

"You don't know anything," I say tiredly.

"Fine. I don't know anything. Just . . ." He sighs. "Come by and see us if you change your mind. Or go to him, and become exactly what you think you are. Ruin your own nature. I guess it's no business of mine." He sounds sad.

I watch him go. He turns back once, when he's far off. And then he turns the corner and he's gone.

158

I go back to the tavern like I said I would. There's a carriage outside with tall gray horses bridled to it. The thug I fought yesterday's there, leaning on the wall by the tavern. Glaring me down. I ignore him. I'm not here for him. The rich man's waiting for me inside the carriage, door open, dressed up fine as he was last night.

The man smiles at me. His mouth widens slowly.

"You may call me Mr. Northwood," he says.

His voice is meant to be kind, I think. His accent's polished up, hard to read.

Most people have voices shaped by home. People always know I'm from Yorkshire—can hear it in the way I speak, the way the words move, sound. Walk round the docks, and there's voices from everywhere. There's threads in them that lead other places.

Not Northwood's voice. His is like his fine coat, or the gold on his buckled shoes. It's got no threads. It doesn't say where he's from. It says what he *is*.

Hearing it makes me wary. I don't think he's a mister. A lord, maybe. Some kind of titled gentleman. Or a merchant so rich that he could own the Heights and the Grange a thousand times over. That's strength I can't beat with a fist or a knife. I should run from it. Him wanting me to think he's friendly . . . that just means he's dangerous.

But I want whatever coin he's offering more, so I pretend to trust him. I nod. Don't quite smile, but say, "Mr. Northwood," obediently. He smiles bigger than me, pleased.

"With me," he says mildly, and gestures for me to join him.

The carriage takes us farther and farther from streets I know, to ones more like the rich place I stumbled on after my first fight. Everything's moving, blurring when the crowd thins out and the horses can go swift. The houses are tall. Pale, yellowish. Grand. Everything's so clean. Do they throw their filth where everyone else lives, to get it this clean? They must.

The house he takes me to is grand as the rest. A servant opens up the door. Northwood strides in.

I hesitate. Hate that I do it, but that door's not meant for my kind. I know I don't fit, with my knuckles bruised up from last night, my jacket old and worn, breeches stained with ale and mud. I even lost my hair ribbon at some point in the fight. Never fixed it, all night through. So my hair's all loose. Wild, no cap to make me decent. My feet won't move.

Some instincts protect you, and this one's telling me going in there will get me hurt. But Northwood's still walking, fading down a corridor. I look over at the servant, who's dressed up strange: a turban peaked with a feather on his head, and big trousers, and shoes that curl up at the ends. He looks like a cartoon in a news sheet of a man out of the Orient.

My unease gets worse.

But the servant's not looking at me—not giving me a hard stare, a once-over, and sending me to the back or turning me away. He's keeping the door wide. So I go up the shining stairs. Through the door.

It's like walking into another world.

Cathy, you described the Grange to me. After the first time

you went, you couldn't stop. I told you I didn't want to hear it. Told you I didn't care what it was like. But you drew it with words anyway: the parlor, all velvet and pale, soft carpets, wood floor that sounded like music when someone walked across it. You told me you wanted to run to make it sing, but you were told ladies don't run, so you didn't try.

This is grander than the Grange. If the Grange made you walk slow, this place would freeze you still forever.

I don't look hard, but I still notice. Vases stuffed full of cut flowers. Chandeliers hanging from the ceiling, big enough to hold a dozen candles each. Carpet so soft, it's silent under my boots, which are leaving tracks. Someone will have to get on their knees and scrub it clean. It's pale enough carpet that it'll be a hard job. Northwood doesn't look like he cares.

"The green parlor," Northwood says to a passing servant. The servant bows his head and goes off somewhere swiftly.

The green parlor's named that way for the reason you'd expect. The wallpaper's leaves, winding, shot through with red roses. The armchair's forest-colored. I stand, awkward, as Northwood sits down on it. Gets comfortable. A maid bustles in, or I guess she's a maid. She's got on a dress that's all folded cloth and beads in her hair. She's as brown as me, hair curling. She brings in tea, cakes, dainty things covered in real cream.

"Sit," Northwood smilingly orders. The maid brings over a harder-looking chair, not half as nice. Sets it down for me.

I sit.

I'm at a new angle, looking straight into Northwood's face. The green silk round his head is patterned gold at the edges, like on his coat. And behind him, set right at eye level, is a paint-ing. He's in it, though he looks younger. There he is, standing up proud by a sitting woman with a wig powdered up even big-ger and whiter than his. On the chair by her is a little girl. On the left, crouching on the floor and looking up at them ador-ingly is an Indian woman. She's got long black hair. Gold in her nose and her ears. White cloth lined red over her hair, and her bangled hand smoothing down the baby's skirt.

I can't look long, but I can't look away either. My stomach hurts when I stare at her face—the trusting eyes, the kneeling. They've painted her like she loves them. That's most mon-strous of all.

The servant pours tea. I look at her, feeling sick. She doesn't look up.

"My man probably told me your name, but I've quite forgot-ten it," Northwood says, no apology in his voice. "Refresh my memory?"

"Edgar, Mr. Northwood," I lie.

"Just Edgar?"

"Yes," I say. Watch as his mouth tightens. "Mr. Northwood," I add, and the anger on his face goes away, melting back into smiling.

"I think of myself as a generous benefactor," he says. "A mentor. I look for people who would flourish with the right guidance, and I provide it to them. Sometimes, I like to go out into the community and pluck an unfortunate with potential up from obscurity. And I make something better of them. Two sugars, Sarah."

The maid—Sarah—picks up a silver spoon. Doles out sugar into his cup. I can hear the clink of metal against porcelain. I try not to look at her, or the painting. Try not to think of picking up the pot of tea and pouring it, scalding hot, into Northwood's eyes.

"You fought very viciously," Northwood says. "And one of my men believes you were—how is it said?—*sharping*. Were you?"

"I was just playing cards," I say.

"You have no need to lie to me," he says indulgently. As if I've amused him. "And call me Mr. Northwood, as I told you. So, you know your numbers?"

"Yes. Mr. Northwood."

"And your letters? You read and write?"

"Yes, Mr. Northwood."

"How well?"

The painting's staring me down. Feels like it's burning through me. But that's what it's meant to do, same as me having to call him Mr. Northwood over and over; same as making me meet him here in this room that screams wealth. Same as the servant pouring tea. It's all meant to grind me down and show me my place. But *nicely*. The niceness cuts crueler than anything. You can brace for pain if you're shown a thing made for hurting. You can't brace for a gentle hand turning harsh.

I think how Hindley did it with fists was better. At least it was honest. At least I could feel pure angry, not small and shamed.

"You can test me if you like. Mr. Northwood." I am already sick of saying his name.

"Another time," he says. He waves the servant off. She bobs a curtsy and moves to the edge of the room. "You've got Indian blood. Or Arab, perhaps?"

It's not a real question. So I don't answer.

"I had great experiences in India," he says in a confiding tone. "My time with the East India Company—it was a great pleasure." He adds more sugar to his own tea. There's so much in there his spoon should stand up. "I was in Bengal. Do you know it? A very interesting place indeed. The people there are a very pleasant folk," he goes on. "Extremely superstitious and ignorant of course, but that is no fault of theirs. I'm sure you would agree. There are so many of them, and their lives so backward. How could they know better?"

"I don't know much of India," I say.

"Is that so?" He looks at me keenly, smiling. "Do you want some tea, Edgar? A cake?"

"No, thank you, Mr. Northwood," I say. I do want them. But not from him.

"You strike me as a model example of your kind, Edgar, my boy," he says. "I saw you and thought, *Ah. Perhaps this one has potential. He has his kind's . . . deceptive nature, certainly. But potential. Perhaps I can help him, as I've helped so many others of his ilk.*" He sips his tea. Lowers it back to the saucer. "You have a good mind, and physical strength. There's something brutish about you, but I believe it can be . . . cultivated."

I shift in my seat. His smile gets deeper.

He's enjoying my discomfort. I look, from the corner of my

eye, at the servant. Her face is blank. If she's feeling the same as me, I can't see it.

Does he want questions or blank gratitude?

I think . . . gratitude.

"That's kind of you, sir," I manage.

"I have plantations in the Caribbean," he says. What he means to say, I know now, is *I own people.* "Interests in India still. Many of my servants were born there. When I left after building my fortune, they begged to follow. Their loyalty warms me."

My mouth is dry. I say nothing.

"I have done good in many corners of the world, young Edgar. And I could do good for you."

I've thought about what use a man like him could have out of someone like me. Strong, he called me. Clever and brutish.

He wants to make you a monster, a voice whispers in my head. It sounds like yours, Cathy. *He'll give you the money you want, and all you'll have to give up is your soul. All you'll have to do is thank him for taking it.*

Don't, Heathcliff.

Don't.

Your soul was mine first.

You're not enough to tip the balance, Cathy. Not after what you did.

It's like a scar in me. The memory I've got of standing in the doorway, you and Nelly sitting together. Your face flushed, your eyes sparkling. Because Edgar Linton had proposed to you. Because you were going to marry him.

Nelly asked about me. *Low*, you called me. You said I was beneath you.

You said you could never marry me.

I thought . . . Hell, Cathy. I thought you loved me. You broke my heart.

My mouth feels like it's full of poison.

"You'd send me to a plantation," I say. I feel like I'm speaking through water. "Or India. You'd send me to . . . do things. For you."

"If you work hard and prove yourself, who knows where you may go?" Northwood says archly. "A man's wealth lies in the quality of his household. Near and far. Prove yourself, and you'll go very far indeed."

I can see the road set out now in front of me:

I'll thank Northwood. Bow and scrape, and make him feel like a big man. That's what he wants: to feel big and special. So I'll do it. I'll be another person he's collected, an ornament showing how powerful he is, how *grand* he is. I'll work hard to convince him to keep me. I'll die a bit inside.

I'll think of breaking Hindley. I'll think of how powerful I'll need to be to do it. And I'll grit my teeth and I'll bow and scrape some more.

I'll get more coin and more power. Bit by bit. And bit by bit, he'll trust me.

Years will go by, and I'll get harder and emptier. Doing what he wants will change me. Make me less a sullen brute and more a rifle, ready to be pointed where Northwood wants it. I'll be his weapon. He'll call me *good lad*, and he'll throw me scraps, and he'll use me. My cruel hands, my cruel mind, all doing cruel things for him.

Northwood doesn't think people like me are properly human. And only someone as human as him could beat him. So he won't see how I'll learn how to manipulate him and other wealthy people like him. He won't see me making plans. Won't see it when I decide to turn on him until there's no stopping me. I'll take all he's got, and I'll do it joylessly, because I won't have any joy left.

Then I'll come back to the Heights, Cathy. Only then. I'll come back broken and twisted, wealthy and vicious. I'll come and break Hindley better than he could ever have broken me. I'll come back, and I won't be low anymore. I won't be beneath you. But my love for you won't be this soft thing that fills me up and bleeds more than a heart ever could. It'll be cold waves, drowning me. And drowning you.

I see all that. Maybe you're not the only one who dreams strange, grand dreams. You see ghosts, and I see them too. My own, coming for me.

But there's another road. Branching off. Dark. I don't know what lies at the end of it.

I think of Jamie, wanting to save me. Hal on the roof, smiling. Annie trying to warn me off coming here. Hetty's mothering.

I want to say, *Thank you, Mr. Northwood.* Want to say, *I'll do whatever you ask.* Want to tell him, *I am so grateful for this chance, Mr. Northwood.* But the words are metal and blood, grating on my tongue. The words won't come.

The words are on one road. And my heart, my fool heart, is already on another.

I look at that Heathcliff—hardened, bitter, ready to die—and I let him go. There's just me left.

"I can't," I say thinly. "I won't."

"Won't what?"

"Prove my worth," I tell him. "I've got none to you. You've read me wrong."

Walls are closing in. The roses round me on the wallpaper look redder than red. Like torn-open hearts.

"You don't want my help," he says flatly.

"I'm not fit for your help."

"Surely that is for me to decide," he says.

I meet his eyes. The cold blue of them.

"No," I say. "I'm sorry, Mr. Northwood. If you kept me round, I'd prove myself no good. Best if I just go now."

The eye contact—that's a mistake. It's too bold.

"I could see you thrown in the jail, or sent to the colonies," he says. His smile is gone. He stirs his tea. Tap here. Tap there. "I could have you hanged."

I could take the spoon out of your hand and stab it through your eye, I think. I'll do it too. If he tries to see me locked up, I'll do it.

But I just say, "I know, Mr. Northwood. But I'm not worth your trouble." I lower my eyes. Fix them on some distant point. I settle on Sarah's hands, clasped tight in front of her, pale-knuckled. "I'm just some lascar's bastard. That's all."

Mr. Northwood sighs.

"Sarah," he says coolly. "Escort the boy out."

Sarah bobs another curtsy and goes toward the door. I stand and follow her.

"You're making a terrible error, boy," Northwood says. Sounding paternal again. Disappointed. "But if you don't see your potential, I cannot help you."

"Perhaps you're right, Mr. Northwood," I say, dipping my head like I fear him. But I don't. I'm looking at his room. The green walls. The painting. Thinking of the blood running through the green, the roses pouring gouts of it out. I think of the coin he's scrounged out of bones to build this room and this house.

I am doing right. I'll hold fast to that. It lets me breathe again, even though there's only a dark road up ahead of me. "But I've got a bad nature. It can't be helped, that I don't know how to learn what's good for me."

Then I walk out. Sarah guides me to the servants' entrance. We pass the kitchens. I hear someone—the cook, I'm guessing—swearing violently and yelling out orders. Steam's billowing under the kitchen door. Sarah ushers me on past it, right out a back door that's not half as grand as the one at the front of the house. She shuts it quickly behind me, not even looking at me.

I keep walking, down the steps and into a narrow alley. No grandness here. And I go fast, striding away and don't stop until the streets are different, and I'm shaking with anger. Shaking with relief. I look up at the sky, tipping my head back.

One road's gone. What comes next, I don't know.

I don't know.

Chapter Fourteen

Catherine

I USED TO THINK EVERY family was like mine.

I thought, surely every girl is afraid of her brother. I thought all fathers stared hollowly out at nothing. And I thought all mothers fretted over everything, working themselves up into a frenzy over their foolish daughters who couldn't behave. Even my body was a rebel, though I didn't mean it to be.

When I was still little I started getting dark hairs on my arms. My upper lip. Mother panicked. She cried. She said it wasn't normal—that it was "showing through," that "people would know."

I thought that was strange. *I* certainly didn't know what it meant, or what was showing. It took Nelly to calm her. They used a straight razor they thieved off Father, one of them pinning me down, and the other shaving the hair away. After that,

Mother made me begin washing my face with chervil water that would "brighten" my skin and insisted I stay indoors, and then insisted I wear a large cap when she realized I couldn't be made to stay inside for anything.

I thought maybe all girls were carefully shaped to look like something they were not.

I didn't know. I didn't know. But now I do, and everything is falling in place and falling apart all at once. If I were truly as fragile as Hindley thinks, then this would undo me and it would be all because of him. But I am what I've always been, so I creep out of my window again to be outdoors, where I can think and breathe and cry if I wish to without anyone seeing me and asking questions I can't and won't answer.

I have an Indian mother. I have my mother who raised me and I have an Indian mother, too. Father was married when he went to India, I am almost sure. So he went to India to make money and also—took a mistress, and had Hindley and me? Was the dead older brother Heathcliff was named after the same as us?

If I had been born as brown as Heathcliff, what would have become of me?

Mother died even before Father did, and I don't remember her as well as I probably should. I just know she was nervous and pale, and she was always moving—always cooking or sewing, or directing servants about, and she found me a trial, because I would never sit still either, but not in a helpful way. I was always causing her trouble, breaking things or climbing where I shouldn't, or escaping outside to play.

But I know she loved me. Better than Father did, maybe.

Why did you do it? I think. Mother, always so tired and thin-lipped, like life was draining out of her as steady as dripping candlewax. *Why did you choose to love us?*

It's morning. Hindley's at the table, nursing a scalding-hot tea and a headache.

"Don't bother me, Cathy," he says tiredly. "My head's pain-ing."

"I want to talk. About." I stumble over my own words, and wet my lips, and manage to say, "About what we spoke of before. Ghosts, and—"

"Shut up. I don't want anyone hearing this," Hindley says back sharply.

In a second, Joseph will trudge through, or Nelly will come in. Or even Hareton will run by, chasing one of the puppies, and then we won't be alone anymore.

"We could talk outside," I tell him.

He rubs his knuckles against his forehead, not answering.

He doesn't want to tell me. I know he doesn't. So I decide I shall be strong and sure, and I will make him tell me by giving him something he wants.

"I want to marry Edgar," I say. I don't even recognize my own voice. When I am with Hindley I often snap, or talk quickly. All my words are like . . . like wood burning in a fire, or carving knives being sharpened. And when I am with Edgar

I am sweet and bubbly and, I hope, easy to love. But now I am trying to be something else, and I sound very calm and like a woman grown. Like I am already married and mistress of my own house, and have nothing to be afraid of. "I want to be Mrs. Linton. I want to make it so we're respectable and no one will question anything about us. But I can't do any of it if I am haunted."

"What will knowing do to end that?" Hindley shrugs. "It's *knowing* that haunts me."

"I know enough to make up stories in my head," I tell him. "And the longer I think about it all, the worse the stories get. I only have half the truth, Hindley—maybe not even half—and that's worse than knowing it all. Please, don't leave me ignorant anymore."

He lowers his hand to the table with a thump. "If I tell you, you'll marry Edgar Linton. No complaints."

"Why would I complain? I love him."

He doesn't look like he believes me. "And you'll forget Heathcliff," he says slowly, cruelly. At least, it feels cruel. Like he's seeing too much of me. Like he's weighing my love for Heathcliff and love for Edgar up against each other, and finding one wanting.

"Yes," I lie.

I don't feel any guilt at all about the lie. Hindley's lied to me all my life. What does one untruth from me matter?

"Come on, then," Edgar says, getting up from the table. "A walk it is."

Outside is warmer than usual, so I don't even need my shawl.

173

The wind is kind, just ruffling my skirt, setting my curls a little askew. It's pleasant, but it would be better if it were cold—if it bit at me, so I could feel some of my own tangled hurt and fear outside, on my skin.

"We're not legitimate," Hindley begins. Then he doesn't say anything for a while.

I try not to speak. I bite on my tongue to keep quiet, and walk by him to the gate, and then out onto the heath beyond.

"It's easier to falsify parish birth records than you might think, if you have the right money and a greedy priest," Hindley says after a long silence. "Or so Father told me. He spent a fortune on both of us, then brought us to the Heights. And now here we are. Is that what you want to know, Cathy? That everything we have could be stolen out from under us if the truth gets out?"

He sounds bitter.

"I want to know about India," I say. "About . . . us. Where part of us comes from. I know Father went there. I know he made a fortune there. And had . . . there was a woman. Not Mother. But—"

"Our Indian mother," Hindley says. "Yes. Her."

"What was she like?" I ask.

"Alive, for a while. Then dead." Hindley's voice is abrupt. "I don't remember anything else."

"You remember her face."

"How could I forget when you're here?"

"What was her name?"

"I don't know," he says.

I hesitate. I don't do it often—measure my words or not know what ones I want to use. But I try now. I say, "The brother who died. The one who was called Heathcliff first—"

"He didn't die," Hindley says.

I think I've heard him wrong. "What do you mean?"

"He didn't die," Hindley says again. "He was too dark-skinned. No one would have believed . . ." He gestures a hand at me, at himself. "So Father left him. Left him with our mother, probably."

My mouth doesn't work for a moment. Then I say, "You said she was dead. She died."

His mouth twists. "How else could she haunt us? She died, Cathy, I'm sure of it. I feel it. I *see* her, and so do you."

"She didn't—she didn't want to come with us to England . . . ?"

Hindley gives an ugly laugh. And I know what that means. She didn't have a choice.

"That's terrible," I whisper.

How could Father have done it? Left the mother of his children and one of his own sons behind, and never spoken of them ever again? *How?* I know I have a hard heart, but even I can't imagine it. I simply can't.

"You don't know what terrible is, Cathy. I've seen more of the world than you have. I went to school. Met real people, people who matter. I learned about money, and I learned about how business gets done. I learned about how men like our father made their fortunes. I didn't want to learn," he says, sounding resentful. "But like it or not, Cathy, the knowing seeps

175

into you. It *finds* you. He was no different from anyone else. Sometimes he was a damn sight better.

"Father was in Bengal, and Bengal was rich," he goes on. "You can't imagine how rich. And the East India Company took it right out from under some native emperor's nose. There were good opportunities there, if you knew how to take them. And Father . . ." Hindley shrugs. "I suppose he knew."

Bengal. I let the word move round inside my head. So Bengal is where I come from, and where Hindley comes from. Bengal is where we might still have a brother living. I wonder what it is like, and all I can imagine is the chinoiserie room. Paintings that aren't real and aren't from there at all. I feel hollow.

"Why did Father leave Bengal behind?"

Hindley laughs again, a broken sound that makes me flinch, shakes his head, and starts striding faster. I have to nearly run to keep up with him, lifting my skirt with one hand. The heath crunches sharply under his boots.

"Because it was hell." He's not looking at me. He's staring off into the distance, his eyes still bloodshot from drinking through the long night. But the haunted look in them is like nothing I've seen before. "Because he and his friends made it hell. We're haunted for a reason."

I remember the clink of shells and the airy cloth under my fingers in the dark—the ghost. A haunting that Hindley has seen, too.

"Tell me," I beg. My heart is hammering so fast it's like it has a dozen wings, like it's going to fly out of me and away. "Tell me why we're haunted."

Slow down, I want to say. But he won't. Hindley's running from something, something that isn't me. I just have to run as fast as him, that's all. So I try, my breath puffing out of me.

"To get a fortune you've got to take a fortune from someone else, so that's what they did." He speaks quickly, angrily. "The Company. Changed the farming, and the way harvests were taxed and sold. Who got what, and who decided it. But then things went wrong. There was no monsoon—no rain. No crops growing. And people started to go hungry. And they started to die."

Hindley rubs his knuckles hard between his eyes, hard enough to make his forehead red. He bares his teeth, pained, but I don't think the pain is in his body. I think it's something else, because I can feel it too—a cold hurt going down through my spirit, separate from my aching lungs. "I don't remember it, but Father told me . . . whole villages were wiped out. More people than you can imagine, Cathy. Bodies in the streets. Children wailing and screaming and hungry. And he said it was his fault."

"Was it?" I manage to say.

"He thought so. He said the Company had no mercy. He said, *If we didn't make the rains dry up, we didn't save anyone after they did.* He said grain rotted, not feeding anyone. He said taxes got taken and taken even if they drained people dry. You're lucky, Cathy." He sounds savage, suddenly. "He never cried to you. He spared you."

I see it in my head: Hindley, young and small, and Father telling him horrors. Hindley, remembering our Indian mother but never speaking of her. Hindley, knowing everything about him was secret, that he could lose everything because of a piece of paper, a lie. The poison of it spreading right through him.

Hindley, looking at Heathcliff. Brown-skinned, dark-eyed Heathcliff, who spoke another language, who wasn't our brother left behind. Who was like all our family secrets with a light shone on them, if anyone knew how to look with care.

I think I'm beginning to understand why Hindley is like he is. I don't forgive him for it—for anything he has done to me or to Heathcliff, to Nelly or little Hareton—but I can see the path that got him here.

If I forgave him, I'd comfort him now. But I just stop, going dead still, and after a moment he stops striding too and turns to me. The wind has grown fiercer. Under the blue sky, it makes the long grass move like wild flame, like a world gone up in fire.

"Did he do anything to make it better?" I ask.

"What?"

"Did he do anything to make it better?" I repeat. "Hindley, you say he saw . . . bodies. And people starving. You say he said the East India Company were responsible for much of it. But did he . . . do anything?"

"He brought us home."

"Do you think we're just here because of guilt?" I ask. "Do you think Father loved us and lied about us, and spent a fortune making us his legal children, because of his guilt?"

"I think that's a stupid question," Hindley said. "I think you need to shut your fool mouth."

I think that must mean *yes*.

"He brought Heathcliff home," Hindley says, voice dripping venom. "Brought him like saving one brown-skinned Indian bastard would be enough to make it all better. That's what he did for his guilt, Cathy, and he destroyed our family by doing it."

I lower my head. I realize tears are dripping from my eyes. I'm not sure I even feel anything, it is like my heart can't carry all the weight and won't speak to me, won't tell me what I feel. But I am crying.

"Don't," Hindley says, sounding furious. He strides over to me and grabs me by the shoulders. It would almost be a hug, but he's shaking me, hard enough to make my teeth rattle, and then his face is up close to mine.

"She used to tell me ghost stories," he breathes out, wine still on his breath, and grief too. It smells like blood. "I think she used to tell me about bhut and jinn and . . . and petni. She used to tell me about . . . bangles chiming, and feet turned backward, hungry ghosts that won't rest. That's what I remember about her: her wild tales. And somehow you know those tales, too. Somehow, even though I didn't tell you. I think she told you. She whispered in your dreams, didn't she?"

"I don't know," I whisper. "Get off me, Hindley."

"I think the dead have their claws in us and they won't let go, because they've been wronged. She's here, but so are they. The starving. The ones he stole from." There's a feverish, hellish light in Hindley's eyes. His grip hurts. "The dead had Father, and they haunted him until he was dead too."

Perhaps I am as cruel and as wicked as Nelly says I am,

because I feel as if my father deserved to suffer for what he did. If a man does terrible things, shouldn't he feel bad? Shouldn't he be haunted?

But he should have done some mending, and bringing Heathcliff home was not enough. Heathcliff had nothing to do with what happened in Bengal. Heathcliff was a starving child in Liverpool, in our own England. And because he had brown skin, because he spoke a few words in a language my father thought he knew, Father dragged him here and thought that would fix all his mistakes. But how could Heathcliff be enough for that? How could anyone be enough?

I thought we had only a handful of ghosts haunting us, but there must be thousands. Thousands of ghosts, carried in every stitch of our clothes, every stone of the Heights. Ghosts in our blood, too.

I do not think I know how to care about people I don't know, people I will never know. But I must, because there is a wave of sickness and sadness coming over me. It is so fierce that I'm not sure I can breathe around it.

Hindley's still speaking.

"The dead have us, and we'll be haunted until we die. Just like Father was. Now you know you'll have no peace, Cathy. Just like me," he says. "Is that what you wanted?"

I blink tears from my stinging eyes. "Then we have to get rid of them."

His grip loosens a little. I take a deep breath.

"We have to lay them to rest," I say. I think of feathers buried under a tree, and how everyone says they keep a soul inside its skin. If something can do that, there must be a way to set a soul free, too. A magic for burning roots, not growing them. "Father's treasures. We have to get rid of them. We have to let them go."

"They're too valuable," Hindley says. But he's listening. Some of the fever's left his eyes. "They're all we've got left of his fortune. Someday we'll need it, Cathy."

True, with the way Hindley gambles.

"But we don't look at them. We don't speak about them. They're . . . proof, aren't they? Now I understand. They're a little proof of where we come from. Like Heathcliff." I feel a pang saying it, but I also know that this will win him over, because hate always drives Hindley better than anything else. "And if they're gone, gone like Heathcliff is—we'll be free."

Finally, Hindley lets go of me. My arms are smarting, hurting.

"Sometimes, Cathy," he says softly. "You're not so foolish after all."

The room with the chests is always meant to be locked. Father used to enter on his own, and no one knew what he did in there. The first time I saw what was in the room, I was very small—it was before Heathcliff came to live with us—and I managed to creep inside when Father forgot to lock up. I cracked open one chest, nudging the lid up with my thumb and peering inside.

That was when I saw cloth patterned with cranes and

peacocks, and women like I saw later in Mrs. Linton's chinoiserie room. That was when I smelled the strangeness on them—a smell sweet and rich with smoke, like peat burning but not quite. I remember gold and gems, all shining bright and strange. Holding cloth to my skin, just to my nose and cheek, and feeling it, softer than water.

Now Hindley strides down the corridor. He kicks the door open, the handle snapping along with the wood. I flinch, but I don't run away. I'm going to let Hindley's anger carry me along with him.

The wooden chests are covered with white sheets to keep them neat; he drags them all off violently until they're piled on the floor. He throws open the chests, and we're surrounded by gold and silk and other beautiful things.

"Gather it all up, Cathy."

Nelly and the others must have heard the door break and the anger in Hindley's heavy footsteps, because I don't see them at all as we walk back outside, arms full. I don't even see them when Hindley uncorks liquor and throws it over all the fortune that's been hidden inside our home, all the silk with gold and silver sewn through it, little jewels winking on their surfaces, and sets it all alight.

We watch the cloth smolder in the fire. We watch it burn up. My eyes are streaming, but I don't look away until everything is gone.

After, we take the jewelry, which is all that's left. It can't burn, so Hindley digs up the soil far back at the edge of our land, under two trees twined together. I stand there, holding bangles and necklaces, long beaded chains, things worked through with emeralds and silver. Then when he throws down his shovel, I pour them in.

Maybe this will set all our ghosts free. Our birth mother, who was left behind. Our father, sent to and fro by his guilt. Our English mother, who chose to love us, who raised us like we were her own. And all those people Father said died, all so he and his friends could grow richer.

I drop the last bracelet into the soil and smooth the earth over it. And as I do it, I feel the past close up behind me. Like a door shut, blotting out the light.

Chapter Fifteen

IT'S YOU I THINK OF, Cathy. After I leave Northwood and the devil's deal he was offering.

I think about how I'll not be coming to see you as an equal. I had a vision of what it'd be like. Me, dressed up like a gentleman. Me, so rich that no one calls me slurs. In Gimmerton they'd tell stories about me instead. *He looks like he's been a soldier. No, he's made his money in trade.*

Can you believe we used to think he wasn't fit to be one of us?

None of that will happen now.

I think of the one time Hindley near killed me. He tried plenty. Threatened it. I always hid, or ran. Mostly, I wasn't afraid. Only angry.

But one time . . . I don't want to remember it, Cathy. I just know I woke after and you were holding me.

"Shh," you whispered. "Don't make noise. Please, Heathcliff."

It took me a moment to realize we were in your bed. Wood closing us in. Wind cutting over my cheek from your window, half open. You were crying. You'd not lit a candle, but moonlight was on you. I saw your tears. They were like silver.

"Hindley," I managed. My mouth didn't want to work. But you understood.

"Not here. Joseph's keeping an eye on him. Hindley, he—he hit you and you fell. He did it so suddenly." Your voice wobbled. "And you knocked your head against the wall, and I thought. I thought . . ."

You stopped speaking and sniffled. Miserable.

I still couldn't speak right. So I touched the end of your hair. Twined it round my finger.

"You have to be quiet," you said. "Hindley wants you gone."

"He almost made me gone."

"*Heathcliff.*" You gripped me tighter. "If he killed you it'd be like he killed me," you said. "All the best parts of me. All the pieces of me that are strong and brave and . . . good."

"You're the one that's good," I managed. "I'm . . . I'm the rest."

"I just know how to pretend to be good," you confessed. "It's not real. Not like it is in you."

"I'm not good," I said. "*Cathy.* I'm not."

You hiccupped a laugh. Then you said, "Fine. I'm not good and you're not either. We're something else."

"Something else," I agreed. Then I fell asleep. Or something like it.

I remember waking up and sleeping and waking, in and out of hearing you and seeing you. I remember you never letting go of me. Not once.

"I know we don't exist without each other," you whispered once, when I woke not knowing where I was. Only knowing you. "If you die . . . Heathcliff, if you die then you must haunt me. You must live inside all my dreams and steal my shadow and my soul, too. You *must* stay, Heathcliff, no matter where death tries to take you. Promise me."

I promised you.

Later, I remember. Half walking, lights shining in my eyes. Your fingers smoothing down my hair. Your voice. Small.

"I'll be rich," you told me. "I'll be the richest woman in Gimmerton, and then I'll keep you safe. That's *my* promise."

I know now. I know what it takes to get coin like that.

It takes dying a little. Making yourself something poisoned and new. I saw that road and didn't take it.

But you did, Cathy. You turned yourself into a lady proper. You learned how not to yell or laugh loud or run barefoot, the way we used to. You learned how to love Edgar Linton and be what he wanted to marry. You walked round family secrets, turned your head away from them, so they couldn't stop you from being the richest lady in Gimmerton. Rich enough to set me free. You hacked pieces of yourself away. You made yourself small. Your road wasn't covered in other people's blood, not like mine would have been.

No. Your road was just covered in your own.

When you called me low, I thought you didn't love me.

But you do, Cathy. You do.

I didn't ask it from you, Cathy. But you did it anyway. And I left you behind.

I think about going back to the attic room. Seeing Jamie. I don't want to say sorry, but I could take some food or buy some ground-up tea leaves for the pot. That'd be enough, I think.

But I don't go. I return to my lodging house instead.

No one's about, so I get a damp cloth. Wash the worst dirt off me. Brush my hair and tie it back. Clean up my jacket, my shirt. Take off my kerchief, and dig for a new one. I've got a pack under my bed with a few pieces now.

The kerchief I pull out is red.

I freeze, holding the kerchief. The red swirls of it. I think of music, and blood on my lip, and a man's voice.

If you need help, then go to Mrs. Hussain.

I've been avoiding that memory, same as I've been avoiding the grand street where I met the lascar. I came all the way to this city, crossed Yorkshire on foot, in the dark and cold, with nothing but stolen coin and a knife to protect me. And still, I'm scared to go one step further. To go where I might learn something about what I am.

Maybe I'm the same as you, Cathy. Afraid of something I don't want to look at. Something inside of me.

I came here because of you. But not just you. I came because I didn't belong at the Heights. Didn't belong with you, where

I'd always be low. Always be what Hindley had made me, and everyone saw me as. I came here because I was a boy from nowhere, with nothing. And I wanted to be *something*. Wanted to be enough to grind Hindley down to dust. Wanted you.

But I'm already from somewhere. I know that. And if I go to Mann Road I might find out where that is.

Cathy, have you ever stood on the edge of a cliff at night? I have. I liked it, the dark in front of me, knowing one step could be the end of me. There's joy in risk like that—it feels like lightning running through you. It makes you feel even more alive. The wind almost lifting me—that's how strong it always was, up high on the moors where the Heights stood. Felt like I could have flown on it.

This is the same. But I'm going to do it. I'm going to step forward. See where I fall. See if I survive it.

Coming to the street's like walking into a dream.

I don't normally dream like you do, Cathy. Big dreams, wild and strange. In some other time, they'd say you could see the future. They'd call you magic.

I just dream of real stuff. Wind through gorse. Birds calling. Someone following me, wanting my blood in the dark. Feels like I've dreamed this road before. Buildings close, bending almost. The stink of sewers. Water creeping in round houses, like the Mersey's being kept back by hope and prayer and luck.

One woman's out on her stoop, shelling peas. I ask her where Mrs. Hussain lives.

"You want Lascar Lily?" She looks me up and down. "Of course you do."

"I'm looking for Mrs. Hussain," I say again.

She snorts, and tells me where to go. She mutters something about brothels and opium dens and "people like that." I don't listen.

I arrive at a lodging house. Not like mine, which is tall but cramped. This one's made of three houses. The doors on the left and right are boarded up, all three painted up the same so they look like one. Some men are sitting out front, caps low over their eyes. They look up at me. No one speaks.

"I'm looking for Mrs. Hussain," I say to them. I take out the kerchief. Can't prove anything with it, but it makes me feel like I've got the right to be standing here. I hold the red in my hand. "I was told to come here. Told I could get help."

One of the men turns to another, words flowing back and forth. Then another nods and says, "She's inside."

I thank him and walk in. My heart's pounding.

It's dark inside. Smells of mold, sweet and sticky. The curtains are sagging. But there's a fire going, warm and steady. A baby's on the floor, knocking some metal cups about. Talking some nonsense to itself. A woman's scrubbing a table clean, her sleeves rolled up, hair sticking to her forehead. She looks up.

"Hello," she says. "Are you looking for a bed to rent?"

I say nothing. Can't speak. It's like my throat's closed up.

She drops the rag she's holding. Says something else—a language I don't know. Then she shakes her head. Gestures at a chair, wanting me to sit.

"Kabir!" She hollers. "Kabir! I've got another that needs you to translate!"

"I speak English," I say, quick. "You're Mrs. Hussain?"

"I am," she says. "Sit down, sit down." She gestures at the chair again. "What do you need from me?"

I can't move. Just stay where I am, rooted, like my fear's got hands around my legs, holding me fast.

"I come from . . ." I hesitate. "Not here. But I think I was born round here."

I feel foolish. Feel small. I don't know how to say it. Don't know how to ask, *Can you tell me what I am? Can you tell me where I'm from? I've lost myself, lost where I've come from. All I remember is hunger, the man who saved me. Feathers buried in Yorkshire soil. Can you help me find what came before?*

"Can you help me?" I ask. That's all I say.

But she doesn't mock or laugh. Only nods, serious.

"What do you need?"

I hear thumping. Stairs creaking. A man comes down. Indian, bearded. He's not dressed much like anyone I've seen before, half sailor and half something else. His hair's up, wrapped in cloth. Maybe that's how lascars look, when they're at home.

"Lily?" he asks.

"Don't worry, love. Actually no, don't go," she says to him, even though he's still standing on the stairs. Looking at me, all distrust. "Put the kettle on for us. This boy and me are going to have a chat."

The man grunts an answer. The baby gives a shriek, and the bearded man goes and sweeps it up, propping the baby up against his hip like I've seen mothers do when they're walking and their children can't keep up. He goes off, and I hear the clank of metal.

Mrs. Hussain's looking at me again.

"What's your name?" she asks.

This time I don't lie. "Heathcliff," I say.

"Well, Heathcliff. You can tell me what you need when you're ready." She sounds like Hetty. Motherly.

She doesn't force me to talk. She brings out one thing, then another, and another after that. Plum cake, cut into thin slices. Cheese and bread. Some dried meat. More range of food than I've seen since leaving the Heights, though the portions are small, being shared out carefully. That's kindness I don't deserve. I don't think she's got much.

The door goes open. Closes again.

"You sit," she says again. So I sit, feeling the draft against my back.

I hear men walk in and out. Stairs creak. She's moving about so I turn and watch them. Some look like me—Indian or something close. But not all. Some look Chinese. Maybe some come from Malaya, like Hetty's long-gone father.

Mrs. Hussain follows my looks.

"It's a busy place to be sure. Not everyone gets on all the

time," Mrs. Hussain says lightly. She thinks I'm nervous. "But most can speak laskari at least, and that helps, though it's a tongue built for talking about life out on the sea and not much else. People keep civil. You'll have no trouble, not here."

I don't know what laskari is, but I can guess from the way words and sounds that don't fit together weave through each other as the men go up the stairs. Some tangle of language that these sailors from all over share.

The kettle's whistling. Another minute goes, and the man—Mr. Hussain—comes in. Baby still on his hip, tea on a tin tray in the other. He sets it down, and she thanks him and starts serving up. Cutting and plating. Heaping sugar into her cup. I think of Northwood and suddenly feel dizzy. His world's so far from this one. Feels wrong there's even a drink in common.

"How much sugar?" Mrs. Hussain asks, then sorts me a cup.

She chatters on, light and easy, her husband walking out with the child. She's trying to make me less tense, maybe, because my body feels like rope knots, tied tight with thinking.

She tells me about lascars from Malaya and China and from India like her husband, all of them coming in and out for a bed or hot meal, paying what they could. Tells me one paid with basket weaving, not coin. She points to a thing high up on a shelf, domed and made of some cloth woven up. "There's not much work for them," she goes on, mouth twisting. "So we only charge what men can pay. And some are generous, because they're grateful."

Then I understand what she's telling me.

"I don't need a bed," I manage to say. Though maybe I do.

Haven't paid my rent yet, after all. But I've not got coin to pay Mrs. Hussain for help either.

Before I can tell her so, she's talking again.

"Not all come and stay, of course," she goes on. "Some just want to ask me a favor. Sometimes others come here looking for an old shipmate, hoping they're alive and safe here, or have passed through. I always share what I remember, and I know everyone who's passed through my door."

She waits, seeing if I'm one of those. But when I don't say anything, she asks, "Do you want a slice of cake?"

I shake my head, but she's not looking. I watch her plate it up. She slides it over. The plate's chipped, yellow flowers painted on it.

"Lascars get in all sorts of trouble, you know," she says. But she's got no judgment in her voice. "When you come to a new country across the world, and you don't know the language, and your ship captain throws you out to fend for yourself with no money or lodging or work . . ." She shrugs, but there's anger in it. "I write letters for the men staying here, sometimes. Letters of complaint, mostly. Or letters begging for what they're rightly owed."

"I can write," I tell her. I bite the plum cake. It's dry, bitterly sweet.

"Can you?" She sounds impressed. "Ah, what good luck! That's always useful, when you're dealing with the law or navy. Or those poxy merchants that never want to pay what men are owed, or treat them right. I was lucky to learn a bit myself, from old friends. It's been useful."

She leans forward, eyes bright. "Sometimes I write direct to the East India Company—you know them, I expect—without anyone asking me, just to try and fix something. Anything. There's so many men not getting what's owed. The Company always blame the shipowners, but they give the shipowners the contracts, so . . ." She shrugs again, all sharp. "I tell them, you think lascars don't know they're meant to be treated proper on voyages? You think they don't know the Company or shipowners or *someone*'s meant to keep them fed and housed? Because they do know, and *I* know."

She goes on chattering, telling me about some letter she wrote last week. How she got some boy up the road who was apprenticing as a law clerk to read over it for her, and all he took for pay was her fixing up his jacket, because he was no good at fixing things and only lived with his father, who didn't know how, either. She tells me about the newspapers passed round the coffeehouses, sold by hawkers outside alehouses, and how she's trying to get the lascars' stories in one of them. Get people to know what's going on. I listen as she trips over hopes and words, quicker than a sparrow. Knots start easing in me.

Now I see why the lascar who played the pipe told me to come here. *Mrs. Hussain can help you*, he said. And that's true, I can see it looking at her. And if she can't, she'll work her way down to the bone trying. She's got something in her that makes her want to *try*.

"I need," I start saying. Stop.

She's gone silent now too. "Go on," she says gently. Turns her mug round in her hands, warming her fingers. "Tell me, love."

A moment passes before I can.

"My father was a lascar," I say. It's the first time I've said it. I'm glad I've got the tea. My throat's all sharp, like getting the words out scraped it raw. I drink. Lower it down. "My mother was . . . Irish. Maybe." I think of how Annie's voice sank through me. Like something I already knew. "I don't remember much. I'm looking for someone who knows more than I do."

She's quiet. I don't look at her. This woman—she seems like the kind to do pity. I don't want to see it. So I look at my tea. Take another bite of cake.

"The city's not small," she says. Gentle, like she's giving me ill news. I want to get ready for the words to hurt. I can take pain. I don't fear it. But I can't make myself ready, bracing for a fight. All the fight's gone from me. This is why I didn't seek out what I was. *This.* "There's plenty of people, and more lascars have children than most know. But—" She stops.

A second goes. She straightens in her seat. Then she gulps her tea like it's ale and slams the mug back down.

"When I was a young girl, before I married, I was a working lady. You understand?" There's a warning in the even way she says it. The warning is that I'd best be polite or I won't be hearing anything more from her. So I nod, not saying anything, and the warning fades off her face. "I knew an older woman from Cork. She took up with an Indian lascar. She wasn't the only one, but I remember her. Nice lady. Not much for smiling, but she'd always look out for the younger girls. And he was good to her, she said, except that no one would give him work."

"What was her name?" I ask.

Her mouth twists up. A sad smile.

"Maeve," she says.

Do you know my *name?* I want to ask. *Do you know what she called me?* But I don't. Truth is, I'm not sure I want to know.

"And my—her lascar? His name?"

She shakes her head. "I'm sorry, love. I don't remember that." She does sound truly sorry. "And I've got more bad news. I'm afraid Maeve died years ago. I heard she had a baby, but I don't know what happened to him, after. I was young then. I couldn't do much."

I swallow. She may not even be my mother. But there's a noise ringing in me, ringing true. Maeve. I think she was.

"And the lascar?"

"Gone long before then," she tells me. "He died, perhaps. Or left. Don't blame him too much, Heathcliff. For either thing. Most lascars are starving here, and death's always calling. Work's scarce for everyone, but especially them." Her hand tightens on the mug again. "My Kabir and I are lucky, because we've got this place, and my uncle gives him a bit of work. Maeve's man had nothing, and he was a burden on her, even if he didn't want to be."

"So he got on a ship," I say. Maybe I'm hoping he did. Maybe that's better. My father being taken by sea, not by death.

"Maybe. Maybe not. I can't be sure. I hear the government or the East India Company—merchants or judges, or something or other—are meant to pay to send men home," she says, all mild. But the kind of mild that's on purpose. That hides strong feeling. "Sometimes they actually do it. But just like many lascars don't make it here, many don't make it back either." She sighs. "I'm sorry, love. But I think your da's long dead, or good as."

I think I already knew. Either I had a bad father who left me to starve, or a dead one who couldn't do anything for me. Either my mother abandoned me or couldn't hold on to me even if she tried. So that's that. I know now, as much as I'll ever know.

But my hands are shaking. Maeve. My mother. A lascar. My father. Both struggling and dying. That's a tale that says I should have died too. Starved on the streets.

If your father hadn't taken me, Cathy, I would have.

I'm piecing things together. Broken things. Me, the night I tried to run back to Liverpool, when I was small. Wanting my ma. She'd loved me. I wouldn't have wanted to run back if she hadn't, would I?

And my lascar father. Maybe he didn't want me. Didn't love me. But even my heart, bitter like it is, doesn't think that feels true. It's not right. I knew his language. I've lost it now, but I had it once. Does a man starving and lonely in some foreign country teach a son his tongue if he doesn't love him? If he doesn't want to give his boy threads that'll carry his boy's soul to the man's home across waters, even if the boy's body never goes?

"I'll get you a handkerchief," Mrs. Hussain says.

"I'm not crying," I grit out.

"Of course," she agrees. Takes my plate and piles more on it. "Let's just sit here for a while, you and me."

She sits, not saying a word. So do I. The door opens and shuts again.

"I don't have money to pay you," I say, throat scratchy.

"You don't need to pay me," she says. "You're just a boy, and you're alone."

"I don't need pity," I tell her. "I pay my debts."

"Children shouldn't have debts."

"I'm sixteen."

"A child," she says, all motherly, and cuts me some bread. "You're taking food with you. Don't argue with me."

She wraps it up in cloth and pushes it over to me. "Take what's left on your plate too," she orders.

I open up the cloth and do what she says. I think as I do it.

"You write letters," I say finally. "I can do that too. I was raised by a gentleman who taught me reading and writing like I was a gentleman's son. I know the way they talk. Their language." I fold the cloth down. "I'll pay my debt by writing something for you. Whatever you need."

"I don't need anything," she says.

But I look at her again, and she's smiling.

"But that's very generous of you, Heathcliff. Very generous. I accept."

I nod. The deal's done. I get up, and the door opens, more men walking in and out. The noise dies, and a man walks up. Mr. Hussain. He's still carrying the baby.

"Heathcliff's leaving," Mrs. Hussain says, like her husband'll know me. He nods.

"I'll walk you back," he says to me. His accent's like smoke round the words. "Some of our neighbors are not very friendly."

"Thank you, darling," she says, and takes the baby from

him. "You come back when you're ready, Heathcliff. There're always letters that need writing."

"I will," I say. Then swallow, some feeling rising in me. "Thank you."

Mr. Hussain pulls on a heavy coat, the kind I've seen dockworkers drag on when the rain gets heavy. He gestures at me: *Follow.* So I follow. We go out.

There's a thin rain falling. I pull my coat tight round me. Hunch my shoulders.

"I heard most of it," he tells me abruptly. "What you said."

"You were spying."

"Not everyone's safe," he says shortly. "And my wife is a giving woman. She thinks well of people even if they don't deserve it."

We keep walking.

"I traveled across the world once," he says. "My ghat serang—you know what that is?"

"No."

"The man who recruited me. Who led us here. Wherever we came from—India, China, Malaya, Ceylon—we were all the same with him. The captain, the farang sailors, they treated us like property. As is their way. But we looked after each other." He pauses. "Only eight of us made it. The ship was too heavy, too much cargo. They threw my friends overboard. When my wife says most don't make it—most men do not. Our lives hold no value to captains, and so we die first." His expression's not changed. But he looks at me, still walking. "That was your father's life."

An old memory. Rolling gray water, cold. Rising and falling. Was it mine, or my father's? Some ghost I carry round, living in my skull?

"You think I want to know my father suffered?"

"Yes." He says it, unhesitating. "I don't know your father. But I know what his life was. And now so do you."

He humphs, and nods. Like we've agreed on something. Then he turns back down the road, past the woman shelling peas, who watches him with suspicious eyes. Down through sewage water, and skinny, skulking dogs. He leaves me at the end of the street. Nods again, and says, "Come back like you promise, boy."

"I will," I say. And the rain starts pouring harder as he turns back, heading home.

Cathy. When we buried the feathers under the tree, I think we buried the old me, too.

I never grieved him. I didn't need to.

But here I am, and I know him. I can feel him, like he's in me. Echo of hunger pangs swimming in my belly. Language he knew. Love he knew, too. He's a skinny, angry thing. He shouldn't live, but he does, somehow. That's his luck. It sees him kicked and bleeding, but it always makes him rise up after. Over, and over, and over.

I feel like I've been cut open, but what's pouring out of me isn't blood. It's memories.

I'll never get all that's lost. But things drift up in my skull, like cloth gone worn and soft: a woman singing songs, holding my hand. A man carrying me on his shoulders, teaching me words. Pointing out things. *How do you say house, beta? How do you name the sea?*

Him, gone. Grief, sitting like stone in my belly. The hunger eating my insides, then eating the grief stone too. My ma shakily kissing my forehead. Her fingers, thin and white as bone, pointing out to the water.

Follow the river and keep going until the water goes silver. Can you dream the water, my love? That's where your father's from. That's what he calls home.

Cathy. I know who I am now. The road behind me's lit up. I can see all the old wounds. The things I've lost that I won't be getting back. The road's covered in the stuff that's broken and made me. And I'm glad I can see it, even though I'm shivering in the rain, soul wounded.

I wish I could tell you, Cathy. Wish I could see you. Hold your face in my hands and say, *I know who I am*. And the knowing hurts, but it's like joy, too. Like being free.

I wish I could press my mouth to your ear, in the dark and quiet, or under tall grass with your head in my lap, and tell you this:

Saagar. That's the word for sea. You asked me once, and I didn't know. But forgotten things can come back to us, sometimes.

Sometimes, lost things find their way home.

Chapter Sixteen

Catherine

Now that the truth is buried and burned, I can breathe again.

Even Hindley seems lighter. He is happier, less angry. Nelly has not hidden Hareton for more than a week. It means Hareton can run around the house, and he starts following me about like a little duckling, even copying my way of speaking, and asking me if I will tell him stories. It annoys Nelly a great deal, because usually she is Hareton's favorite. It makes me smug.

I still don't have much patience for Hareton, but now the world is brighter I can do things with him that are truly fun, without worrying what Hindley will say or do. I take him horseback riding, carrying him with me as he begs me to go faster and faster and whoops like a little devil. I tell him so. "You sound like you're straight from hell," I say, tickling his ribs, and he shrieks in delight. I tell him stories too, but he is sad about the ones I don't tell. There will be no more ghost tales. No more fairies either. That's in my past.

I don't have to think of who I am anymore. Not once. The fabrics are all burned. The jewels are buried.

And Heathcliff is not coming back. He thinks I don't love him.

So I am Catherine Earnshaw again, but Catherine Earnshaw with the heart scooped out of her. She didn't know what her heart was before she learned the truth about herself—she didn't know her history, her blood, even her own secrets. And now she does, and knows they mean she's cursed and haunted. So she won't keep her heart or the truth.

I open a book of sermons by my bed. I've written in this one most of all. I write in the space between one line and the next, so small and so surrounded by neat print and my own wild hand that even if someone stumbles on my books I don't think they will see this. Their eyes will move over it like it's a little drip of ink, nothing as important as what's around it. And that's how I want it to be.

I have taken out my heart, I write.

I have taken it out and buried it. I am a stranger now. I don't know myself anymore.

I go to the Grange to see Isabella, or so I tell everyone. I say I don't need Nelly to chaperone. Isabella will do enough.

I tell Hindley we're going to embroider, and he finds this funny enough to laugh. But then he shakes his head and says, "Embroider to your heart's content, Cathy."

It's strange hearing Hindley laugh. It makes me go tense and still, even though he was only laughing from humor, and there was nothing malicious about it. But still, my pulse hammers long after we stop talking. Like I am relieved to escape some terrible thing that could have happened to me, and by pure chance did not.

I don't enjoy embroidery, and I have no skill for it. Everyone knows that, even Isabella. So when I arrive at the Grange and she meets me, she says, "Do you *really* want to embroider?"

I tell her I certainly do, and she cannot convince me otherwise.

"I could play the pianoforte for you," she suggests. "I'm really getting very good!"

It's possible she's improved since last time, but I doubt it. When Isabella last played, her parents were still living, and they and Edgar sat very politely as she mangled some sonata or other as I turned the pages for her. She asked me how she had done, and I told her honestly she sounded like two cats fighting over a sausage.

She didn't like that very much.

"Embroidery," I insist. And then I steer her to the parlor that doesn't have a pianoforte in it but does have long windows that let the sunshine in.

But I grow bored very quickly, once we're settled. I sigh and lower my embroidery hoop and say, "When is your brother finally coming to see me?"

Isabella giggles. "Cathy! He'll come soon. He promised he would." She wriggles in her seat like an excited pup, then leans forward. Her eyes are sparkling as she whispers, "I should ask a maid to come in and chaperone. But if you want to go for a walk, where I can see you . . ."

"What if we go where you can't see us?"

"Cathy!"

"Oh hush," I say. "Edgar would never do anything inappropriate and you know it. He *loves* being a proper and honorable gentleman."

I roll my eyes, and Isabella laughs again, hard enough that she snorts. She slaps a hand over her mouth, and that makes me start laughing at her, doubling over and dropping my hoop onto the floor. That makes her laugh again in return.

"What are you both laughing so much for?" Edgar's voice asks. He's standing in the doorway, dressed in his riding habit. His mouth is curved into a smile. His golden hair is in disarray.

I know, looking at him, that he's very handsome. I know I am very lucky. Becoming Catherine Linton will be a coup for a girl like me, who should not even have what she does. There should be pleasure in that—thinking he's something I've stolen, something I shouldn't have.

And yet. And *yet*.

I look at him and for a moment I feel absolutely nothing. It is very strange. Like my entire body is empty and the light could shine right through it, like through water or a piece of clear glass. Then Isabella laughingly says, "It's none of your business, Edgar!" and I lean down and pick up my embroidery and make myself feel the kind of gentle love I know I should.

Why do I love him? Nelly asked me. And I was honest. I love him because marrying him sets me free. Not the kind of setting free that Heathcliff gives—*gave*—me. When I was around Heathcliff I felt like I was all myself—all wild, all joyful and thorny. Edgar gives me a different kind of freedom. The kind that's built on money.

When I am Mrs. Linton, I won't be under Hindley's control. I'll be here. I'll be safe. No one will ever turn up out of the woodwork and say, *That Catherine Linton is illegitimate!* They wouldn't dare. I will never hunger, or worry about my home being gambled away, and I will never wash the bruises of someone I love from a basin I've dragged into a stable. I will be free to ride my horse across the heath, or run whooping across the gardens like Hareton loves to do.

Well. I will not *actually* be able to race my horse, of course. Or run in the gardens, or go barefoot on the moors. And I will not be able to go to the crags or the fairy caves again. I will not be able to write my secrets into books. Catherine Linton will not be that kind of person. She won't want to do any of the things that Catherine Earnshaw yearned to do. I will have to be a good wife and a proper lady, and one day I will have to be a good mother, too.

I stand up and walk over to Edgar and lean in. I feign a whisper, though I keep my voice loud enough for Isabella to hear.

"Isabella says we can wander off alone and she won't say a word."

"I did not!" Isabella shrieks.

Edgar laughs, a little nervously. He's blushing.

I take his hand. Wrap it up in two of my own. "I want to go look at the roses," I whisper. Really whisper. "Can we?"

He looks over my shoulder at Isabella.

"Catherine and I will sit in the garden," he says.

"I don't want to go to the garden," Isabella says immediately. "I want to stay here."

"You'll be able to see us through the glass. How is that?"

Isabella makes a noise that could mean absolutely anything but must be meant to irritate Edgar, because his eyebrow twitches a little.

"This is ridiculous," I say. "Who are we proving our respectability to? There's only the three of us here. Come on, Edgar."

I grasp his arm and take him out to the corridor so we can head to the gardens. He doesn't protest, and soon we're out in the sunshine, the birds singing overhead and the perfectly manicured lawn under our feet.

I have a new gown on. It's plaid and it's vibrantly pretty, all oranges and yellows and greens that shimmer in the sunshine. I ask Edgar if he likes it, and he immediately says, "It's beautiful." But he isn't looking at the gown. He's looking at my face.

I should feel something. I should.

Instead, I skip forward, soaking in the sunshine. Maybe there's too much of it. I feel too hot in my gown, like I am beginning to sweat, and I expect I will have to use creams and special waters to make me paler. And even though my heart feels dull, my brain is racing like a starling.

I think of the time when we were small, when Heathcliff and I crept over these grounds and looked in the window, and I got my dog bite and got Edgar too. I look at the roses and lean forward to smell their scent, and think of the time I made Heathcliff let me garnish his hair in flowers: purple feathery heather and bursts of yellow-white asphodel. I never asked him to do the same to me in turn. I bullied him into tying my hair like a sailor's in a tight, snaking queue. I said we should build a ship by weaving grasses, and Heathcliff said he would help me.

I stand up again, the scent of flowers in my nose. Edgar is looking at me with such fondness.

"Do you love me, Edgar?" I ask.

"You know I do," he says earnestly.

He does not ask if I love him. Does he know that I am not entirely sure? That sometimes I think I love him, and sometimes I think how I feel about him—this sweet, airy thing—is no more than plain liking, or something I have brewed up, like a bitter tonic I have to drink for my health? My love is a thing that will fade and drift over time. It's so flimsy. But my love for Heathcliff—

I can't think of my love for Heathcliff.

But now that I have, I feel the heart I thought I buried suddenly beat. It's an awful feeling. Like a specter beating its fists against a casket lid. I curl a hand up against my chest.

"What's wrong?" Edgar asks. His forehead is furrowed. "Catherine?"

My face feels stiff. I force a smile.

"Nothing is wrong," I say.

He looks my face over and walks closer. He clasps my clenched hand. "Something *is* wrong."

"It's not. Why won't you believe me when I tell you it's not?"

"Catherine," he says. "I know you." He stops and thinks, and then he says carefully, "You're going to be my wife one day, and I'll be your husband. Shouldn't we trust each other? Be truthful with each other? That's how it was with my parents."

"Would you still love me," I ask, my voice wavering a little, "if I were not . . . perfect?"

"You are perfect," he says. "But of course I would."

He is trying to unclasp my hand, to open my fingers. But I only hold them tighter. My nails are cutting my palm.

"But what if something out of my control made me . . . not like you think I am? What if I were . . ." I shouldn't say it, I know it, I do. But my mouth moves anyway, like it is on strings, but I am not the one pulling them. I am just the doll stitched to them. "What if I were illegitimate, Edgar? What then? Would you still love me and marry me?"

I am a coward. I should just say it. I want to say it.

I have an Indian mother, Edgar. My father took all sorts of things from India, before he became a landowner here, and my brother and I were just two of those. I did not know until recently, but only because I did not wish to know. The knowledge was all there for me if I'd wanted to take it. My parents whispered strange things sometimes, and had cloth and jewels from India we didn't dare touch, and my brother thinks the mother who gave birth to us has haunted us for years.

I hear her sometimes on the wailing wind, and I see her in my own face, and when I sleep sometimes I still hear the clink of her shell bangles and the glide of her feet, which can't touch earth, but rasp like silk all the same.

I don't say the words. I don't get a chance.

Linton has gone terribly pale. His mouth firms. He lets go of my hand. He takes a step back.

"Don't say such things, Cathy." His laugh is forced. "You have such an imagination. I don't know how you think of these things!"

I know what I should do. I should smile.

I don't.

"You know I'm not making up tales, Edgar," I say, my voice oddly calm. Shouldn't I be shaking? I'm not. "You know I am trying to tell you something true."

"Don't," he says, more sharply than he has ever spoken to me. "Don't tell me something true if . . . if—"

"If what?" I demand.

"If it means I must do the right thing!" He inhales and clenches his fists and takes another step away from me, and closes his eyes. "I love you, Catherine," he says. His eyes are still closed. It's as if he can't bring himself to look at me. "I've lost so much. My—my mother. My father." His voice breaks, and he swallows. "I'm all that's left. I must make sure Isabella has a good future. And I must preserve my family and be the son my parents wanted me to be. I must be a good master to my servants, and I must be generous to the parish poor." He says it is like he is reciting something he was taught. "I must take care to be honorable and to be a gentleman. And I must marry a girl who is also kind and good and will help me in all these things. I must marry a lady."

He opens his eyes. Looks at me. I have never seen Edgar look so vulnerable before.

"I can't stand to lose you too," he whispers.

You've never had me, I think. *Only a shadow of me that I made especially for you.*

There are probably many things I could do. But what I do is this: I look down at the grass like I'm ashamed of myself. I say, "Oh, Edgar, I'm so sorry for being foolish. I didn't mean it."

I hear him swallow.

"I know," he says. "I knew that."

I walk up to him, close, and I raise my head so I'm looking into his eyes.

"I can't help but be a little mischievous, Edgar," I say. "I'm sure I'll grow out of it one day."

"There," he says, softly relieved. "There's the Cathy I love."

I smile back at him, exactly as wide as he smiles. I feel the empty feeling seep through me again, all the way from my heart to the tips of my fingers, down to my toes.

This is how I will always feel, every single day, when I marry him.

If I marry him. If.

Chapter Seventeen

Heathcliff

I'VE GOT NO MONEY LEFT. I'm going to lose even my half of a bed. The landlord who owns the lodging house tells me he'll give me a day. After that, I'm on my own.

John must feel sorry for me, because he offers me his pipe. I say no. But I do sit with him on the bed while he gets the pipe ready, then lights it.

"You could go fight again," he suggests.

"Maybe," I say. But I'm not sure I need to. I can pick pockets now. I can't go back to the place Northwood's men saw me, but the city's full of other alehouses and taverns where I can sham someone out of coin. Might be harder without Annie to charm them, but I could still try.

John taps tobacco ash out of his pipe. "You have friends in this city, don't you?"

Maybe not anymore. But I nod anyway.

"Maybe you should go stay with them instead, huh?" He pats my shoulder. "Ask them to look after you for a while."

I shake my head. "I'll get the money."

He's going to say something more when I hear a noise from outside. Earsplitting.

"*Heathcliff!*"

Hal's voice. I know it, even though it's gone strange—piercing and panicked.

I don't think. I'm on my feet. Going down the stairs fast. Out the door.

Hal barrels into me, grabbing my arms.

"Heathcliff," he pants. "You—you need to come. Please."

I set my hands on his shoulders. Press down. Steadying him. He goes quiet, shaking. Calming a little.

"Tell me what's happened," I order.

This time his voice is smaller. Steadier. "A press-gang got Jamie. They're going to force him to join the navy and he'll be gone. They came and broke the door. Annie was screaming, distracting them, and Hetty shoved me under the bed so they didn't see me. But they grabbed Jamie. They took him. They—"

"Stop," I say. I've heard enough. "Let's go."

"Where?"

"To Annie and Hetty. Show me where. Now."

We take the stairs to the attic room. The door's broken. Table cracked, the beds on their sides. Annie and Hetty are standing there, waiting, Hetty holding a rifle.

"Heathcliff," Hetty says. Nothing else. Just stands there, holding the gun.

"Someone followed Jamie," Annie says. Voice hoarse. "He . . . he was watching, when you met the merchant. I told him the tavern I'd been at, so he could make sure you were safe. But one of the merchant's men must have seen him, because they followed Jamie."

"And came back with a press-gang," Hetty says grimly.

"He said—the man, the one you fought . . . he said they were looking for you. He said he wanted to punish you. But the recruiter took Jamie instead, saying he'd do."

"The press-gang came in with guns." Hetty's voice is trembling. "They threatened Jamie. They threatened all of us."

I don't ask where she got her own rifle. Don't ask what she plans to do with it either.

"They've got him with them. With others they've taken. They'll . . . they'll make him sail for the navy. Take him away," Hal says. "Before I came to you I followed them on the rooftops. I couldn't go all the way but I think I know where they've got him."

"Jamie doesn't like violence," Annie says. "You know that, Heathcliff."

"I do," I say.

"You need to talk to that merchant and get him to save Jamie," Annie says. "You have to."

"What did you do to make his men so angry, anyway?" Hetty asks.

"I said no to him. Like Jamie told me to." I grind my teeth. "I should have done it sooner."

"If you speak to the merchant, if you—"

"No," I say, shaking my head at Annie, who's gone red-faced. Fear's got her flushed. "That man doesn't care about us." Keep my voice sure, even. "We've got to get him out ourselves."

"I'm ready to try," Hetty says. Her hands are shaking on the rifle. But not a nervous shake. More like she wants to hurt someone and she's trying not to. The people she wants to hurt aren't here.

I'm used to Hetty being in charge. But she's rattled.

This time, I'm needed.

I go into my own head. Go to the place I do when Hindley's deep in rage. When he's got a knife or gun ready, and I know my life's in danger. I go there, and my body goes all calm, but alert. The way hunted animals go.

"Hal," I say. "Grab any weapons you've got, and coin. We're getting Jamie back."

Time's tight, but we go back where we started. The others don't complain. Just follow. Maybe I look more sure than I am.

I'm relieved: John's smoking out the front of the lodging house this time. Like he's been waiting. Might be that he has. He heard Hal's yelling. Maybe heard more than that.

I ask John for help—Hetty, Annie, and Hal with me. I lay out what's happened.

He listens, eyes narrowed. Then he nods.

"I know people who can help," he tells me. I guessed he would. You don't know boxing rings, or fixers, without knowing *people*. "You can't trust gangs," he warns. "But you're lucky. No one likes navy press-gangs, and dangerous folk will do you the favor of fighting them just for the pleasure of seeing a press-gang go down. I'll ask around. I can find out where press-gangs have holed up. *If* they've holed up, and not taken your friend straight to a ship."

Hal makes a miserable noise. John's face softens.

"No need to cry over it, son," he says. "The navy's hell, I hear, but he'll live. Either you'll get your friend out or he'll get himself out someday. Maybe he'll be wiser for it."

John goes and talks to the people he knows. Time goes. Half an hour. An hour. Hal stops crying, letting Annie hold him. Hetty keeps on pacing, gripping her rifle. And me, I stay still and wait for John to get back. There's not much else I can do.

Two hours go, maybe more. Then John comes back with three friends.

Two men, one woman. The woman's dressed up like the finest lady I've ever seen, wrapped in a silk gown and jewels, but a man's coat thrown over her shoulders, her smile wolfish. I've seen the two men before, round the prizefighting ring. One's the fixer. The other's the pockmarked man who tested my fighting. I nod at them, showing respect.

John doesn't introduce them. Just says to them, "These children have got a friend taken for impressment."

"My girls had some gossip for me," the woman says. "I don't think we'll have any trouble finding your friend."

I say, "I hope the joy of fighting the press-gang will be enough payment. Because if it's not, we'll find our own way."

She laughs. "You're a cheeky thing, aren't you?"

Hetty makes a strangled noise. Don't think anyone's called me that in my life, and I never want them to again.

"Just making clear where we stand," I say. "We don't need more trouble. Just want to get our friend out of it."

"Don't worry, darling," she says, with another throaty laugh. "The pleasure of a good fight'll be enough for us. Hating press-gangs's as close to a hobby as we get in these parts. Don't you worry your sweet head about it."

Jamie was right when he said I could have joined a gang. I don't regret not doing it now, but I look at them and wonder how it would've suited me. What it would've made me.

Hours have gone since Hal came screaming to me. It's getting dark. Hal may have seen where Jamie was taken, but he's probably been moved since. Annie's near in tears now, though she's holding them back. She thinks we'll be too late for Jamie. But turns out we're lucky: the press-gang tried to grab a man on Atherton Street too, a butcher. He had a cleaver with him and there was scuffling and blood, and one navy man got out his rifle and made a show of shooting it. A handful of shipwrights drinking outside an alehouse nearby spotted them and started threatening them back. Someone threw bricks, and one shipwright had a rifle too, and now the press-gang have holed up in an alehouse farther up Atherton and can't get out.

"We'll deal with the press-gang," the fixer says. "You get your friend. But if he gets caught up in the fight. Gets hurt or dies . . ." He clucks his tongue, once. Tightens up his cravat, and touches his rifle. "Don't blame us."

It's a big tavern. Three floors high. But the door's shut tight and someone's peering out the window, ducking back when they see eyes on them. They're hoping to sneak out, maybe. But they don't stand a chance.

They're well surrounded. The gangs John called on, but men and women from nearby streets, too. Shopworkers and more, peering out windows, standing in doorways, looking vicious. More than one brick's already been thrown. The tavern's windows are mostly broken. Someone's boarded some of them shut.

We stand with the gangs, me and Hetty. Annie and Hal are back at the lodging house. "We don't all have to be foolish," Hetty snapped at them both when they were arguing, saying they should come, too. But then she kissed Annie soundly and said, "Do it for me, please." And Annie blushed, saying she would.

One of the fixer's men goes out on the road and walks forward. Sets his rifle ready, then shoots at one boarded window.

The wood splinters and he does it again. There's a shriek from inside, and suddenly the whole gang of people's surging forward.

Hetty and I look at each other. Then we run too, me with a cutlass someone threw me. Hetty with her rifle. She holds it steady, sure. She told me she hated violence. Meant it, too. But she cares about her people more, and Jamie's one of them.

A gunshot breaks out of the tavern, and Hetty flinches, but the bullet goes into the opposite wall, not into any of us. That's good. Can't think, after that, not even to worry. We pour in. Someone kicks open a window, boot through wood, shutters cracking, and we're inside.

The tavern's chaos. Bottles are breaking. Hetty's pressed closed to my side. She won't get a chance to use the rifle. She's got it in front of her like a shield.

The men in the press-gang are near the back. Their rifles are out, waving around. They're yelling. They've got the men they've caught behind them. I can see Jamie. His hands are tied, and his jaw's gritted.

I nudge Hetty's side. "I see him." She follows my eyes. Sees him.

"Jamie!" she yells. "Jamie, *Jamie!*"

His head snaps up. His eyes go wide. He looks left and right, men from the press-gang surrounding him. He's trapped.

Someone's going to get killed here. There's too much chaos. I feel the crowd press forward, some people punching, fighting. There's no getting near to Jamie.

I see why the fixer's man warned me. Getting Jamie won't

be easy. I look at him and wrench my head left. Hoping he understands.

He sucks in a breath. He nods.

One press-man lifts his gun up to shoot. Jamie moves fast. When the navy man from the press-gang's distracted, still holding his aim, Jamie shoves him. The man stumbles, shoots. The bullet lodges in the floor. Jamie scrambles free, hands tied up but he's running toward us, and the other caught men are following. One gets grabbed by a navy lieutenant and curses, but the rest are out.

I turn. There's no getting to the door. The crowd's too thick.

"With me!" I shout, and go for the stairs. Feet pound behind me, and we're going up, through a narrow staircase to the next floor.

The second floor's mostly empty, but there's some bedding up here. Maybe the workers use it, or the tavern owner, for sleeping overnight. I don't know and don't much care right now. Breathing hard, I go for the window and slam it open.

The window opens out onto a window that juts out. The roof around us is sloped sharply. Dangerous. It's a risk we'll have to take. Muttering a curse, I turn to say something—

I hear a cough from outside.

I look. On the right, Hal's clinging to the roof tiles.

"Hi," Hal says, sheepish.

"What," I say flatly, "are you doing here?"

"Watching from the other roof," he says, gesturing. "And now I'm on this roof."

"I can see that." Doesn't mean I like it.

"*I* didn't promise not to come," Hal says, which is true.

"Hal?" Hetty's coming up behind me. "Where's your shoes?"

"Bare feet stick better," Hals says. Wind gets in his hair, making his short curls fly about. He's breathing hard. Don't know if it's the strain of the climb, but he doesn't look fearful like he should. "I've got rope. There's a garret room next to this. If people can hold the rope and not fall, they should be fine to climb in that window and run out."

There's a dirty bloodbath of a fight going on downstairs.

"We'll try it," I grunt out. The caught men are coming up, too. Jamie's bruised round the face. I go over with my cutlass and start sawing the rope off his hands. The next man's a sailor, hair in a tight queue. Another's still on the stairs, head in his hands, breathing hard.

Don't think we've got long, but Hetty's already clambering out, following what Hal says and holding the wall. She's shaking, but she's got a stubborn look on her. Hal's saying something comforting to her.

"What're you doing here?" Jamie asks me.

I keep sawing. Concentrating. I don't want to cut flesh. "I said no to the merchant," I say. "Hal came and told me what happened to you. Now I'm here."

"You said no?"

"Talk later," I say. "Let's go now."

"There's something you've got to know first," Jamie says. He tilts his head at the other men.

There's the sailor, looking between us. And the man on the stairs. He stands when we go silent. Turns.

Hetty left her rifle when she went out. Wasn't safe to carry it, I expect. That's good for me, because I grab it now and aim at Northwood's lackey. He's still got bruising from when I fought him in the tavern, and new marks from the press-gang on top of that.

"He got taken with the rest of us," Jamie mutters. "He looked so bloody smug when the press-gang broke into our room. That faded fast when they tied him up too."

"Go," I say to Jamie.

He hesitates. I kick him in the foot.

"Fine! I'm going."

I don't let the rifle move, but I speak to the sailor next.

"You're going out there after my friend," I say to him. "Follow what the rest are doing and you'll be fine."

"You want me to climb on the roof?" the sailor says weakly.

"Yes."

"I might fall and break my neck!"

"Would you rather fall to your death," I say steadily, "or join the navy?"

He blinks once. That's all the thinking he does. "I need my ropes cut," he says weakly. "Or I won't be able do it."

I hold out my cutlass and tell him, "Ask the boy on the roof to do it."

I trust Hal will get it done.

Northwood's man's not getting untied. Not by me.

I turn back to him now. "If you try to lie to me," I say evenly, "I'll shoot you dead. So you'd best answer me. What does

Northwood know about me? What's he going to order done to me next for offending him?"

"Mr. Northwood knows nothing, nothing," he says quickly.

"Liar."

I can hear more gunshots downstairs. A crash like furniture breaking.

"I'm not, boy, I swear it. He doesn't know where your people live," he says, sounding terrified. "He doesn't know where to find you. He's not trying, I swear. But he said you offended him. I thought I'd impress him."

"You were trying to prove your worth," I say flatly. "Is that how you do it, when you work for him? Bring him dead boys like a cat bringing home rats?"

"Yes, yes," he says, like that'll make the rifle in his face disappear. "Please, don't shoot me."

"Fine," I grit out. I walk backward toward the window. He looks more panicked.

"Don't leave me here!"

"I don't owe you help," I say.

"I don't even like sailing," he says. "Don't let them take me."

"I heard the navy don't take lascars," I say. "Guess that was wrong."

"I'm not a lascar," he says, voice a wisp. Like he doesn't have the energy to be proper angry, now he's here.

"They don't know what you are," I say back. "They don't care. Maybe I would have. But not now." Turns out, these are my friends after all. They matter. I want them safe, and I want people that hurt them to suffer a thousand times over.

There's footsteps coming up the stairs. Loud. I hear one of the men from the press-gang. That cut-glass voice shouting isn't from here.

"Don't leave me here," he says desperately. "Boy, don't leave me. I'll pay you. I'll do whatever you need. Please."

He tries to take a step forward. I shoot the floor at his feet, and he freezes. Despair creeps over his face.

"I would have shot your leg," I say, calm and cold. "But that would have saved you from service. Enjoy the navy, friend."

And then I slip out the window, and I go. I take the rifle with me.

We get through to the garret, no bones broken. Run down the stairs, back out on the street, and go the opposite way of the fight in the tavern. We only stop running when we're far from it all, down a narrow street. The sailor says this way will take him back to his own family, his wife and his girls, so we say we'll leave him there. He collapses to his knees.

"Thank you," he says. "Thank you. What will I owe you for that, lads?" He's sweating, his hair matted. He's clutching his hat hard against his knees as he breathes. "And lady," he adds, tipping his head to Hetty.

"It's fine," she says.

"You don't owe us," Jamie says.

"Yes, you do," I tell him. I crouch down in front of him. Meet his eyes. "If you hear anyone's looking for someone who looks like me, or like my friends, I'd like to know," I say. "If you want to honor your debt, that's what I want."

Something's bound us. Whatever he sees in my face makes him nod slowly, not looking away.

Maybe the bond will break. Maybe it won't. Me, I think he'll keep his word.

"Where would I find you?"

We don't have the stolen attic anymore. But I know where he can go.

Chapter Eighteen

Catherine

I GO HOME.

Hindley asks how my day went, and I tell him it was lovely and that I thoroughly enjoyed embroidering. I pinch Hareton's cheeks and chase him around the house until I'm breathless and he has collapsed into a tired heap. Then I give him to Nelly, and I eat, and then I prepare for bed and hum as I brush my hair. I put down my brush and shut my door. And then I go to my bed, lie down, and feel all the strength leave me.

I'm shaking. My teeth are chattering. I draw the covers over me, wrapping myself up as if I am in a cocoon, but it makes me no warmer. The cold is coming from inside me.

My mother was a stranger, and I am a stranger. My mother's ghost is a stranger, and I am a stranger too. The words string through my head like beads. *Strangers, strangers*. This is my home and I belong here, this is *home*, but I also saw how Heathcliff was treated even though the Heights was his home too. How people looked at him, and spoke about him, and how he learned to vanish even when eyes were on him. He learned it so well that now he is gone, gone so far that I can't find him at all.

The past is burned and buried, but I am still bringing it back from the dead. I was the one who told Edgar, after all. He would never have known, if I hadn't told him. Maybe I couldn't help myself. Hindley always said Heathcliff was trouble because he was an outsider. I am a stranger, bringing destruction into my own life and my own home. I don't know myself anymore.

No. No, that's not right. I've brought no trouble that wasn't given to me by my father's choices. By Hindley's choices, too. The only trouble I made for myself is the one that lost me Heathcliff. Only that.

I start crying then, thinking of Heathcliff. I cry like I always cry—small and miserable. And then suddenly I am not crying like that at all. I am sobbing awfully, inconsolably, like someone has died and left me. I am sobbing like my heart is broken. And it's all true. My heart is not buried after all. My heart is in my chest, and it *aches*.

I'm safe to cry in my own bed, so I don't stop until the crying fades out of me all on its own. When it does I just breathe in and out, in and out against my bedding. I can hear my heartbeat in my ears. And also . . . something else. Tapping. Whispering.

There's a storm, I realize. It's come without warning. The sky looked the same as ever when I came home. Or maybe I wasn't looking. I was very distracted.

I slide back the covers and sit up. The window frame is rattling, from wind and rain and the touch of the tree branches. My bedside candle is flickering wildly.

I shove open the window, pushing it as wide as it will go. The wind gusts in. The candle snuffs out.

Without the candle, I can see only shifting darkness outside. Flashes of the colors of the moors. The silver white of the tree. I see a flicker in the distance, like pale cloth moving. Like something or someone drifting across heath. The wind is singing, long and mournful. My face stings from the rain, my own old tears.

"Mother," I whisper.

The white in the distance moves and turns, and the branches of my tree are scraping my cheek, whipped by the wind. They're cold fingernails, scrabbling, trying to get through my skin.

"Come back!" I wail. "I didn't really want you to go. I didn't. Shouldn't you know, if you're my mother? Shouldn't you know I need you?"

The spindling branch of the tree grasps at me like fingers. Not clawing—holding, or trying to. It *is* fingers—the white bones of a fleshless, bloodless hand clinging to my face, then my own hand as I grasp it tight.

"Mother." I'm weeping again. "Mother. Ma. Don't leave me. Don't go."

I don't know if ghosts can hear or speak or answer. All I know is that I fall backward. The window is still rattling, but my oak closet is open, and I am on the floor. My hair is dripping wet. My hands are cold.

I scramble to my feet and get back onto the bed.

If she won't stay or can't stay, if my mother's ghost is drifting, lost because of what *I* did to her, burying or burning everything that tied her to me, to Hindley, to the Heights . . .

I grasp my pillow.

Birds can fly, but feathers, plucked or lost, pin your soul down.

The pillow tears almost too easily. The cloth hisses, ripping open under my fingers. And then a cloud of feathers bursts up between my hands.

Pigeon feathers, most of them. But here—ah. White and black, faintly curved, are lapwing feathers.

Once, Heathcliff and I were out hunting. Or Heathcliff was hunting and I was distracting him. We watched a lapwing overhead, soaring, and I said, "Won't you shoot it?"

He shook his head and said to me, "I think it's going back to its nest."

So we followed it, both of us. Stumbling through high grass, tracking it with our eyes.

We found its nest on its side. Broken, like a predator had already found it. It had been ruined a long time ago, but the lapwing had gone back to it anyway, maybe many times, over and over again. Maybe that's how birds grieve, just like people.

We found the bones of those little birds inside the nest, and I sobbed. Heathcliff stared at me at first. He was too shocked to move, I think. But then he hugged me, fierce and strong with his knuckles digging into my spine, his face in my hair.

"Come on, Cathy," he said, low and gentle, coaxing me back

down as if I were a sweet pup with a wounded leg. "Come on, let's go home. Let's go."

I made him promise to never shoot a lapwing. "Never, ever," I said. "Promise me. It would be like shooting *us*. Like shooting a thing that can grieve. I can't stand it, Heathcliff."

"I promise, Cathy," he said, brushing away my tears with his fingers. "I promise."

The lapwing's feather is caught by the wind. I try to grasp it but it's too late. It's gone. Losing it awakens me, and I feel like myself again. Less wild. I breathe shakily, and move, and carefully draw my window shut. The storm is outside now, and I am not.

There are no ghosts, and I must put my grief away. I must accept how things are, and stop weeping. I know that's what Nelly would say, so I must try.

A handful of feathers have drifted to the floor. I kneel down on my hands and knees to gather them all up.

There is something beneath my bed.

I see a hint of it. At the base of the oak closet. A piece of wood that is not like the rest, that had been pushed under there a long time ago. I flatten against the door, slide my fingers under the bed, and drag it out.

It's a thin wooden box. So thin it fit without being visible. I feel along the edges, until I find a clasp. It's stiff, but I force it, and I manage to open it.

Inside is cloth. But it's not just simply cloth.

I pull the material out.

It's—oh, how can I describe it? It feels like I imagine clouds must feel. But there's nothing airy about it. It is smooth, glowing like ivory. There's a light inside it that makes it shine. I know without being told that it is part of the fortune my father brought with him.

And I know it belonged to my mother.

This is what has kept my past and my heart alive somehow. One scrap of cloth so beautiful that it shines like moonlight.

I get back onto my bed. I don't think. Ink, and a quill pen— all the things I keep at my bedside—I grasp them. I light a candle with shaky hands. I barely know I'm doing it.

The wind is still howling.

I open one of my books, full of a stranger's sermons, and peel the pages open. There are words on them already— printed words and my own old words, but none of them matter.

There is ink on my fingers. Dripping onto my skin, my bedding. I don't care. The moon fabric is on the floor and safe from me, and I must spill the words out. They are like a howl—a thin, high thing, piercing, and it must be heard, and written, and heard again.

Once. Once . . .

Once and now, there is a woman. She looks like me, or I look like her. She has long hair, very black and shining. A long nose and fierce eyebrows, and a full mouth. She has Hindley's eyes and his slightly out-turned ears.

She is brown. Brown like the peat, or bark, or the moors that roil up like waves far out beyond my window— brown like everything I love. And she is my mother.

Maybe this is my memory. Maybe I am spinning a tale. I don't know. I only know it is not Heathcliff's story. It is my own.

Water. A woman crying. She tells a man that she wants to keep her children with her. Her baby's eyes—my eyes—are barely open. Please, he can't take them from her.

"You can take everything," she says. "Everything. But you can't take them."

She says it in a language I don't know, but you don't need words to know what grief sounds like, not really. I think there was room carved in my ears and my head for that language when she had me, and the room's still there; it shifts inside me like the noise wind makes on a dark night, like a warning. Like life.

"You want them to have a better life, don't you?" he asks. He says it without even really looking at her. He's already far away in his soul, back in England with his English wife. He tells her he will leave her eldest with her, and a generous payment to tide her over, and that will have to be enough.

She does want them to have a better life, so she lets them go.

She stands at the dock when they leave. Her second son, so much lighter skinned than his brother, howls and howls as he's carried off. Her baby sleeps the whole time, not knowing that a goodbye is happening at all.

She watches them cross the water, roiling and gray and green and black as a night with no moon or stars, and dreams of it for years after. And then she dies, somehow, and of course she becomes a ghost. Because what else can she do, when her heart has grieved so fiercely that even death can't snuff the pain out?

How far can England really be for a ghost? she thinks. And off she goes, gliding over strange waters to stranger lands. And she's here, here watching her children grow, here in their dreams whispering tales, here carrying love with her, trying to give it where it can't be seen or felt or heard, but . . .

But I hear. I hear, and I see.

I let the book fall from my hands. Still open, so the ink can dry. The ink on my fingers has settled into my skin, blue swirls of it that won't shift or fade without water and scrubbing. Then I take up the cloth from the floor. My hands are trembling. I drape it over my face, like I am a bride or a body under a shroud. I go over to the mirror. The glow of the candle, still by my bed, follows me.

I look up, look at my mirror . . . and finally I see her.

My mother.

Silvery fabric over dark eyes and the slope of a nose; the shadow of a face. A parted mouth, always trying to say words. I stare and stare, and the dark coils around me, and she stares back.

Then slowly, my mother fades. I feel the cold of her, loving and sweet, drift out of me.

There is a ghost, and she has my face, and there is a ghost under my skin. She's the me I don't know—the me who was born in another country and had another mother. The me with a father who helped people die, and filled his pockets with coin, and brought me here, to this stone house where the wind wails, so that I could become someone else.

And the ghost is the me I know, too. The me with wild curls and her feet always bare and dirt on her hands. The me who gathers up feathers and buries them, and creeps into caves and up crags, and lies back in the heath listening to the wind until she feels like she is flying or floating, angels holding her up by the arms.

I lower the muslin and there she is, still in front of me. The me I am.

If I stay here I will become a ghost. I know it. I hold the scraps of pearly white cloth in my hands and I know it in the same way I know Heathcliff's dreams.

I'll spend years and years thinking I am alive. I will marry Edgar and wear the finest gowns and I will be loved and cosseted and adored. I will walk down the beautiful corridors in the house I will be mistress of and look at my very fine gardens and my paintings, my beautiful looking glass and my own face set perfectly inside it, staring back at me, and I will think, *I am happy. I am so happy and so alive! What more is there to being alive than this?*

I won't have nightmares of the smell of stale wine. I won't remember the way the stairs creak under light, careful feet, or the way they sound when Hindley hurtles up them in anger— the crash like splintering, like a tree struck through the heart by lightning. I will never, ever think of how it was when I was a girl, *this* girl, weeping and weeping in my bed until I could not breathe for wishing that Heathcliff was lying beside me. I will not remember leaning into his body, the time we almost kissed each other. Or all the times I pressed my ear to his chest and heard the wind across the moors, or the crash and pull of the sea.

I will be silent inside, a sweet silence, and Edgar will love me and I will love him. I will be Catherine Linton. *Mrs.* Edgar Linton. Scratch out the *Earnshaw* and the *Catherine* both, and make something new of me. Why not?

But murdering Catherine Earnshaw and Heathcliff's Cathy, blotting her out . . .

It will only work for a time. I know her. She doesn't take well to being contained or silenced, and she'll find her way out. She will go mad, utterly mad from being confined inside me, and one day she will rip Catherine Linton apart and run, run, run as fast as she can, out of my skin, out into the moors, out into the wind, out onto the Heights, and I will be free, a hardy and free ghost, my turned-around feet never touching the moors again—

Death and oblivion. I know the road ahead of me. And I hate it, knowing. I don't like to see myself so clearly.

I look in the mirror. I am not smiling. I had not realized how often I smile—how I always carry my mouth curved upward, in challenge or in joy or in something that looks a little like it. I do it because I think I should smile. I am not doing it now, and I think . . . I think I like the face I see.

I will die if I stay like this, and I don't yet want to die.

I don't know where I will go or what I will do. But I take my hair in my hands—all my wild, tangled curls—and I scrape them back from my face so no one can look at my unsmiling mouth and my firm nose and strong eyebrows and see the pretty, laughing girl I work so hard to be. I pick up a ribbon, a black ribbon I stole from Heathcliff, and I tie my hair back low at my nape, like boys wear it. Like he wore it.

I look at my face again. And, oh. I *am* Heathcliff. And I am myself. More myself, maybe, than I have ever been.

Heathcliff.

Heathcliff, I wish you could hear my voice. I wish my soul could call yours across miles and worlds. Our souls are one thing, after all. You should always know where I am. Always hear the sound of my voice, like I should hear yours. But my head's been silent, and my life's been hollow. Even if I had the power to reach you, I don't think this grieving girl I've been could have done it.

It is strange, so strange, accepting that our souls can be the way they are, entwined like two old trees, and we can still be two separate people. We can still be so far apart that our dreams no longer touch, so distant that we can hurt each other and run from each other. You cannot hear me, Heathcliff. And you can't know my heart if I don't tell you what's lying inside of it.

If I could, I would send flocks of birds to you. I would send you my shadow in glass, in windows and mirrors, watching to keep you safe. I would send gentle dreams, and kind people, and all the things you deserve and never had, here in the Heights where you should have been safe.

I know now, that I'd send my soul to you wherever you are. Because wherever you are is where I belong.

Chapter Nineteen

Heathcliff

THE DOOR OF THE LODGING house on Mann Road opens.

I know how we look. Bruised, bleeding, tired. Still holding weapons, though we don't look fit to use them. Mrs. Hussain stares back at us. Eyes wide, mouth open.

"Heathcliff," she says. "What happened to you?"

"I'll write you a hundred letters," I say, "if you help us."

She looks calmer already. Recovering herself.

"So many as that?" Mrs. Hussain says mildly. She opens the door wider. "Come on in, Heathcliff. Bring your friends. Do any of you want a cup of tea?"

Everyone does. One of the lodgers says he'll make it. Mostly, I think he's curious and wants to listen in.

But Mrs. Hussain doesn't care. So we all sit at her table, and I talk.

I tell her we've got no home, and no place at my old lodging house. When we got back, Annie was out on the road. The landlord had kicked her out. Said it wasn't a place for "loose women," which made me and Hetty consider setting the whole place on fire. Only thinking of John made me stop. He'd done us a good turn. So we left, and I slipped my last coin under his pillow as thanks before going.

"We stole a room," Hal says. "Up in an attic. I found it. I nailed the door shut, and we moved in."

"It was a slum. The landlord never checked what was up there, so we were safe." Annie looks down, brushing her hair back from her face. "I didn't love the climb," she admits. "But it was ours, and it was fine."

"A press-gang came and broke everything, and now we don't have it anymore," says Hetty. "But we're all safe, so that's something." She pauses. Then says, "Safe and homeless."

"There's always cellars," Hal says.

"I'm not living in a cellar," Hetty says, sharp. "And neither are you. You get sick as it is."

"We can't go back," Jamie says eventually, as Hetty goes on scolding Hal. Jamie's eyes are rimmed dark. Tired. "We're going to have to start over again."

Guilt's got no worth. If it won't fix anything, I won't bother feeling it.

"We just need somewhere to stay a day or two," I say. "Until we can find something else."

I don't mean to say that. *We.* Like we're bound together. Like what happens to them happens to me, too. Jamie looks at me, but I don't take it back. That's set in stone now—truth I won't unravel. We're together now. I'll see them safe.

Later, it's just me and Jamie sitting together. The girls are sleeping on makeshift bedding in the parlor. Hal's curled up on an old armchair, head to knees, snoring like a tin whistle.

"You shouldn't have gone with the merchant," Jamie's saying. "But you didn't stay and do what he wanted. And it's not your fault." He sighs, and leans forward. Lowers his head down on the table. "Those rich shits," he mutters into the wood. "They'll take any chance to ruin it for the rest of us."

"If I hadn't walked away from him, none of this would have happened," I observe.

"Shut up," Jamie says tiredly.

"If I worked for Northwood, I could have helped you all," I say. "I could have sent you money. Could have got you somewhere to live."

"Are you trying to torture me, or torture you?" Jamie asks. "For what? What're you saying this for?"

I stretch in my chair. My body's hurting. Tired.

"The world's uncaring, mostly," I tell him. "Most rich men use people. Pick clean their teeth with our bones, then say they're saving us."

Jamie sighs again. Lifts his head. Rests his chin on his hands.

"We have to rely on people like him," I observe. "Because they own everything."

"You're not making me feel better," he says. "If that's what you're trying to do."

"It's not."

"Ah," he says. "Go on, then."

But I don't. Not straightaway. I'm thinking. Tiredness has got my brain, and now my thoughts are slow treacle. I look at Jamie. He's frowning at me, mouth turned down. Outside there's lodgers talking. Three men from somewhere in India, who wear high turbans and steel at their wrists, speaking words that half make sense. My hearing keeps turning to them. There's threads there pulling me.

I don't follow them now.

I think of Annie's charm. Her cards, flickering so fast through her hands. Hetty, hard as iron, keeping folk together. Hal, light on his feet, hellish brave. Jamie, too softhearted, gathering people up.

I look at this place: curtains sagging with mold. The fire in the grate, welcoming heat. Voices, speaking words I know and words I don't, carving out something in me.

With coin, we could build something. The Hussains. The people living here, who've got to face death if they want to go back to where home was. These four who taught me and saved me. Maybe I'm a fool. But I was bone-sure, once, that I could make a fortune and break Hindley's soul and heart, and get a vengeance no sailor's bastard, no orphan who should have died hungry, gets to have. Not in this world.

Used to be, when I'd dream, I'd dream of getting my hands around Hindley's throat. I'd dream of tearing everything down. The Heights. Hindley. Edgar Linton. I thought I wouldn't be happy until it was all ground to dust around me.

But now I think maybe I don't want to unmake everything.

I look at all these broken things and people, trying to live, and I want them to keep on living. I want to build them defenses that'll cut men like Northwood to blood and ribbons. But I'll settle with making it so that when someone like Northwood turns up, a boy has somewhere else to go to, and another road he can walk. I want it so a boy like me can say no without feeling like a knife's twisting inside him.

I've never dreamed of building something before. Turns out, when I do, the same cruel hunger that makes me want to raze everything makes me want to build whole new worlds.

"We could make something for ourselves," I go on finally. But it's not easy to say. It wrenches out of me, like a stone pulled from earth. Under it is something soft and squirming I don't want light on, but I let it happen anyway. "Something different from them. We could make something for us."

"Us," he repeats.

"I owe you all."

"We don't want debts," he says, mouth twisting. "Not anymore. I didn't ever want them."

"You helped me," I say. "That debt's not cruel. You're not asking for it. That debt's . . ." My words die out. Seconds go past. I think of how to say it.

Debts that bind people together. Debts that keep them living. When the world's cruel, those debts are reliable.

Like you, Cathy. How you cared for me. How you cleaned my wounds and loved me. You loved me and I loved you, and love was like a debt we were always paying and calling in. It kept me alive.

I say to Jamie, "That's what friendship is. Debts that don't end. They just go back and forth between people. So don't say no to mine."

He looks and looks at me.

Finally, he says softly, "Go on then, friend of mine. How're we going to make enough money to make something?"

I'll tell him everything. Or most of what I'm thinking, at least. But first I'll start with this.

"To make something for us, we'll need money," I say slowly. "To make something better, we'll need some justice. And I know how to get some of both."

It shouldn't be so simple. Turns out though, it is.

We don't need to climb a roof or even pick a lock. We borrow some clothes from one of the lodgers staying at Mrs. Hussain's. We go to a grand, rich street, all shining houses. Go round to the servants' entrance.

Northwood collects people from the Orient and Africa, anyone who's got a speck of blood he looks down on. Two boys walk up to the servants' door, dressed like he prefers—turbaned in tunics and trousers. If their clothes are less neat and shining than most of Northwood's servants, no one notices. They're carrying boxes up the stairs. A bit of dirt's not strange. One gasps, "We got to get these to the kitchen quickly, we're already late."

The maid by the door hesitates. Frowns. She doesn't know them. But one boy says, "The cook'll skin us." And they must be from here, if they know what the chef's like, always shouting and swearing. So she stands aside, and mutters, "Good luck." And in they go.

Still, I almost laugh over how easy it is. We don't go to the kitchen. On my way out last time, I saw an alcove down the servants' corridor. Luggage lying in it, and boxes. We drop the box there.

Then we walk. Going slow, watching, until we get to the green parlor. We step in.

Jamie crosses the room. Stops.

"You're right," Jamie whispers. "It's awful."

The painting's right ahead of us. I go up to it. Put my hands on the frame, and take it off the wall.

"I hear footsteps," Jamie says suddenly.

I hear it too. Someone's coming. We sink back against the wall. In my head I'm cursing.

A servant comes in. She's got a cloth for dusting. Starts straightening cushions, then goes still. Raises her head.

The maid looks me straight in the eye.

I recognize her, by her jaw shape. Her beaded hair. The way she tilts her head, looking at me. She poured the tea when Northwood tried to make me one of his.

Sarah.

I stare at her, and she stares right back at me. One long moment of looking at each other, not blinking. I wonder if she'll yell. Wonder if she'll make other servants come running, and it'll be the end of me. End of Jamie too.

I don't look away, when slowly I touch a hand to my own

clothes. Touch the frame. Then I let my gaze move, marking her clothes. My costume, her costume, the painting. *Look*, I say, using no words, just my own eyes, my own face. Hoping she'll understand. *Look at the lie Northwood's told himself about us. That we're these clothes, and that kind of kneeling. Look at the lie he's got us telling for him.*

But you and me, we know this isn't what we are. Under all this— you and me, we're the same.

Sarah, I mouth then. I look at her steady. *Please.*

I don't like begging. I beg now. Trusting her.

She's still frozen. One long moment, I don't know what she'll do, or what I'll have to do. Then her shocked face goes firm. She looks brave and flinty, ready to do what she must.

She nods her head. Squares her shoulders, and glides out.

When we go out in the corridor, it's empty. More empty than it should be.

Thank you, Sarah, I think.

We put the painting into the box. Carry it the way we came in. We go out the back. Then we walk sedately for half a minute before we run for our lives.

I think it'll be Hal, Jamie, and me. But Hetty joins us for the burning. She brings rags and alcohol and sets the fire up herself. I don't interfere. I just do what I'm told, when she asks me to fetch and carry. We're on the roof of Hal's favorite building, right where we can see the water move. Hal's worried we'll set the whole building on fire, but Hetty sucks her teeth like she's looking for patience, then ruffles his hair, and says not to worry. It's not even a big fire.

She takes out her own tinderbox and hands it to me.

"Set it alight," she orders, the way she does. "You stole it. It's yours."

I stay still for a second. Jamie was the one who got us in. I look at him, and he shakes his head, crossing his arms.

So I kneel down. Use the tinderbox, and send the whole thing up in flames. Fire catches the soaked cloth, and I leap back. The painting curls at the edges. Black, white, orange, gold. It smells sick—turpentine paint, peeling up, dying. In minutes the painting's gone.

It's not justice. Not revenge for this woman, or for anyone else. Northwood's not special. I've seen his kind of cruelty everywhere. Seen the seeds of it in myself, too.

But they're staying seeds. I'm growing something different. Making something else out of me. I don't know what yet. And it's something, taking the painting away from him. The next time Northwood takes some boy into his house and tells them they should be grateful he can make a monster out of them, at least they won't have to look at that painting of how he thinks they should look at him too. How he thinks the world *is*.

I'd rather see him burn, but this will do. It'll do fine.

"How's Annie doing?" Jamie asks.

"She's got it done," Hetty says. She means Annie's taken the frame. Had it melted down, so the gold's ours. We'll sell it for coin. Get started. "We won't go hungry yet. Also, here," Hetty adds roughly. Shoves something forward. I look down.

They're currant buns, burned, nearly bitter. The baker sells the burned ones cheap. Sometimes you can find them thrown out, but it's harder to get those. Everyone fights over them.

"Are we celebrating?" Hal sounds eager. He jumps forward and holds out his hand. Hetty drops a bun into it.

"Annie insisted," Hetty says, resigned. Like she'd never do this if she hadn't been strong-armed into it. She holds out one to me, and I take it.

"I'll give her my thanks," I say. "Have you got one?"

"I didn't want one," Hetty says.

I break my bun in half. It's not easy. The burnt parts don't want to crack, but I force them. Hetty takes it, almost smiling. Then Jamie mutters something and does the same, so Hetty's got a whole and we've both got halves. And we eat the burned bread, the sweet-sharp currants, in a cloud of smoke and ocean air washing right over us.

"What will you do now?"

I look up. Eyes stinging. I blink the feeling out of them. Mr. Hussain's face looks back at me.

I've written ten letters. The last's drying now, ink blotting. I won't do more. It's getting dark. Candle glow's not enough, and Mrs. Hussain's off with baby. I hear it fussing. Some lascars are sitting round us, quietly eating or drinking tea. Ale's forbidden to some, who can't have liquor because God told them not to, so tea's always being drunk here. The kettle's whistling again on the fire.

"I don't know," I mutter. Got ideas. Got plenty of them. But putting them together . . . that'll take time.

"You could make something of yourself. People says Liverpool's full of chances for smart young men," he observes. "That's why people come every single day."

And get their money stolen in alehouses. And rent space on half-beds. Or die robbed, or thrown onto ships they don't want to be thrown onto. Liverpool's full of ways to die. But most places are.

"That's not how the city is for most," I say.

"True," he replies. "But I wondered if you knew it."

"Your wife says I could do anything."

"My wife has a generous heart," he says. "And she knows how hard the world is. But she does not live in the world we live in." He looks at me silent. A long moment. Fire crackling. "You understand."

I nod. I do understand.

"Without her family, I would have nothing," he says. "But you . . ." Creaking wood. He's moving a chair. Sitting down. His shadow's over my paper. I slide the letter to the side. "You can read. You can write. That's a lot more than most boys can do."

I hear his arms go down on the table. Settling in.

"You can't do *anything*," he says. "But you can do very much."

"You're thinking of something," I say. "Tell me. I'd like to know."

"You could help men like your father," he offers. "Fight for them with words. Do my wife's work, but more. Many terrible things happen to lascars. But the navy, the merchants, the East India Company, the lawmen here—don't care. You could tell them and make them care."

"I can't make them care if they don't have hearts," I mutter.

He laughs, low. "All men have hearts," he says. "Sometimes they're good. Sometimes bad. That's God's will."

I don't believe that. I keep my mouth shut.

"It's your choice," Mr. Hussain says. "But you must think what you want. You have a bit of time," he says finally, and stands. Grunts. Grimaces.

"My bones hurt," he grumbles. "More and more, in this weather. I miss heat."

He goes away.

I sit until the candle gutters.

What next? I've got plans. We've got money. Enough to start. We've all agreed we'll stay here. Get the place sorted. Make it nicer for the Hussains and the lodgers. Make our home here, too. I'll keep writing letters. We'll get everyone to pitch in money—Hetty's idea. She'll get a handle on ledgers. Keep track of what comes in, and make things better. More hearth fires. Better windows. Curtains that have got no mold on them.

More rooms, for more lascars. Room for families, too. That'll take time. Time, and more coin coming in.

What Mr. Hussain's suggesting—that's not wrong. But my

teeth itch. I've still got a want in me, a hunger. Not just violence and anger. Not anymore. But it won't rest.

I light a new candle. Walk along to the parlor. Annie and Hetty have got a proper cot now. They're practicing letters. Chalk on a board. Annie looks up.

"I'm going somewhere," I say. "Tomorrow, probably. I'll be gone a while."

Annie's face is calm. She nods. "Where?"

I look out the parlor window. It's smeared with hearth soot. No matter how often it gets cleaned, it clouds up again. So I can't see out. And if I could, I'd see the same road. The water settling on it.

"I don't know," I say.

"Heathcliff," Hetty says. Exasperated. "How can you not—"

She goes silent. I look back. Annie's holding her arm, quieting her.

"Okay," Annie says, and smiles. She looks me up, down. "We'll all be here when you come back."

Annie's a sharper. Can't sham people if you can't read them. So I know she's looked at me and understood me more than I understand myself.

I step out, pulling on my coat.

The road's not quiet. There's a man out, one of the lodgers. He's playing a pipe, some winding music. I lean against the wall. Listen. Then I turn.

I know his face.

"I've got your kerchief, still," I say. "If you want it back, it's yours."

The music stops. He looks at me and grins.

"You!" he exclaims. "You listened to my advice?"

I nod. "I did."

"You look better now you're not bleeding."

"Thank you," I say.

"Keep the kerchief," he says, waving me off. "No, no. Keep it. Look at you. It brought you good luck. I hope it brings you much more."

I nod, then stand straight. I walk. Go down the road, past houses. It's evening, but most are still lit. Candles, lamps, and people sitting out on doorsteps.

The roads are narrow. I walk down to the docks. Quiet's around me. Just the creak of wood. The slosh of river water, rising. Falling.

I know. That's the truth. I know where I've got to go, even before I see something falling. It catches my eye, so I raise my head. Sky's dark, but there's moon glow, and light from the houses behind me. So I see it fall, slow and easy, and hold my hand out to catch it.

The feather lands right in my palm. It lands soft and then it stops. No wind catches it and sends it flying off again. It's like it was meant for me.

I look down.

I'd know it anywhere. A lapwing's feather.

My head goes up. But I can't see a lapwing. And why should I? A bird like that, over this city—that's not right, not true. But it must be, because I have its feather in my hand.

Moments pass. But the sky doesn't change. So I look slowly

down at it without breathing. It's still there. White, black. Curving. I look at it, and remember: a nest of bones. You weeping. And me, wishing even one had survived. Thinking I'd have kept them all living if I could, so you wouldn't cry. So I'd know the world wasn't near always cruel, and nature not always harsh, and small things could grow up, winged and free, and able to leave their nest behind. Like maybe if birds had hope, so did you and me.

I promised I'd never shoot a lapwing. Promised you and promised myself. And I never have.

My face is wet. I've never cried like this. Gentle tears. Easy. They don't feel like grief. Don't feel like anger.

I think of gray, roiling waters. I think . . . some waters are for drowning in, or going far from home. But some wash you clean. That's how I feel. Like a thing washed clean. Some old grime stuck to my soul's been carried off.

I want to think you're calling me home, Cathy. But maybe I'm calling myself.

Cathy, I have been speaking to you. Speaking in dreams. Speaking in my own skull. But you haven't heard me. Turns out we're two people after all. Two bodies, two memories. Two roads, and mistakes enough between us. More regrets than one soul can hold.

But I have a lapwing's feather. And soon enough you'll know this, because you'll see it with your own two eyes. A bird across the sky. Or a dream. Or just me, walking to you, grass up to my knees and the sky blue behind me.

I'm coming back for you.

Chapter Twenty

Catherine

I WON'T RUN OFF WILDLY this time.

I feel so calm.

I have let days pass. I have told Hareton tales. I have been nice to my brother. I've seen Hindley's mood darken, and seen him turn back to drink, as he realizes we haven't been able to bury the past after all. He stares into space sometimes, like all he can see are the things that still haunt him—what was stolen from him and from me. What Father stole.

I start to tell Hareton stories of ghosts again. All the stories that are mine and Hindley's, that I did not know came from our mother, because he should have them, too. And perhaps, one day, he'll have his own ghosts to face, and he'll need to know what to do.

"You mustn't forget," I whisper to him, as I tell him a tale by the fire, the pups tumbling around our legs. "Do you promise you'll remember, Hareton?"

"Mm-hmm," he says, distracted by trying to pull the dog's tail. But it's the best answer he's given me yet, so I decide it's enough.

Storms have come and gone these past days like warnings. But this morning, the sky's clear.

Today Hindley will be out until the late afternoon. So I have taken all the jewelry I have, and all the coin I've hoarded in my room. I've packed it tightly between handkerchiefs and tied them off, and put them in a bag I can carry easily on a long journey, slung over my side.

I have dressed in Heathcliff's clothes. I have tied my hair neatly back. I put no gowns in my pack, except the simplest one I own. I would like to take no gowns at all. Whoever Catherine Earnshaw is, she likes these breeches and stockings, the cuffs of her shirt and the buttons that line her waistcoat. She's pleased to sit on her oak bed holding the last piece of her mother in her hands. She loves how it feels like holding the ocean, which is just like holding her first memory and all her dreams, right in her own palms.

I hear the door open. I don't even feel fear jolt through me. I'm ready.

"Miss Cathy," Nelly says. She looks around, left to right, and then closes the door behind her. I hear it fall into place with a soft thud. "Why is your room like this? And why are you dressed like that?"

Nelly sees far better than most people do, so I know she's only asking me so that she can scold me for my answer.

"This cloth's like water," I say, instead of what she wants to hear. I move it back and forth between my hands, feeling its lightness, the softness of it. It's white. Time should have stained or yellowed it, but somehow it hasn't. I thought maybe it looked luminous because of my mother's ghost, because of some strange, deathly magic that had breathed its way through me in my bedroom when I'd gazed into my silver mirror. But it still shines now that I'm holding it in front of Nelly. "How do you think it's made?"

"Why," Nelly says, "are you dressed like that, Miss Cathy?"

"I think it must take magic," I murmur. "Or weavers so skilled that no one can even imagine how they do it. See? You can see my hand right through the cloth, it's so thin."

I hold my hand up. It's visible through the muslin, like a pearly shadow. Nelly doesn't look impressed.

"It must be like weaving glass," I muse out loud. "Mrs. Linton would have adored it. She would have made curtains of it. Or bedding."

"Miss Cathy."

"No, you're right, Nelly. Dresses. She would have made dresses. Though I think they would have looked a little indecent, don't you? Maybe it would have started a new fashion."

"Catherine Earnshaw," Nelly says sharply. "Stop it now. Talk seriously to me."

"You talk to me like I'm a child, Ellen Dean," I reply, using her full name. If she wants to be formal and she wants to be sharp with me, I can do the same in return. "But I'm not. If

I'm old enough to be thinking of marrying someone, I'm old enough to respect."

"I'll treat you with respect when you stop doing such childish things," she snaps. "Answer my questions."

"I didn't think your questions were worth answering," I say sweetly. I lower the muslin, folding it up tenderly and putting it by my side on the bed. "You can see what I'm doing."

"Please," she says. "Not again. You keep running and keep coming straight home. There's no need for it, Miss Cathy. Put your things away, and this can be forgotten."

"It can't," I say back. "I've learned I don't like forgetting. And I don't like that I keep coming home too. I have to go, Nelly."

"Miss Cathy." She sounds despairing. "Talk sense. You're not fit for the world."

"Then I must go, and make myself fit for it."

"You'll perish," Nelly says.

"Then let me perish," I say calmly. "I won't be convinced to change my mind."

Nelly must see in my eyes that I mean it; a haunted look flickers over her face.

"Hindley has been better," Nelly says, in a careful, gentle kind of voice. "He's given no one any trouble. Not even gambled. Hasn't the household been better for it?"

I nod. It has. Even Joseph has looked less sour.

"If you try to run off again, all of that will be undone," she tells me. "He will drink more. He'll be violent. Hareton will suffer even more than he already does, poor thing." I hear the love she has for him in her voice. It's warm in a way it never is when she talks about me or to me. "If you won't behave for yourself, then do it for us. Do it for Hareton."

"I'm not responsible for the things Hindley chooses to do," I say. "Isn't Hindley a grown man? Can't he decide not to hurt his own people without my help?"

Nelly exhales and shakes her head. "Oh, Cathy," she says. "If only *shoulds* could shape the world. But that isn't how things are. Hindley is as he is."

"If I marry and go to the Grange, I won't be able to do anything to calm him down," I say. "It will just be you and Joseph and Hareton, and he'll kill one of you eventually, and you won't be able to blame me for it."

"You silly girl," Nelly says despairingly. "You may not be able to fix him, but you can make him worse. You *do* make him worse." I watch her hands clench and unclench. "Why can't you be good? Do you truly lack the heart to love your own family as you should, or even your Edgar? I have never known such a cold-hearted girl!"

"Do you even like me, Nelly?" I say it curiously, peering into her eyes.

"Of course I do," she says.

And I know she is lying. All the lies of my life are unraveling around me, and the truths are glittering, hurtful and sharp. I did not think anyone particularly disliked me. I did not think I would care even if they did. But the truth stings me. It feels like something sharp, twisting about in my chest. Like I'm an apple being cored.

"If I let myself love everyone the way you think I should, it would kill me," I say. "Who shall I love that way? Tell me, Nelly. Edgar, when he is my only hope of riches, and I must handle him with care? Hindley, when he is liable to turn to rage and drink at any moment? You?"

Nelly says nothing. I raise my chin, defiant.

"Sometimes love is about running from people who hurt you and starting again," I say. "I think you should run too, Nelly. I really do. You may say you don't fear Hindley, but having a knife aimed at you . . . it's frightening, isn't it? You can admit it is!"

"I can bear it," she grits out.

"You shouldn't have to just bear it," I insist.

"And what else shall I do?" Nelly demands. "Leave? You may forget, but I was only a young girl when I began working here. This is my home too! You may not be family, but you're all I've known! And who shall care for Hareton if I go? Who will keep him safe? When even his own aunt isn't willing to protect him?"

"I won't die for Hareton, and you shouldn't either!" I am standing, suddenly. I realize that Nelly and I are the same height, that we can look furiously into each other's eyes exactly. "We should take him. Nelly, we should run—"

"And go where? Feed him with what money?"

"It would be better than remaining here and suffering," I say.

"You don't know real suffering, Miss Cathy," Nelly says sharply. "By God, you don't know anything about it. Have you ever been hungry? Have you ever been hopeless? You have not! You know nothing about what it means to suffer."

"That may be true," I say. "Maybe my griefs don't matter at all, and other people suffer much more than I ever shall. But my griefs will still kill me if nothing changes. I would rather they kill me, if nothing changes." Tears are pricking again at my eyes. But I feel fierce, and I am not ashamed to weep, and I am not ashamed of being what I am. Even if I am selfish, even if I am unlovable. "And Hindley's griefs may kill me, or you, or Hareton at any moment. I'd rather choose my own way than his. That's what I feel, Nelly, and my heart won't be changed."

Nelly is breathing hard, and as I keep speaking, her face goes from flushed red to an awful white—a bleached-bone kind of anger or despair that I can barely look at.

"Go then," Nelly says finally. "Go, if you want to go. Perish, if you like. I've done all I can for you."

She storms out.

I go back to packing the few other things I'll take. My hands are shaking, and there is something sad in me, but I don't regret anything that I am choosing to do. I reach over to my window ledge. I adjust all my books until they are lined up perfectly, looking like they've never been touched or written in at all. And then I put the muslin carefully in my pack. The moonlight fabric slithers from my fingers, neatly folding away.

It's only after that that I get up and pick up my pack, and walk down the stairs. Out the gate, and away.

Where am I going? I don't know yet. I still remember all my fears as a small girl, that a person lost on the moors would become a ghost. I'm not afraid of that anymore, but I do wonder if my body is going to suddenly turn to silver and dust, and I'll glide over the moors forever.

It doesn't, of course, although the wind is fierce enough again that it feels like my skin's thinking about it. The day has grown colder than it was this morning, the chill sharp.

My feet start taking me toward the fairy cave. There are birds wheeling wildly overhead, carried on wind currents. It's going to storm soon. This time I'm not distracted, so I can tell. Even the air feels heavier. I stick out my tongue, and it's like I can taste the coming rainfall on the wind. It tastes like metal.

If I must, I can hide in the fairy cave until the storm passes and then continue my journey. It's still early enough that Hindley will not be back home for hours, so I will have a head start. And since I don't know where I am going, neither can he.

I am halfway up the crags, under piercing sunlight and the first thin rain beginning to fall. Everything is shining, glowing with light through water.

That's when I see him.

I am sure I'm dreaming. Absolutely sure. Because Heathcliff is standing in front of me. His back is to me, but I would know him anywhere. I know the way he holds his shoulders, the way he always holds his face forward even in the sharpest wind, as if daring it to try and hurt him. His hair is longer. He has on the same greatcoat I saw him wear last, but there's a new kerchief around his neck, red as blood.

I try to speak. But my throat is just an airless thing, like I can't make sound, never mind words. But somehow he hears me—of course he hears me—and he's turning. And he's looking at me. His deep, dark eyes are wide and fixed on my own, and his mouth is parting.

"Cathy," he says.

I've missed his voice—like wood smoke, like warm fires. Home, home, his voice is my home.

"Cathy," he says again, and we're running toward each other, crashing into each other. I bury my face against his neck, against his hair and his skin, and he's lifting me up, holding me tight enough to hurt.

"I didn't know if you'd come back to me," I manage to say, and my voice is all muffled by his skin, my tears. "I didn't . . . didn't think you would."

"I didn't know if you would want me to come back, Cathy."

"Of course I would!" I burst out. "Of course. I thought of you every day, Heathcliff. Every single day, and I couldn't search for you. I couldn't go and find you. I . . ." I'm crying, and I don't know if the tears are happy or full of grief. I only know that they flow out of me and I can't stop them, no matter how much I would like to.

He doesn't try to make me stop crying. He looks down at my face like he's starving and he wants to drink every part of me in, but I keep ducking back down against his shoulder.

"You're so strange," I force out, voice wobbling. "Looking at me like that."

His thumb under my chin nudges my head up. We stare for

a long moment, me through tears and him through fierce eyes, blazing like fire.

"Now we're both looking at each other," he says. "That makes us both strange."

"That's nothing new," I whisper. I'm transfixed.

I frame his face in my hands. His face that isn't handsome, but better than handsome. You wouldn't call the crags handsome, or the view over the edge of a cliff, or the place where the sky meets the moors and collapses into one shimmering blue-gold sea. You'd call them all *breathtaking*. That's the word I think of when I look at him.

I press my thumb to his lower lip and he inhales sharply. I think about leaning forward.

And of course, the rain suddenly starts pouring.

It's cold and heavy, and we both begin turning at once, running toward the fairy cave. We worm our way through the narrow entrance, and then we're inside, within the shadowy white stone.

I am soaked. I can feel the way my hair has come down, unraveled, stuck to my head. But the moment's broken, when I almost kissed him or he almost kissed me. There's water in his hair too, and I watch him take off his cap with damp fingers, face shining.

He's still holding my arm with one hand, and I am holding his.

"Where have you been?" I blurt out.

"In Liverpool," he says.

"You were well? Safe?" I ask. "You left with *nothing*."

"Not nothing. I took a knife."

"Heathcliff."

"Cathy." An almost smile tugs at his mouth, darting over his face, then gone. "It took time, but I was fine eventually. I had work. I had friends. It was . . . good."

There's something in the way he's speaking that makes me sure he's thinking of that city and the thought makes him happy. Friends. Work. He's had a whole life away from me, a whole life I can't imagine. I can't be jealous of a place, but I am.

I am shivering from cold. It reminds me of the dark, and running. Being soaked through with rain.

There is so much I want to tell him.

"I tried to chase after you," I confess. "When you left, I . . . it was raining."

"I remember the rain," he says, after a second of silence. Maybe he's remembering what it was like that night. What he heard. What I said.

"I got sick," I say. "Fell ill with fever. Can you believe it? Just from a little rain. Then I tried to chase after you again, but Joseph and Nelly caught me, and Hindley thought I was fragile and falling apart for sure." I laugh through my chattering teeth. "Maybe I am fragile, or at least more fragile than you are, but I don't think so. Does breaking from holding too much anger inside you make you fragile? I don't think it does. I think breaking is just . . . breaking is taking everything that locked you up and turning it into knives you can use, instead of walls pinning you in." I feel suddenly nervous, and my tongue is all clumsy, and I push my wet hair back from my face and say uncertainly, "Does that make sense?"

"You were sick?" Heathcliff says instead, a question wrapped up in his voice. "How sick?"

"Sick enough to worry everyone, but what does it matter? I'm fine now."

We can't stop touching each other. Even as I try to wring the water from my hair, I clutch his sleeve with my fingertips. And then his hand is in my hair.

I close my eyes, feeling his warmth seep through me and say, in a quick tumble of words, "I should never have said what I said about you, Heathcliff. I should never have called you low. I didn't mean it. I know it's no excuse, I know, but you know how I am, how I always talk and talk, and half my words are vicious for nothing. Because *I* am vicious." I am trying to be grave and honest, but my voice is wavering.

"I know how you are, Cathy," he says, much more evenly than me. "I know why you said it. But you did break my heart."

He says it so simply. I swallow.

"Has it mended?" I ask.

He cups my cheek. "It's mended enough," he says. "I'll always forgive you, Cathy. Don't you worry. That's how it is with you and me."

You shouldn't, I think. *You shouldn't forgive me.* But I am just so grateful that he has, that I don't say so. "Are you happy now?" I ask him instead. "You look happy."

"Happy enough," he says, which isn't yes. I know it. "You said you've broken. Said you're all shards."

I shiver again. His hand is against my neck.

"I went on a journey of my own," I murmur. "I . . . learned the truth. About myself. About where I come from." I put my hand over his on my neck. Layers of warmth, and my pulse under us both.

"I always said we were the same inside," I say. "I just didn't know how. But you did, didn't you?"

He nods, wordless.

"You've always known," I prompt, and he nods again. "Why didn't you tell me?"

"I used to think you knew," he says. "Then I thought it didn't matter."

"It does matter," I manage to say. "My father . . ." I exhale, shaky again. And I tell him, or try to tell him, what guilt my father carried with him from India. Because it's Heathcliff's story, too. His life was saved for that guilt, after all.

He listens, wordless, his thumb against my jaw as I explain. As I say, finally, "I was leaving. That's why I'm here. I was running again. I knew I would die if I stayed home and pretended to be something I'm not." His grip tightens. "There are things I want to do," I confess. "Father had things he should have put right and paid for. And now he can't, and Hindley never shall, and I want to be the one who tries. I want to make the world better. I know I'm not . . . I'm not good. I will never be good, and I don't care to be. But I want to *do* something good." It is foolish, so foolish, so my voice gets smaller. "I want to change the world."

Heathcliff makes a rasping noise. I tense as I realize he's laughing.

"Why are you laughing?" I ask him.

"Because we've been so apart, Cathy, and not at all. Seems we've been walking the same road this whole time." He presses his forehead to mine, a brief and sure pressure. I relax. He's not mocking me after all. "But that makes sense," he says fondly. "Since we belong to each other."

He tells me what he's been doing in Liverpool. The lodging house where sailors from across the Orient live, sailors like his father was. Lascars. He tells me about his friends, who're smart and good at thieving and want more from the world too. He tells me about letters, and courts and the East India Company, about an apprentice law clerk who may help change things, and a newspaper that may share their stories; things that should be dull but are not when I think of men surviving maybe because of what Heathcliff does. He tells me about building a safe haven where people can do more than merely survive.

Listening to what he's doing is like lightning running through me.

I think of how Father should have mended things. This . . . listening to Heathcliff, is like being handed a needle and thread full of some kind of ghostly magic, so that I can do the mending myself. My fingers itch and my heart is like a bright thing inside me.

"Let me come with you," I say. He freezes and becomes silent and I ask, "You came for me, didn't you? To take me with you?"

"I came to see if you were well."

"Just that?"

His breath out is controlled, his grip on me sure, but not so strong that I can't slip free.

"I thought you were marrying Edgar Linton," he says finally.

I could explain to him exactly why I am not. I could tell him the last look Edgar turned on me, when he came near to understanding the truth about my past, and how I knew then that he didn't really love me and I didn't love him. I could say how light and hollow the Grange made me feel, but I don't.

I just say, "No. Even if you hadn't come back . . . no."

There's still rainwater on his eyelashes and on the ends of his hair. I think of having a home with him. A home where we're not afraid, and I can bring a cloth, and dry the water from his hair ever so carefully, and touch the cloth to his skin, light as kisses, until he is warmed through. I want it so much that it sends warmth through my rain-cold body, my beating heart a hot coal.

"Cathy," he says. Regret colors his voice like ink. "I wanted to come back to you as a wealthy man. I wanted to come back and show you I could keep you safe, that I didn't need you to protect me. I wanted to come back and prove you wrong. But I've done none of it. I'm not wealthy. I can't promise you riches. I can't even promise you we won't starve."

I put my hands in his. "Then we'll go make riches together. I'll make sure you don't starve, and you'll do the same for me."

"Cathy," he whispers. He doesn't sound comforted, and maybe he's right not to. "If I could, I'd lay the whole world at your feet. But all I've got is myself. And God help me, I'm not enough."

"You think you're not enough for me?" I laugh, and it's a sound like cracking my own heart open and letting all the tenderness and awful strength of my love pour out of it. It brings words with it—all the words I have never said to him. All the words he deserves to hear, even if letting them out leaves me vulnerable, barer than if I were in nothing but my naked skin. "Heathcliff, don't you know what you are to me? You're the earth that holds me steady, and the sun that wakes me in the morning. You're the moonlight folding me in sleep. You're the way the wind fills my lungs when I run across the moors, and the sea that fills my heart when I dream. You're the birds overhead, and the deep roots of trees. You are . . . oh, you're the night sky that holds the stars up." I inhale a deep breath, and say shaky but so sure, "To me, you're all the wild and true things that are everlasting."

He's silent. Staring at me with the hungriest look, drinking in my words and my face. I hope my words are like a mirror. I hope he sees himself the way I do. I look back at him, and let him see my soul, every part of it.

"I'm not enough for *you*," I tell him. "I have no skills. I don't know how to soothe any suffering. I only know how to make my own worse. I'm spoiled and cruel and I've never loved anyone half as well as I love you, which is just the same as loving myself. But if you love me anyway, Heathcliff, and if you'll have me anyway, then I'll go anywhere with you. I promise you. And I'll never regret it."

He looks at me with those dark eyes of his, his jaw tight, hands still on me. Then his hand on my neck goes down to the first point of my spine, warm and large and cradling me. I shiver, not from cold.

"Before we go back, Cathy," he says. His fingertips trace circles, then spread out, sending shivers with them. "Before we go," he says again, his voice warm and low. And I am already rising on my tiptoes, already wrapping my arms around his neck, when he dips his head low, and presses his mouth to mine.

Chapter Twenty-One

Heathcliff

I DON'T TELL CATHY, *I came because you called.*

I came for a feather. Came and found you, like I knew that I would. I came because it's everlasting things that tie us. The wind, the sky. The rocks, and the birds. And when you're gone, everlasting things won't have meaning anymore. Not to me.

I would tell her, but I'm kissing her and kissing her, and I don't want to stop.

I kiss Cathy the way I've always wanted. First gentle, seeing what it is—the brush of noses and then lips, getting the angle right. The cold of her lips, wind-chapped. Then I kiss her fiercer, pouring all my love into her. I know how my love is— too much, too harsh. Loving Cathy was what I learned when I was grieving and forgetting, then ignored, then hated. The whole world turning on me, and only Cathy to love—it's no surprise I love her like there's a storm in me harsher and more wild than what keeps us in this cave.

But Cathy kisses me back fierce, wrapping her arms round me. She kisses like she loves me the same. Like a wave's come, huge, ready to drag her under and she's holding her arms out for it. Welcoming it as it takes her right under.

She takes my hand. Hers are cold from the rain. Softer than mine. Presses one to her side.

She breaks the kiss. Says, "My shirt. It's—" Then she squirms, and tugs at it, and touches my hand again, moving it. I feel her. Skin of her stomach, the curve of her hips. I'm suddenly warm, too warm and feeling wanting, tender and overwhelming. The wave's taking me too.

"I don't look pretty," she whispers, laughing. "I'm sorry."

Pretty's not enough of a word for her. But I know she means she doesn't look pretty, dressed up in my clothes. But I like the look of them on her—the way they don't fit, too big for her. But still, they've got a rightness to them all those gowns of hers never had.

"You look like you," I tell her. "More like you than I've ever seen."

"Silly?"

She knows that's not what I mean. But I tell her anyway.

"Wild," I say. "Hardy and free."

"Not beautiful?"

"That too," I say. "But wild most of all."

I feel her side with my hand. Dip of her back. She looks at me, laughing eyes.

I make myself pull back, putting distance between us. I've got no shame over wanting Cathy, or her wanting me. I know I want to do everything with Cathy. I have forever, since I knew what wanting was. So I can wait longer, until we're somewhere else. Somewhere warm, safe. Light pouring in the window, so I can look at her and she can look at me. That's what I want.

She grins at me. With all her teeth, cheek dimpling up. Her lips are redder. I want to kiss her again. So I look away, and breathe careful, and put my clothes back how they should be. But then she reaches for me again and presses a quick kiss on my mouth once more. My cheek. Steps back.

"Do we go now?" Cathy asks.

"If you're ready," I tell her.

"I am," she says.

I think of Cathy back at the lodging house with me. Meeting the others. Don't know what they'll make of her, but if they like me they'll learn to like her too.

I tell her we need to get dry before we go and she laughs wickedly, but still takes off the shirt when I do. We wrap up in my coat, the two of us leaning against each other to get warm. Cathy presses her cheek to my shoulder, staring out the fairy cave with half-closed eyes.

"What could you do," Cathy says slowly, "you and your friends, and the lascars you know, if you had more money?"

I remember again, how it is with me and Cathy. Sometimes I don't know her at all, or she me. But sometimes we're just the same. Where we meet, it's like a song twining.

"Protect ourselves," I say. "Protect more people."

I look down at her face. The look in her eyes . . . it's distant.

"What are you thinking, Cathy?" I ask.

A shiver runs through me when she looks at me again. There's something faraway there. Something looking where I can't.

"We need to go back to the Heights. My brother owes a debt," she says. "I think it's time he pays it. Heathcliff . . . Will you come with me?"

Of course I go.

The Heights hasn't changed. Same dark stone. Same wind howling round it, and the same trees, bent out of shape by the window beating them day in and day out.

I don't see Nelly when we get in. No Hareton either. Cathy, meeting my eyes, shakes her head.

"Nelly's hiding," she says. "I told her I was leaving. She'll be worried what Hindley will do."

Most likely she's up in her room, door barred with Hareton sleeping in her bed. I follow Cathy, going through the kitchen. On the way I stop. I see Hindley's rifle. It's propped against the wall, all readied for hunting game.

I pick it up.

Cathy looks at me, face solemn, hair like a cloud from the rain and wind.

"What're you going to do with that?" Cathy asks.

"Nothing." Unless I have to. "If I've got the gun," I tell her, "Hindley can't use it. That's what matters."

The parlor's ice-cold, chilled through. Cathy kneels down and gets the fire going. I stand up, waiting like a soldier.

We hear noise. Door creaking. Both of us freeze.

It's not Hindley.

"Come back, have you?" Joseph asks. He's frowning, beady eyes all black.

"I have," I say.

"The master's going to kill you," he clucks, ambling through. "Kill you stone-dead."

"He can try. He's not managed to kill me yet."

"Bullet straight through your chest. Stone-dead," he mutters. Seems like it's more to himself than me, but it gets Cathy's anger up.

She stands quick, yelling, "Get out, you beast! This is no business of yours."

Joseph barely takes notice of her. He keeps on muttering. Stomps about, back and forth, then finally heads up to his own bed in the garret. We watch him go.

"I hate him," Cathy mutters. "I'll be glad to never see *him* again."

I look at her. Hold out my hand. She takes it, frown going soft, and sits down on Hindley's armchair. I stand by her, still holding the rifle. Fire keeps on crackling. We wait.

We feel the cold of the wind first, now that the fire's warmed us through. The door opens, and there's footsteps outside. Then Hindley, coming into the parlor, still damp from outdoors. He freezes on the threshold. His eyes set on me and get a look of hell in them.

"I'm not here to kill you," I say low.

Hindley waits a beat. Another. He smiles. Before he smiles he looks disappointed. Like I've failed somehow to be what he expects.

I'm not the brute here, Hindley Earnshaw. Not me.

"Hindley," Cathy says. Speaking first. She sounds calm, though I know she's not. Her hand's trembling in mine. "Remember what you said to me? About Heathcliff coming back?"

His eyes dart between us. Back, forth. He sees the state of us—clothes still drying, wild-haired. Cathy dressed up in shirt and breeches. His lip curls, a sneer that's more snarl.

"Stop touching her," he says to me.

I grip Cathy's hand tighter. Keep my eyes fixed on him. *Try it*, I think. *I've got the gun. Not you.*

"Leave him alone, Hindley," she says sharply. Scared as she is, she'll try to protect me like always. "We're here to talk about what you owe."

"I told you I'd let him come back," Hindley says flatly. "Well. I see he's back. Now he can go, and I'll do him the favor of not slitting his throat."

"I was wrong to ask for just that," Cathy says. Her voice doesn't even tremble. "I want proper money for him, Hindley."

"No."

"It's what Father owed him. And Heathcliff will use it for good. If you'd listen, I can tell you."

"Good?" He laughs, an ugly noise. Rubs knuckles against his brow. "That savage has never done anything good in his life."

I know that word like I know hunger. Felt it melt through my bones, all my years at the Heights. Now, though, I say quietly, "I'm no more savage than you are, Hindley Earnshaw. What's in my blood and flesh lies in yours too."

Hindley goes very still. The fire throws light on him that's hellish. His eyes are burning up inside like coals.

"Damn you, Cathy," he says softly. Viperous.

"She didn't tell me," I say. "I knew from the start. You're a bastard with Indian blood, and I'm a bastard with Indian blood. There. It's said. So let's talk like equals now. I could use this to ruin you, Hindley. But I don't want to. I don't even want your coin."

"What do you want then?" Hindley grits out.

"I saved your son, it's true. But it's not me you owe. It's your sister." I nod my head at Cathy. "Give her enough money to start over, and we'll leave you with all you've got. Your land, your house, all you've inherited. You'll never see me darkening your doorstep again."

"Pay my sister and then—what? You'll take her?" he spits.

"Cathy," he says, turning on her again. "I said I'd pay the devil his debt. I didn't say I'd pay with *you*. You're not like coin, Cathy. I won't give you to him."

"Am I not? Isn't that why you really want me to marry Edgar Linton? So you're tied to him as family, and he might cover your gambling debts? You can admit it, Hindley. I know every time your friends come you lose worse and worse—"

"Shut up," he says back. "Shut up, Cathy, I swear."

"What do you swear? Do you swear you'll beat me and show me my place? Is that what you swear?"

"If I have to, Cathy," he says. "I'll beat the brain out of your skull."

I let go of Cathy's hand. I aim the rifle.

"Heathcliff," Cathy says to me. "Ignore him. You don't need to protect me."

But I do.

I think of all the times I feared he'd hurt Cathy too. All the times she insisted he hadn't. When I'd looked for bruises on her, not seen them and thought, at least I've got this. At least Cathy's safe.

There's more ways to hurt someone than skin. I know that now.

"There's a thing I dreamed of," I say. Grip on the gun steady. "To come back here a rich man. To kill you. I wanted to kill you slowly. Take everything from you, until there was nothing left of you, and you were degraded, crawling on the floor in front of me like the animal you are. I knew it'd be my greatest pleasure. But I *will* settle for shooting you."

Cathy's hand goes on my arm. Holding.

"Put down the gun, Heathcliff," she says. "And, Hindley, sit down. Let's talk properly."

For a long moment, I hold the gun steady. I know it'll shoot easy—know it's ready, clean. It's Hindley's own gun. I've seen him with it, night after night, keeping it in killing form. If I stay steady, if I aim right, I could kill him swift.

His death's mine. I'm owed it. I look at him, thinking it, and my arm doesn't shake.

But there's Cathy next to me. She's stiller than lake waters. Stiller than night.

She doesn't want him dead.

I lower the rifle. Warily, Hindley settles himself down into a chair. Cathy makes a noise of approval and goes to stand by the fire. She picks up the poker, moving it in the grate, getting the fire merrier.

"Better," she says. Sounding relieved. "That's better."

"Well," Hindley says impatiently. "Are you going to talk more about wanting to kill me, boy?"

"I want what Cathy wants," I say.

And Cathy says, "Just give me some money, Hindley. I know you have some hidden around the house. Think of it as giving me my inheritance."

"You should have just stolen it," Hindley says.

"But then you would have come after me," Cathy says. "I was willing to risk you looking for me if I ran. But now . . ." She looks at me, eyes tender. "Now I want to know you won't. I want a devil's pact of my own."

"Money, and in return no one knows what our father did?" Hindley asks bitterly. "Money, and I leave you be, to die wretched in some gutter with this savage? No."

"Yes," says Cathy. "That's the pact I want."

Hindley looks at Cathy. Then his head sinks, tipping forward. He looks pained.

"I thought things would be better now, Cathy," he whispers. "I thought we'd be done with being cursed."

"The ghosts are never going to go away, Hindley," Cathy says. "They live in your heart, and in mine. So we just have to live with them. And . . . decide what we'll do. This is what I want to do."

He nods with his head lowered. Long seconds go by and he's not moving. Just breathing, those shoulders slumped, spine going up and down with his breathing.

"Cathy," he says. "I love you."

Then he lunges. He goes for me. I see it, but I can't move fast enough. I lift the rifle, but I think again to myself, *Cathy doesn't want him dead*. I falter. And then Hindley's brandishing a hunting knife, almost on me. I can't twist away. The chair's blocking me.

He's got it aimed at my gut. I know it'll sink in, and I know then I'll die. Slow, painful. The kind of death I wanted for him.

Everything goes slow. I see Cathy, six years old. Looking at me, ghosts on her tongue. Cathy, twelve, dressed shining and strange. Her and me, in her bed, as she begs me to stay awake. *I'll die if you die*, she told me. *I'll die—*

I hear a thud. And there's Cathy, standing with the fire poker in her hands. Her hands don't tremble either. Hindley's on the floor. She kicks the knife away from him.

"We'll have to take it," Cathy says. Her face is blotchy. Red cheeks. Eyes dark like coals. "Come on."

Chapter Twenty-Two

Catherine

I WORRY I'VE HURT HINDLEY very badly, but he starts waking up seconds later. "Quick," I say to Heathcliff, and I see he's already moving, striding out of the room. He comes back with rope, and we lash together Hindley's hands and then his legs.

"Someone will come find you soon," I murmur to Hindley, though I am not sure if he can hear me yet, or if he would even want to. "You'll be fine."

I realize when I was not wary of Hindley—even when I thought everything was normal and safe—I was afraid. There's a fear that makes your heart race and your hands tremble, and then there's another fear that lives inside you constantly. I have been like . . . like a hare, knowing it is prey, just waiting for a trap to spring or a predator to swoop down on me.

I wish it wasn't like this between us. But I am glad I am leaving him behind.

I stand and Heathcliff stands with me. I say, "We're going to do good things, aren't we? We're going to help people?" I hesitate. "People like us?"

"Yes," he says. He sounds so sure, and I am so glad of that. Goodness is like a coat that doesn't fit me, a costume that sits wrong on my skin. But perhaps the longer I wear it, and the harder I press it over my skin, the more it will become my own.

My heart is racing. I feel oddly light-headed. I have never hit anyone before. Not like I just hit Hindley. I am not sure if I never want to do it again or if I hunger to do it some more. But I'll worry about that another time.

"In that case," I say to Heathcliff. "I know where we can find our fortune."

I love the Heights. I love the howl of the wind. The way the moors change color with the movement of the sun, and the birds that fly over them. I love the lakes and waterfalls, the wetlands, the crags, the sparse trees. I love how it looks like a place nothing should live, but everything does.

But the Heights is also the place I've been most hurt.

How can home be somewhere that's written in your bones, and also a place you're afraid of? Does that mean I am afraid of my own bones? Is the very stuff that holds me together my enemy?

I take a shovel, and show Heathcliff to the place where two trees are twined. The soil is still unsettled, and nothing's growing upon it yet, which is how I know we're in the right place.

"Dig here," I say to Heathcliff. And although he looks curious, he is so used to my schemes that he just starts to shovel the dirt. "Carefully," I warn. "It won't take long—look."

There, in the dirt, I see the first of my mother's jewelry pieces.

It isn't exactly where I buried it. I remember.

"Don't dig anymore," I order, and fall to my knees. I scrape the dirt up, cupping it between my hands and discarding it. I do it quickly, my hands blackening, my nails going dark. My heart is pounding again.

Heathcliff sucks in a breath after a moment, then kneels with me.

It is like we are unearthing a grave. I suppose in a way we are. But when Hindley and I buried the jewels, we only tipped them into the soil, in one deep pile close together.

These are placed like they're being worn—like they're the echo of a body long gone. Earrings, fanned out below a headpiece like a gilded crown. Necklaces below that. Some short, and some long. A chain, that I thought was a necklace, but is placed where a waist should be. Rings. And bangles, at the edges where arms would lie. So many bangles, some made of gold, some made of shell, white like bones. A fortune.

"They're my mother's jewels," I whisper. It feels wrong to be loud. "My Indian mother. Hindley and I buried them."

We've folded the soil like cloth, and now we can see all that's left of her. The shape of a body where there's no body, all marked out in shell and silver and gold, all of it gleaming like the soil never even touched. We stare silently for a moment, as if we both feel the strangeness of what we've found deep in our own bones. I feel like grief is spilling through me, running through every bit of my body.

"I think her ghost did this." My voice splinters up a little. But I don't want to cry. "I think . . . she was here."

Heathcliff murmurs something. I don't know if it's a prayer, or something else. Then he says, "Like feathers."

I swallow. I nod.

"Yes," I say. "Yes. Oh, Heathcliff. Do you think she'll forgive me? For taking her jewels, for using them to . . . to do good? To help us?"

"I think," he says slowly, "that she will be glad for you. And I think . . ."

"What? Tell me. Honestly."

Silence. And then, "I think you'll be setting her free."

I exhale. I go for my pack, and I take out the muslin that shines like moonlight. I spread it out on my lap. Then I look up at Heathcliff and I say, "Give me the jewels."

He does. One after the other. He lifts them up reverently, and carefully places them on the muslin in my lap. I listen to the clink of gold and metal, and Heathcliff turns his back as I touch one bracelet, tracing the patterns in the gold. The bangle is warm, like it's been touching skin for longer that it can possibly have been touching Heathcliff's.

Perhaps it should frighten me, but it doesn't. I know my ghosts have taken care of me.

When it's done, and the grave of jewelry is empty, I wrap the muslin up. I place my hand over it, closing my eyes, and let Heathcliff close the soil up again.

Ma. We'll use them for something good.

I don't know if she can hear me, but that's what I think as he works. And I think of all the other ghosts that my father made, him and his Company, in a land far away where part of my soul comes from.

Heathcliff is near. I can hear his breath. It's comfort, and it's hope.

"If you are still here," I whisper out to the night. Calling my ghosts. "Then come with me. There's nothing here for you anymore."

I think of Father, and Mother who raised me and loved me, and wish I could ask them . . . oh, anything. I think of my other mother, with her clinking jewelry, her loving ghost. All of them gone to rest. I think of carrying the rest of the ghosts here away with me, to a new city, and how I might mend their torn souls a little day by day and year by year, until they can rest, too.

I feel the wind whirl around me. I wonder if it's all those ghosts answering me. If they're choosing to come with me, to follow me to Liverpool and to the water's edge so they can drift back to the land where they were born.

Maybe all I feel is the wind, the same wailing wind I've grown up with all my life, and nothing more than that. Either way, I close my eyes and feel it on my skin and in my hair, and wish it goodbye.

I will miss the Heights forever, I think. But I've left a piece of myself here, in the walls I've traced with my fingers and the floorboards I've run over, and the bed where I dreamed of the dead. And there are still books at my bedside, full of my words. I have a feeling Hindley will never touch them. He'll never touch my room at all.

But maybe one day Hareton will. I hope he'll read what I left behind, and know his aunt Cathy has gone far away, but she still loves him. She still hopes he'll survive what our family is, and find his own way to live, just like I have.

I open my eyes, and there's Heathcliff. Waiting for me.

I'm ready to go.

Chapter Twenty-Three

TWO PEOPLE FROM NOWHERE KNEEL under two twined trees. The moors are all around them. It's nighttime. Everything's leeched of color. Wind's moving the grass, the trees. All of it blue or black or tumbling gray. Like everything's waves and water. A place fit for nowhere people, readying for a long journey.

I close up Cathy's mother's grave. There's nothing resting in it. No jewels, no bones. But something put those bracelets and necklaces out like they were on a body, put them out with care. So I close the soil up with care too.

I think maybe the moors did it. Laid out a goodbye for Cathy, and laid out a fortune for the both of us. If anything's ever loved me and Cathy, it's the moors where we played and laughed, and cried over bird bones, and let each other go. If they did, I'm grateful. Maybe that's a debt the world owed us, and now it's paid.

Used to be, I'd tell myself a tale. Not like Cathy's tales, but something small. The tale went like this:

Once, there was a boy from nowhere. He carried nowhere with him, inside him and on his skin, like a curse. Best he goes back where he belongs. Best he goes before he ruins it all.

But that tale's just a tale. A false thing I can let go. I'm not from nowhere. I never have been.

"Heathcliff," Cathy says, and holds out her hand. "I'm ready."

Someday people round here will tell stories about ghosts. They'll say, Catherine Earnshaw vanished into the night. They'll say, the dead servant boy who ran off, the one who came from nowhere and nothing, turned up and whisked her off to join the dead with him. They'll say, there's fairy creatures that took her. They'll say, it was a foreign devil who did it, hell in his eyes. I know how people spin lies, stronger than truths, bending the world silver and strange like mirror glass.

I don't mind being a ghost. Don't mind being remembered wrong. I've got Cathy, and Cathy's got me.

A bird flies overhead, soundless. Somewhere there's still feathers with me in them, locks of hair tangled up, hidden in the dirt. So the Heights will stay with me, and I'll stay with the Heights too. I don't mind it, knowing I've got roots. Threads that cross England, and cross the sea. That's what makes me.

There's still earth on my palms. Marking me.

I reach out.

The boy from nowhere takes the girl's hand.

They stand up, the two of them. Weighed down with a small fortune. The girl smiles, brighter than the moon. The girl says, "If my feet hurt from walking, I'm going to make you carry me."

"That's fair," the boy says, lightness in his heart.

"It's not fair at all!"

"I don't mind," he says. "I like holding you, Cathy."

She blushes, then laughs, and curses him as a fiend.

He loves her so much.

They turn away from the Heights, the twined trees, the buried feathers, the inked tales in books. The old hurts and bruises. The people who gave them.

They start walking the long, lightless road that'll take them to somewhere else. Although they know where they're heading—to friends and a wild city and hoping for something better—it doesn't really matter where they go. All that matters is they've got each other.

They're already home.

Author's Note

In *Wuthering Heights*, a boy overhears the girl who grew up alongside him—the girl he loves—call him unworthy of her. And he runs. Three years later, he returns dressed up like a gentleman, and in possession of a mysterious fortune. By then, the girl has married another man. The boy destroys person after person, in vengeance for his violent and humiliating childhood, and the loss of his love. Ultimately, out of fury and heartache, the girl destroys herself. Their love story and their lives end in tragedy.

That isn't even half the story contained in Emily Brontë's novel, of course, but it is the part I chose to change. *What Souls Are Made Of* takes place during the time period when Heathcliff first runs away, and Cathy is left behind. It's a reimagining in which they discover things about themselves that set them on a different and more hopeful path.

The original *Wuthering Heights* is a story about violence and childhood trauma, and how those hurts can twist you. It's also a story about a girl who ignores her own true nature and tears herself apart, and a boy who is *other*. A boy who comes from nowhere and nobody. He's an outsider, the story says, and dangerous for it. Foreign, dark, speaking a language no one knows. Nelly once says to him: "Who knows but your father was Emperor of China, and your mother an Indian queen"— but we can never be sure if Heathcliff *is* Chinese or Indian, and likely neither can Heathcliff. He is a stranger even to himself.

We never get to hear Cathy's true voice, either. Her story is always told by other people. In this book, I wanted to give them both the chance to speak. And I wanted to give them roots.

I suppose, in a way, I decided to give them mine.

I grew up in a loving Punjabi family, in outer London, in a very South Asian area. The Britain I knew was, and still is, culturally diverse. It was a place I belonged to, and that belonged to me. But when I learned history in school, I only saw white faces. I thought families like mine were new, that immigration was a recent development, a wave that hit post–WWII with the British Nationality Act. Today, there's a sense in politics and the media that immigration is something modern and strange, altering or eroding whatever makes up British (or frankly, specifically English) national identity.

It was only when I started doing my own research that I realized the white vision of British history was a flattened version of the past that ignored nuance. At school, we learned about the British Empire without learning its atrocities; learned about the textile industry, or the historical crazes for tea and sugar without learning where tea and sugar and cotton came from, or how they were harvested or provisioned to the British public at low cost. It was history without dimension.

South Asians like me have a long old history with Britain, but let's focus on the period *What Souls Are Made Of* is set in. The eighteenth century was a time when European powers, Britain among them, were vying with each other to take control and ownership of the wealth of Asian and African countries. By 1757, the East India Company, a British trading company, took control of Bengal. The British East India Company went on to seize a significant portion of the Indian subcontinent along with other parts of Asia, monopolizing trade and laying the groundwork for the British Raj.

Against this backdrop, many East India Company officers and soldiers wed Indian women, or took Indian mistresses. Some of those children were brought back to Britain and separated permanently from their mothers. Others were left behind.

Meanwhile, Asian sailors were being recruited to work on ships, some of which were contracted by the East India Company. Lascars were paid a sixth of what British sailors were paid, and were heavily mistreated. Many died on voyages to Britain. Others died on arrival in Britain, where they were often abandoned without payment or lodging, or died later, on journeys back to their home countries. But some settled in Britain, marrying British women, and lascar communities grew up in portside cities like London and Liverpool.

Atrocity and empire went hand in hand. Sugar, rum, tobacco, and cotton were regularly brought into Liverpool on ships, and made Liverpool—and Britain—rich. But those riches were the result of the triangular trade: the movement of goods and enslaved people between Africa, the United States of America, the West Indies, and Britain. By 1786, when this story takes place, slavery was not legal on British soil but was still the backbone of the British Empire, and was not officially abolished by the British until 1833. Although that was, of course, not the end of slavery in its entirety.

The 1770 Bengal famine—a source of horror and guilt for Cathy's father—was initially caused by a poor harvest brought on by poor weather, but East India Company policies, including high taxation, exacerbated the food shortage and resulted in mass starvation. It's hard to assess how many people died, but sources suggest up to a third of the population of Bengal perished.

In this novel, Cathy is an East India Company officer's daughter; Heathcliff is a lascar's son. Both of them are tangled up in the real history of migration, displacement, and identity that make up British history.

Cathy's moonlight cloth from her ghostly mother is Dhaka muslin—a precious cloth that was produced via a laborious, highly skilled process in Bengal, and was all the rage among British and European elites. Cathy is right to think it could be made into clothes. Similarly light, airy muslin was worn by Marie Antoinette and was key to the Chemise à la Reine fashion. But the cotton industry was strangled under the Company's purview, and the skill of making a cloth described as "woven air" has been long lost. Heathcliff's gifted red kerchief is made of kantha cloth, a fabric style also from Bengal, though his fragments of language and likely his father came from nearer to what is now New Delhi.

Both of them discover scraps of the past: words, cloth, ghosts. And with those scraps, they come to understand who they are, and in the process, save themselves.

I hope this book gives you a few scraps to hold on to, as well—a glimpse into one vision of a multicultural, complicated past full of pain and exploitation, but also of small kindnesses, and resistance, and people helping each other in ways big and small even when the odds are stacked against them.

If you want to read more about this period of history or some of the topics raised, I have a few recommendations that may help you begin your own search:

Dalrymple, William. *White Mughals: Love & Betrayal in Eighteenth-Century India*. London: Harper Perennial, 2004.

Fisher, Michael H. *Counterflows to Colonialism: Indian Travellers and Settlers in Britain 1600–1857*. Delhi: Permanent Black, 2006.

Macilwee, Michael. *The Liverpool Underworld: Crime in the City, 1750–1900*. Liverpool: Liverpool University Press, 2011.

Mortimer, Ian. *The Time Traveller's Guide to Regency Britain*. London: Vintage, 2020.

Olusoga, David. *Black and British: A Forgotten History*. London: Pan Macmillan, 2017.

Visram, Rozina. *Ayahs, Lascars and Princes: The Story of Indians in Britain 1700–1947*. London: Pluto Press, 1986.

Acknowledgments

I never want to write a book during a global pandemic again, thanks very much.

I would never have been able to do this without the support of good friends. Thank you, Nazia and Cat, for encouraging me to take this chance. Thank you, Shuo, for celebrating with me in the middle of an Imogen Heap concert many moons ago when I found out I was going to get to remix *Wuthering Heights*. You were there through my goth teenage years, so you know how much this means to me. Much love to Kate, whose impression of ghost Cathy yelling at Heathcliff in a proper Yorkshire accent haunted me the entire time I was writing this. To all the friends and family who immediately started singing Kate Bush's "Wuthering Heights" when I told them I was writing this: I categorically do not thank you.

To my mother, Anita Luthra-Suri, I send the warmest thanks, for always encouraging me to read and love even the books you hated. Ritika, my favorite big little sister—we've read so many romances together. I hope you enjoy this one half as much. And huge thanks to Carly, who is always the best of me, and helped me source approximately a dozen academic articles and also bullied me into reading Engels' *The Condition of the Working Class in England*. I get it now.

Thank you to my wonderful agent Laura Crockett, who loves the Brontës as much as I do. Every dream book I get to write is thanks to you. Thank you to Feiwel and Friends for giving me this opportunity. Particular thanks goes to my wonderful editor, Emily Settle, for helping me whip this book into shape. Big thanks also to publisher Jean Feiwel, managing editor Dawn Ryan, production editor Lelia Mander, and copyeditor Erica Ferguson for making this book shine. I am very grateful to Rich Deas for designing the beautiful cover, to Jonathan Barkat for photography, and to the models Niva Patel and Usman Habib, who brought Catherine and Heathcliff to life.

Thank you Dee Hudson and Sahrish Hadia for helping me write this book with the care it deserved. And I must extend my thanks to other authors in the Remixed Classics series, including Bethany C. Morrow, C. B. Lee, Aminah Mae Safi, Anna-Marie McLemore, Kalynn Bayron, Caleb Roehrig, and Cherie Dimaline. It's a privilege to be published alongside you all.

Finally, my thanks goes to every teacher, librarian, or educator who has looked at a library collection or history curriculum devoid of the real diversity, pain, nuance, and power of the past, and decided young people deserve better. It was people like you who made me a writer. Thank you for continuing to throw those doors wide open.

**The sea and those who sail it
are far more dangerous than the
legends led them to believe.**

This remix of *Treasure Island* moves the classic pirate adventure story to the South China Sea in 1826, starring queer girls of color—one Chinese and one Vietnamese—as they hunt down the lost treasure of a legendary pirate queen.

**They will face first love, health
struggles, heartbreak, and new horizons.
But they will face it all together.**

In a lyrical celebration of Black love and sisterhood, this remix of *Little Women* takes the iconic March family and reimagines them as a family of Black women building a home and future for themselves in the Freedmen's Colony of Roanoke Island in 1863.

**There seems to be no such thing
as home in a war.**

A ragtag band of misfits—two loyal Muslim sisters, a kind-hearted Mongolian warrior, an eccentric Andalusian scientist, a frustratingly handsome spy, and an unfortunate English chaplain abandoned behind enemy lines—gets swept up in Holy Land politics in this thrilling remix of the legend of Robin Hood.

Thank you for reading this Feiwel & Friends book. The friends who made *What Souls Are Made Of: A Wuthering Heights Remix* possible are:

Jean Feiwel, Publisher

Liz Szabla, Associate Publisher

Rich Deas, Senior Creative Director

Holly West, Senior Editor

Anna Roberto, Senior Editor

Kat Brzozowski, Senior Editor

Dawn Ryan, Executive Managing Editor

Celeste Cass, Assistant Production Manager

Emily Settle, Associate Editor

Erin Siu, Associate Editor

Foyinsi Adegbonmire, Associate Editor

Rachel Diebel, Assistant Editor

Lelia Mander, Production Editor

Follow us on Facebook or visit us online at mackids.com.
Our books are friends for life.